Samuel Tayl

Letters, Conversations and Recollections of S. T. Coleridge

SALZWASSER
VERLAG

Samuel Taylor Coleridge, Thomas Allsop

Letters, Conversations and Recollections of S. T. Coleridge

Reprint of the original, first published in 1864.

1st Edition 2022 | ISBN: 978-3-75259-242-9

Verlag (Publisher): Salzwasser Verlag GmbH, Zeilweg 44, 60439 Frankfurt, Deutschland
Vertretungsberechtigt (Authorized to represent): E. Roepke, Zeilweg 44, 60439 Frankfurt, Deutschland
Druck (Print): Books on Demand GmbH, In de Tarpen 42, 22848 Norderstedt, Deutschland

LETTERS, CONVERSATIONS,

AND

RECOLLECTIONS.

LETTERS,

CONVERSATIONS AND RECOLLECTIONS

OF

S. T. COLERIDGE.

WITH A PREFACE BY THE EDITOR,

THOMAS ALLSOP.

Pliny writ his Letters for the Public; so did Seneca, so did Balzac, Voiture, &c. &c.; Tully did not: and therefore these give us more pleasure than any which have come down to us from antiquity. When we read them we pry into a secret which was intended to be kept from us. That is a pleasure. We see Cato and Brutus and Pompey and others such as they really were, and not such as the gaping multitude of their own age took them to be, or as Historians and Poets have represented them to ours. That is another pleasure.—BOLINGBROKE TO SWIFT.

THIRD EDITION.

LONDON

1864.

PREFACE

TO THE

THIRD EDITION.

A NEW Edition of this work appearing, the Publisher asks of me some words of Preface.

I have little to add to the literary remains of this wonderful intellect—the very sweepings of whose mind have been foisted on an indulgent public by men whose passions, prejudices, professions and profits have found a reflex in their books, and have rendered the name of Samuel Taylor Coleridge a puzzle to this later generation.

All that is really Coleridge's own, even the abstruse musings in the *Biographia Literaria*, grows in value—like good wine—with age. Before its time, fresh and new when said, it is ripening for this and future ages. Thus the reader of this day finds the name of Coleridge so often recurring—now more than ever—that a right appreciation of the inner mind of this extraordinary man is more needful than when his cotemporaries were more numerous.

He was a thinker so profound that the men attracted by his rare eloquence were often the most impressed by his affluence of thought and the extent of his research: whilst those who sought him for aid to their intellect were led captive by the felicities of his diction and the charm of his voice.

In the first edition of this work I had purposed to have entered at some length into the esoteric views entertained by Coleridge, but was compelled by my publisher to relinquish this purpose. I blame him not. He was influenced by his *patron* and by his patrons. This indirect species of *surveillance* of the Press, of the liberty of printing, has escaped the notice of John Milton, and finds no place in the instances or applications of John Stuart Mill's great work "On Liberty."

I now distinctly state that Coleridge ever retained the convictions of his early, earnest youth. That he often repeated the saying of Plutarch, quoted so often with approval by Bacon: "*That it was better to believe that there was no God, than to believe in a God who eat* (or roasted) *his children*:" that it excited in him one only feeling, to see men full grown, and apparently sane, thinking, first, that they needed salvation; second, that they had been saved before they were born; and lastly, that they had to seek forgiveness for sins they had never committed.

It is true that in later years, when his health failed, when his bodily sufferings were great and constant, that he leant to a system, a scheme rather, which should, if it might be, reconcile religion with philosophy; that as the Mosaic dispensation of denunciations and punishment was superseded by the Christo-Platonic, so the contradictory dogmas of the existing Christianity needed a complement to fit it for the present era. This he diligently sought in the German philosophers of the past century, in Lessing, Kant, Fichte and Schelling, as well as in Hegel and the Neo-Christian writers of a later period. To this he alludes in that most beautiful and most affecting poem "Dejection," in which more entirely than in any other of his writings may be traced the habit of his soul—

"And haply by abstruse research to steal."

This research availed nothing; yet he became deeply interested in the views of these metaphysical writers, and when interrogated by men who had grievous doubts and wanted their minds propped, gave them these gatherings for a staff.

Finding little in these writers to strengthen his faith, he sought to purify the existing Bibliolatry, or blind Bible worship, in the hope that hidden harmonies might be discovered. Hence, though *he* aimed chiefly to aid his readers to enquiry and research, they were led by their own previous study, by the pre-occupation of their minds, to conclude that he had faith in a Clergy, whilst he avowed his belief in a *Clerisy*—in the advantage gained by a system which secured one educated man in every parish in the kingdom.

His wont to dilate on the fallacy of the Unitarian

system, to expose its coldness, hollowness, and the want of earnestness to which it led *or attracted* its adherents, was often mistaken for faith in the church creed, than which nothing was farther from his inmost conviction.

That he urged his doubts in later years, in the midst of great suffering, less decidedly, is less to be wondered at—rather to be admired, that in such pain he should still earnestly urge upon all who approached him those eager questionings which in earlier days he uttered in sarcasm, repeating the saying of Pascal: "*Since nothing is certain, let us believe in the absurd;*" or, quoting the well-known aphorism of Tertullian, that oddest of Fathers and father of oddities: "*I believe, because it is impossible.*"

To think of Coleridge, the myriad-minded, believing in, as he phrased it, "the raw-head-and-bloody-bones" jumble which it pleases the mystery-men who profit and those who from habit adhere to them, to call Christianity, would be to affirm that it was midnight at noon.

To utilize a system existing, since no better might be, was

> "His sole resource, his only plan;"

and if, in attempting to give life to a corse he caused some of his hearers and even some careless readers to misconceive the scope and tendency of his teachings, the most charitable conclusion is that they were self-deceived. And yet, when they heard him state, as was his wont, *that he should have been a Christian had Christ never lived; that all that was good in the teaching of Christ was to be found in Plato, in Zoroaster, Confucius,* *and the Gymnosophists;* that the miracles had no force as affirming truths, were of no more weight than so many conjuring tricks, it must have been a heavy draft on their bank of faith. Speaking of the Church of England, he repeatedly asserted that it was incapable of defence on the ground put forward by Churchmen, and that had Lord Byron, with his great facility and command of language, only had patience to understand its weakness, he could easily have demolished it.*

In speaking of St. Xavier, the great Apostle of the Indies, of his great powers and perseverance, he often referred to that intrinsic perception of truth belonging to Asiatics, which led the Japanese to reject at once and with one voice the doctrine of eternal (or everlasting) damnation, crying out "Annihilation! annihilation! annihilation!" repelling by an impulse of nature and conscience a doctrine as abhorrent to the universal feeling of humanity as it is baseless in fact, and opposed to all known facts.

That there was ever an earnest striving after truth, and a hope of reconciling truth with Christianity, is clearly to be found in all his later works. In the later years his sufferings were terrible. Enough is shown in the letters to shadow forth the causes of this agony. Evil and pain and strange calamity, concurred to render

* The two notices from the *Quarterly Review*, at the end of this Preface, are not given as examples of consistency, but as samples of the judicial and of the priestly mind. The one written, I have been told, by a Barrister of eminence, the translator of Gœthe's *Faust*, who probably does not see any reasonableness in the belief of a devil and everlasting damnation, by which priests profit and prosper; the other, by the Rev. John Moultrie, is given as a sample of the courtesies of clerical criticism.

his late years very painful. I may not dwell on this picture farther than to say that though in the last years of his life he was not "a drivel and a show," his mind was enfeebled and his surroundings were not entirely suited to his state. May we not say, in his own affecting words,—

> "Oh! first the age and then the man compare;
> That age how dark, congenial minds how rare!"

To show his love of liberty, his hatred of despotism, it will be enough to know that he justified Brutus and Cassius, whilst admitting the wonderful gifts of Cæsar, just as he would have justified tyrannicide at the present day.

The last written work, "The Confessions of an Enquiring Spirit," humble as is its tone, bears unmistakable evidence of the author's doubts as to the everlasting fire and brimstone of, what he was wont to call, the vulgar Christianity.

The respect for free-thought, as contra-distinguished from so-called belief, is well shown in his rejoinder to William Smith, of Norwich, who on his secession from Unitarianism had accused him of Atheism.

Opposed from habit and conviction to theological controversy, he ever maintained that the best road to real progress, until truths have made some advance in the public mind, was by enquiry and suggestion; feeling confident that in the present era, the philosophy of one generation would become the common sense of the next. He used to affirm that as reeds which bend before the blast recover their upright form, whilst the oaks which resist are laid low, so the Reformation owed more to Cranmer, who yielded to the King, than to the Martyrs who stood firm to their new creed. In conclusion, I cannot do better than to transcribe the last or nearly the last words he ever wrote:—

"Proposed preface to the first volume of my work, the 'Magnum opus et labor mea vita.' In my judgment there are but two schemes worthy the name of religion; and I believe that the first is to the second, as the acorn to the same acorn expanded into an oak. The first is that of Lieutenant Bowling in his reply to the zealous Romish Priest: 'As for me, friend, d'ye see, I have no objection to what you say. It may be either true or false, for what I know. I meddle with nobody's affairs but my own; the gunner to his linstock, and the steersman to the helm, as the saying is. I trust to no creed but the compass, and do unto every man as I would be done by; so that I defy the Devil, the Pope, and the Pretender, and hope to be saved as well as another.' The second scheme the reader will find in the following system of Faith and Philosophy, or *Catena veritatem, de Deo, Homine et Natura.*—S. T. COLERIDGE."

T. A.

"A book of considerable interest."

—QUARTERLY REVIEW, No. CX.

"TO THE ANONYMOUS EDITOR OF COLERIDGE'S LETTERS.

"A gibbering ape that leads an elephant;
A dwarf deformed, the presence heralding
Of potent wizard, or the Elfin King;
Caliban deigning sage advice to grant
To mighty Prosper in some hour of want;
Sweet Bully Bottom, while the Fairies sing,
Braying applause to their rich carolling,
But feebly typify thy flippant cant,
Stupid defamer, who for many a year
With Earth's profoundest teacher wast at school,
And notwithstanding dost at last appear
A brainless, heartless, faithless, hopeless fool.
Come, take thy cap and bells and throne thee here,
Conspicuous on the dunce's loftiest stool."

—QUARTERLY REVIEW, No. CXVII.

PREFACE

TO THE

SECOND EDITION.

The following admirable and instructive Letters, forming portion of a Correspondence between Samuel Taylor Coleridge and his friend and favourite disciple Thomas Allsop, were originally printed in the year 1836. Although published in a very expensive form, the first edition was quickly exhausted, and the Work has now been for some time out of print. Being impressed with a conviction of the great value of these reminiscences of the Great Thinker, I have for some time had it in contemplation to reprint the Work in a form accessible to the majority of readers—an intention of which the execution has been hitherto prevented by the ceaseless claims of an engrossing and anxious occupation. Probably this might have been still longer deferred had not recent circumstances rendered it incumbent on me, for reasons of a different nature, to lay this correspondence before the public.

It having been stated that Mr. Thomas Allsop was cognizant of and sanctioned the attempted tyrannicide of the 14th January, which resulted (as it could hardly have failed to do) in the death of innocent persons, I deem it my duty, by the republication of this work, to show to the world what manner of man he is, and in what estimation he was held by one of the greatest Philosophers and most profound Thinkers of this or any age.

Independently of all personal considerations, I have a high gratification in giving increased publicity to this work. The vigorous manliness of tone and independence of thought with which it is pervaded, contrast markedly with the great bulk of *conventional* literature, and cannot fail to be appreciated by those who are accustomed to think for themselves, and not blindly to adopt the ideas and habits of mind prevailing at the time and place of their existence.

R. A.

STOCK EXCHANGE,
April 19, 1858.

PREFACE.

HAVING for more than sixteen years enjoyed a large share of the affectionate regards, sympathy, and inmost confidence of the most variously gifted and extraordinary man that has appeared in these latter days, it has been to me a most melancholy, though not unpleasing, task, to arrange these materials, so as to give to you, my dearest children, some idea—alas, how poor! how inadequate it *must* be—of that friend for whose sake you are, if possible, more dear to me.

To you, my dearest Elizabeth, the Fairy Prattler of the Letters, and to you, Robin, the still meek Boy, I am especially desirous to convey, through these fragments, some better, some more entirely individualised, notion of the earliest friend, best, and first lost.

Of the no less loving, not less to be loved Charles Lamb, having been house-mates, your recollections need not this aid. I stood beside the Grave, and saw when it received their loved forms, and, since then, I seem to have lived on their memories.

Lamentation and regrets for the loss of such men

would be felt by all who knew—and were worthy to be known by—them, as a grievous wrong done to their memories. If we have not learned from, and for, these men, that boisterous grief, grief of which the signs are external and visible, is an inadequate and unfitting tribute; then, as relates to the manner in which they would be remembered, they have failed to make themselves understood.

Thoughts that are indeed too deep for tears mingle with all our recollections of that grey-haired Old Man, that mightiest Master of Poetry and of Philosophy in its truest and only valuable sense.

To have known such a man, to have shared his many sorrows and sufferings, and to have partaken of the few and far between gleams of glad and joyous sunshine which fell to his lot, are recollections to be cherished in the inner sanctuary of our hearts. Few indeed as were the gleams of genial and warm and cordial uprising of that noble and pure-minded Spirit in later years, still to him it was an ever new delight to impart all he had learnt, all he had experienced, and much in which he could only have been his own teacher, to those who sought him in sincerity and simplicity of heart.

I seek most earnestly to make you know the minds of these, to you, Ancient of Days; and I think I shall best effect this by allowing them to speak for themselves. "Of the Dead," says the old adage, "nothing but what is good." I say to you "*nothing—or what is true.*"

Of the first of these friends, both lost in the past year, I shall chiefly speak to you; more full and sufficient records of the last I earnestly hope to see from the Pen of one every way fitted, both by love and fine appreciation of his Character, to the task.

I have given with the Letters such brief Notices and Recollections as seemed likely to enable you to appreciate that great and extraordinary mind, that greatest and truest philosopher, in the highest and only true sense of that term, in its combination with Love.

Upon the Letters and Conversations, however, I chiefly rely for conveying to you some slight image, though vastly inadequate, of the mind of this wonderful, this myriad-minded man, whose loss is however far too recent to admit of just or adequate Estimation.

Cherished and sustained by his extraordinary Intellect, and still more by the Love and Sympathy in which, like a vast reservoir, he always superabounded, and the fullness of which seemed to arise from its overflowing, I have been able to arrive at settled and definite conclusions upon all matters to which I have heretofore attached value or interest. When I say that I have arrived at settled conclusions, you will not for a moment believe that my opinions can or *ought* to be received by others of a totally different experience, as truths for *their* minds; still less that matters which depend upon individual experience and temperament can be permanent truths for all time. You will find, and this it is which I wish to impress upon your minds, that a spirit of pure and intense *humanity*, a spirit of love and kindness, to which nothing is too large, for which nothing is too small, will be to you, as it has ever been to me, its own "exceeding great reward."

This, my dear Children, and I do not now address you only, nor your younger brothers and sisters, but I would fain speak to, and, on this point at least, could wish to be heard by, all young and confiding minds,—has been to me a solace in sorrow, an unspeakable reliance and support when all outward has been lowering and overcast. This indeed it is, in the language of an early letter, "Which, like an ample Palace, contains many mansions for every other kind of Knowledge (or renders it unnecessary); which deepens and extends the interest of every other (knowledge or faculty), gives it new charms and additional purpose: the study of which, rightly pursued, is beyond any other entertaining, beyond all others tends at once to *tranquillise* and *enliven*, to keep the mind elevated and stedfast, the Heart humble and tender." In this is the purest source of mental self-reliance, of self-dependence, and thence INDEPENDENCE, under all circumstances.

LETTERS, CONVERSATIONS,

AND

RECOLLECTIONS.

LETTER I.

DEAR SIR, *Jan. 28th*, 1818.

Your friendly letter was first delivered to me at the lecture-room door on yesterday evening, ten minutes before the lecture, and my spirits were so sadly depressed by the circumstance of my hoarseness, that I was literally incapable of reading it. I now express my acknowledgments, and with them the regret that I had not received the letter in time to have availed myself of it.

When I was young I used to laugh at flattery, as, on account of its absurdity, I now abhor it, from my repeated observations of its mischievous effects. Amongst these, not the least is, that it renders honourable natures more slow and reluctant in expressing their real feelings in praise of the deserving, than, for the interests of truth and virtue, might be desired. For the weakness of our moral and intellectual being, of which the comparatively strongest are often the most, and the most painfully conscious, needs the confirmation derived from the coincidence and sympathy of the friend, as much as the voice of honour within us denounces the pretences of the flatterer. Be assured, then, that I write as I think, when I tell you that, from the style and thoughts of your letter, I should have drawn a very different conclusion from that which you appear to have done, concerning both your talents and the cultivation which they have received. Both the matter and manner are manly, simple, and correct.

Had I the time in my power, compatibly with the performance of duties of immediate urgency, I would endeavour to give you, by letter, the most satisfactory answer to your questions that my reflections and the experience of my own fortunes could supply. But, at all events, I will not omit to avail myself of your judicious suggestion in my last lecture, in which it will form a consistent part of the subject and purpose of the discourse. Meantime, believe me, with great respect,

Your obliged fellow-student
of the true and the beseeming,
S. T. COLERIDGE.

The suggestion here alluded to was, if I remember rightly, as to the best mode of re-exciting that interest in and for mental cultivation and refinement, which, from lapse of time, had in most men actively employed, become dormant. This was fully treated in the last lecture.

LETTER II.

DEAR SIR, *Sept. 20th*, 1818.

Those who have hitherto chosen to take notice of me, as known to them only by my public character, have for the greater part taken out, not, indeed, a poetical, but a critical, license, to *make game* OF me, instead of sending game TO me. Thank heaven! I am in this respect more tough than tender. But, to be serious, I heartily thank you for your polite remembrance; and, though my feeble health and valetudinarian stomach force me to attach no little value to the present itself, I feel still more obliged by the kindness that prompted it.

I trust that you will not come within the purlieus of Highgate without giving me the opportunity of assuring you personally that I am, with sincere respect,

Your obliged,

T. Allsop, Esq. S. T. Coleridge.

LETTER III.

My Dear Sir, *Dec. 2nd*, 1818.

I cannot express how kind I felt your letter. Would to Heaven I had had many with feelings like yours, "accustomed to express themselves warmly and (as far as the word is applicable to you, even) enthusiastically." But, alas! during the prime manhood of my intellect I had nothing but cold water thrown on my efforts. I speak not now of my systematic and most unprovoked maligners. On *them* I have retorted only by pity and by prayer. These may have, and doubtless *have*, joined with the frivolity of "the reading public" in checking and almost in preventing the sale of my works; and so far have done injury to my *purse*. *Me* they have not injured. But I have loved with enthusiastic self-oblivion those who have been so well pleased that I should, year after year, flow with a hundred nameless rills into *their* main stream, that they could find nothing but cold praise and effective discouragement of every attempt of mine to roll onward in a distinct current of my own; who *admitted* that the Ancient Mariner, the Christabel, the Remorse, and some pages of the Friend were not without merit, but were abundantly anxious to acquit their judgments of any blindness to the very numerous defects. Yet they *knew* that to *praise*, as mere praise, I was characteristically, almost constitutionally, indifferent. In sympathy alone I found at once nourishment and stimulus; and for sympathy *alone* did my heart crave. They knew, too, how long and faithfully I had acted on the maxim, never to admit the *faults* of a work of genius to those who denied or were incapable of feeling and understanding the *beauties;* not from wilful partiality, but as well knowing that in *saying* truth I should, to such critics, convey falsehood. If, in one instance, in my literary life, I have appeared to deviate from this rule, first, it was not till the fame of the writer (which I had been for fourteen years successively toiling like a second Ali to build up) had been established; and, secondly and chiefly, with the purpose and, I may safely add, with the *effect* of rescuing the necessary task from Malignant Defamers, and in order to set forth the excellences and the trifling proportion which the defects bore to the excellences. But this, my dear sir, is a mistake to which affectionate natures are too liable, though I do not remember to have ever seen it noticed,—the mistaking those who are desirous and well pleased to be loved *by* you, for those who love you. Add, as a more general cause, the fact that I neither am nor ever have been of any party. What wonder, then, if I am left to decide which has been my worse enemy, the broad, pre-determined abuse of the Edinburgh Review, &c., or the cold and brief compliments, with the warm *regrets*, of the Quarterly? After all, however, I have now but one sorrow relative to the ill success of my literary toils (and toils they have been, *though not undelightful toils*), and this arises wholly from the almost insurmountable difficulties which the anxieties of to-day oppose to my completion of the great work, the form and materials of which it has been the employment of the best and most genial hours of the last twenty years to mature and collect.

If I could but have a tolerably numerous audience to my first, or first and second Lectures on the History of Philosophy, I should entertain a strong hope of success, because I know that these lectures will be found by far the most interesting and *entertaining* of any that I have yet delivered, independent of the more permanent interests of rememberable instruction. Few and unimportant would the errors of men be, if they did but know, first, *what they themselves meant;*

and, secondly, what the *words* mean by which they attempt to convey their meaning; and I can conceive no subject so well fitted to exemplify the mode and the importance of these two points as the History of Philosophy, treated as in the scheme of these lectures. Trusting that I shall shortly have the pleasure of seeing you here,

I remain, my dear Sir,

Yours, most sincerely,

T. Allsop, Esq. S. T. Coleridge.

This letter, as well as some more specific allusions and charges in after letters, I have thought it a sacred duty to publish; no admiration or reverence for the Great Living being for a moment to be placed against the higher duty to the greater, or, perhaps, I should say, the more greatly various, Dead. The conclusion to which I have come, from an intimate and thorough knowledge of the circumstances, is, that judged by all received rules, my much-loved friend had not *generous* usage. Far from me, however, be it to attribute blame; I am rather inclined to ascribe this seeming want of generous feeling of sympathy, to an incompatibility of adaptation. How expressive is this passage:—"In sympathy alone I found at once nourishment and stimulus; and for sympathy *alone* did my heart crave," coupled as it is in my knowledge with the mention of his labour for fourteen years to build up the fame of his friend; and how affecting the allusion to the mistake of having supposed "those to love him who were well pleased to be loved by him."

LETTER IV.

My dear Sir, *Highgate, Sept. 30th*, 1819.

Returned from Ramsgate, I hasten to assure you that, next to seeing you, I have pleasure in hearing from you: and wish the former in preference, not merely from the greater mutual enjoyment, but likewise because one can convey more, and with greater assurance of being understood, in an hour, than one could write in a day. On the other hand, letters are more permanent, and an epistolary correspondence more endearing, like all marks of remembrance in absence.

My sentiments concerning the expediency, and both moral and intellectual advantages, of a trade or profession, for such as fix their ultimate end on objects nobler than trades or professions can bestow on the most favoured of their followers, may be learnt from the eleventh chapter of my Literary Life, which, though addressed to a small and particular class, yet permits a more general application. To you, my dear young friend, I should say, temptations and preventives—the poisons and the antidotes—are pretty evenly dispersed through all the different accredited paths of life. Nay, those temptations which are foreknown and foreseen as most appertinent to our particular calling, are commonly least dangerous, or even cease to be temptations to a mind forearmed by principles and aspirations like yours. The false step is more likely to take place in the recoil than the advance; in the neglect rather than in the too eager pursuit of the means; in under, rather than over, valuing the advantages of wealth and worldly respectability. The true plan on which you should regulate your conduct and feelings, (that at least, which to me appears such) is the following. Propose to yourself from the present hour such views of action and enjoyment, as will make the leisure attached to independence, and honourably earned by previous industry, the fair object of a wise man's efforts and a good man's desires. Meantime, let the chosen *employments* of the years in *hope* be the *relaxations* of the time present, of the years devoted to present duties, and, among these, to the means of realising that hope; thus you will answer two great ends at once. Your inward trains of thought, your faculties, and your feelings, will be preserved in a fitness and, as it were, contempered to a life of ease, and capable of enjoying leisure, because both able and disposed to *employ* it. Secondly, while you thus render future affluence more and more desirable, you will at the same time prevent all undue impatience, and disarm the temptation of poisoning the allotted interval by *anxieties*, and anxious schemes and efforts to get rich *in haste*. There is yet one other inducement to look on your existing appointment with complacency. Every improvement in knowledge, and the moral power of wielding and directing it, will *tell for more*, — have a wider and more benignant influence,—than the same accomplishment would in a man who belonged to one of the learned professions. Both your information and your example will fall where they are most wanted, like the noiseless dews in Malta, where rain comes seldom and no regular streams are to be met with. As to your present studies, for such portions of your time as you can prudently appropriate to reading, without wrong to the claims of health and *social* relaxation, there is one department of knowledge, which, like an ample palace, contains within itself mansions for every other knowledge; which deepens and extends the interest of every other, gives it new charms and additional purpose; the study of which, rightly and *liberally* pursued, is beyond any other *entertaining*, beyond all others tends at once to tranquillize and enliven, to keep the mind elevated and stedfast, the heart humbler and tender: it is *biblical theology*—the philosophy of religion, the religion of philosophy. I would that I could refer you to any *book* in which such a plan of reading had been sketched out, in detail or even but generally.

Alas! I know of none. But most gladly will I make the attempt to supply this desideratum by conversation, and then by letter. But of this when I have next the pleasure of seeing you at Highgate.

You have perhaps heard that my publisher is a bankrupt.

*   *   *   *   *

*   *   *   *   *

*   *   *   *   *

All the profits from the sale of my writings, which I should have had, and which, in spite of the accumulated disadvantages under which the works were published, would have been considerable, I have lost; and not only so, but have been obliged, at a sum larger than all the profits made by my lectures, to purchase myself my own books and the half copyrights. Well, I am now *sole* proprietor, and representing my works by cyphers, and the author by I, my emblem might be 0000I. I have withdrawn them from sale. This is rather hard, but perhaps my comet may some time or other have its perihelion of popularity, and then the *tail*, you know, whisks round to the other end; and for 0000I, lo! and behold, 10,000. Meantime, enough for me to thank God that, relatively to my fellow men at least, I have been "sinned against, not sinning;" and relatively to my Maker, these afflictions are but penances of mercy, less than the least of my forfeitures.—I hope you will soon take pot-luck with us.

Believe me, with esteem and regard, yours,

T. Allsop, Esq. S. T. Coleridge.

Leaving out the particular expression of *biblical theology*, liable to be interpreted, or, rather, misinterpreted by every believer in belief according to his own particular faith or delusion, and keeping constantly in mind what the writer intended to convey, viz., the philosophy of humanity, the humanity of philosophy, I am not aware that I can recommend to your perusal, or press earnestly and affectionately upon your attention, any letter, essay, or advice, so beautifully expressed, or, when applied to practice, so well adapted to secure that happiness which surpasseth understanding; far, very far, surpasseth adequate expression. Often do I dwell upon the recommendation, to "let the chosen *employments* of the years in hope be the *relaxations* of the time present, of the years devoted to present duties, and, among these, to the means of realising that hope: thus you will answer two great ends at once. Your inward trains of thought, your faculties and your feelings, will be preserved in a fitness, and, as it were, contempered to a life of ease, and capable of enjoying leisure, because both able and disposed to *employ* it. Secondly; while you thus render affluence *more desirable*, you will prevent all undue impatience, and disarm the temptation of poisoning the allotted interval by *anxieties*, and anxious schemes and efforts to get rich *in haste*."

I would fain hope that, not only for you, but for all others, riches, *as such*, will be better appreciated ere your career commences; this is my anxious hope for others—for all. For you, it shall be my care to place before you irresistible examples and illustrations of the frightful evils of contemplating riches, power, fame, as *ends* to be sought and valued for their own sake, not as *means* to greater and higher *ends*,—the high aim and purpose of destroying these fruitful sources of crime and misery, or of subjecting them to *general* not *individual* advancement. Alas! could I but recal

"The time when, though my path was rough,
The joy within me dallied with distress,
And all misfortunes were but as the stuff
Whence Fancy made me dreams of happiness;
When hope grew round me like the twining vine,
And fruits and foliage, not my own, seemed mine:"

I might then have some hope of conveying to you with good effect the results of my experience.

"But seared thoughts now bow me down to earth,
Nor care I that they rob me of my mirth.
But, oh! each visitation
Suspends what nature gave me at my birth,
My shaping spirit of imagination.
For not to think of what I needs must feel,
But to be still and patient all I can,
And haply by abstruse research to steal
From my own nature all the natural man,—
This is my sole resource, my only plan;
Till that which suits a part infects the whole,
And now is almost grown the habit of my soul."

LETTER V.

MY DEAR SIR, *Dec.* 13*th*, 1819.

Accept my affectionate thanks; and, in mine, conceive those of my housemates included. Would to heaven I had more than barren thanks to offer you. If you, or rather your residence, were nearer to me, and I could have more of your society, I should feel this the less. It was, for me at least, unfortunate, that, almost every time you have been here, I should have been engaged in the only way that I should have suffered to be a pre-engagement, viz. the duties of friendship. These are now discharged; and whenever you can give me a day, henceforward, I shall have nothing to do but to enjoy it. I could not help "winning an hour from the hard season," as Milton says, the day before yesterday, by surrendering my reason to the detail of a day dream, as I was going over, and after I had gone over, a very pretty house, with beautiful garden and grounds, and a still more lovely prospect, at the moderate rent of £60 and taxes proportionally low, discussing the question with myself, as seriously as if it were actually to be decided, how far the rising at eight, breakfasting, and riding, driving, or staging to London, and returning by the stage or otherwise, would be advantageous to your health; and then the ways and means of improving and enjoying our Sundays, &c. All I can say in excuse of these air-built castles is, that they bring with them no bills for brick and mortar, no quarrels with the masons, no indignation at the deceits and lures of the architects, surveyor, &c., when the final expense is found to treble the amount of the well-paid and costly calculation: in short, that if they do no honour to the head, they leave no harm in the heart. And then, *poeta fuimus:* and the philosopher, though pressing with the weight of an Etna, cannot prevent the poet from occasionally changing sides, and manifesting his existence by smoke traversed by electrical flashes from the crater.

Have you seen Cobbett's last number? It is the most *plausible* and the best written of anything I have seen from *his* pen, and *apparently* written in a less fiendish spirit than the average of his weekly effusions. The self-complacency with which he assumes to himself exclusively, truths which he can call his own only as a horse-stealer can appropriate a stolen horse, by adding mutilation and deformities to robbery, is as *artful* as it is amusing. Still, however, he has given great additional publicity to weighty truths, as *ex. gr.* the hollowness of *commercial* wealth; and from whatever dirty corner or straw moppet the ventriloquist Truth causes her words to proceed, I not only listen, but must bear witness that it is Truth talking. His conclusions, however, are palpably absurd—give to an over-peopled island the countless back settlements of America, and countless balloons to carry thither man and maid, wife and brat, beast and baggage—and then we might rationally expect that a general crash of trade, manufactures, and credit, might be as mere a summer thunderstorm in Great Britain as he represents it to be in America.

One deep, most deep, impression of melancholy, did Cobbett's letter to Lord Liverpool leave on my mind,—the conviction that, wretch as he is, he is an overmatch in intellect for those, in whose hands Providence, in its retributive justice, seems to place the destinies of our country; and who yet rise into respectability, when we compare them with their parliamentary opponents.

I am commanded to add an especial request, that it may not be long before you make yourself visible on the banks of Lake Superior.

Ever, my dear sir,
Yours faithfully and affectionately,

T. Allsop, Esq. S. T. Coleridge.

The tendency of the age is now decidedly practical, and the advocates of abstractions will do well to admit the superiority of practical knowledge; and to lay claim to it as springing directly from their speculations, from their generalizations. The very opinions here said to be heretical and damnable, are now held (such is the rapid advance of public opinion) to be stale and common-place, and have already given way to a far more searching inquiry into the nature and uses of *all* property. When we see a man so highly gifted, so far differing from the common sense of his contemporaries and immediate successors, stigmatize as a wretch, one of the most extraordinary writers of the day, for holding opinions which those contemporaries have for the greatest part adopted, and many gone far beyond, we are forcibly struck with the absurdity of all ille-isms or affirmations. If we confine ourselves to the expression of an opinion, or, if more honest, we confess our ignorance of the matter at issue, we shall be more likely to *approach* true conclusions.

Neither is it the fact, that Cobbett claimed himself to be the discoverer of any or all of the principles he advanced or advocated; he combined the scattered truths of Paine and the preceding writers into a practical shape; and in that form he has brought them forward *so clearly*, so often, and in so many ways, that he has forced the attention of his countrymen to the CAUSES of the evils by which they are environed; so impressed with the importance of those principles, that he will take no denial; but, at the sacrifice of ease, and that loved country-life, and those rural pursuits, in the midst of which he is so happy, and so fond of creating happiness, he prostrates opposition, and is determined that what he has devoted his whole life to make easy to the meanest capacity, shall not perish for want of a fair trial. That Cobbett himself commits the same injustice towards others, I well know; but this proceeds in his case from an impatience of any remedies but his own, *until his own has been tried.* To you, to whom personal controversies will, as I hope, be pitiable, if not painful, I would say, that speculation upon the cause of an evil, is, like the punishment of a crime, useless in remedying *that* crime, and is only useful, *if useful at all*, in preventing *future* crimes or evils. The direction of *existing* powers and combinations, and the formation of new combinations, upon scientific and practical principles, are the matters of most importance at this time; and the knowledge necessary to the attainment and application of these principles, does not to me appear likely to be attained whilst men are in a state of social warfare; whilst the immediate or apparent interests of one man are constantly opposed to those of another, and *both*, impediments to the well-being of the whole.

LETTER VI.

MY DEAR SIR, *20th March*, 1820.

You must have thought it strange that I had taken no notice of so kind a letter from you; but the truth is, I received the little packet supposing it to contain the Cobbett only, put it in my pocket for my reading at a leisure hour, and had not opened it until the day before I last saw you. Within a few days, I hope to lay myself open to you in an express letter; till when, I can only say, that the affectionate interest you have taken in my well-being, has been not only a comfort but a spur, when I needed both, and was almost yielding at times to the apprehension, that I had sacrificed all that the world holds precious, without being able to do any effective good in a higher and nobler kind. I have sent the three volumes of the Friend, with my MS. corrections, and additions. The largest, that towards the end of the last *philosophical* essay in the third volume, had a two-fold object—to guard my own character from the suspicion of pantheistic opinions, or Spinosism (it *was* written, though not so much at large, before the work was printed, and omitted by wilfulness, or such carelessness as does not fall far short of it); and next, to impress, as far as I could, the conviction that true philosophy, so far from having any tendency to unsettle the *principles* of faith, that may and ought to be common to all men, does itself actually require them as its premises; nay, that it supposes them as its ground.*—I was highly gratified to hear, and from such a man too as Mr. John Hookham Frere, that a man of rank, and of a highly cultivated mind, who had become reluctantly a sceptic, or something more, respecting the Christian Religion, wholly in consequence of studying Leland, Lardner, Watson, Paley, and other defenders of the Gospel on the strength of the *external* evidences—not of Christianity, but of the miracles with which its first preaching was accompanied—and of having been taught to regard the arguments, and mode of proof adopted in the works above mentioned, as the only rational ones, had read the Friend with great attention, and when he came to the passage in which I had explained the nature of miracles, their necessary dependance on a credible religion for their own credibility, &c., dropped the book (as he himself informed Mr. Frere), and exclaimed, "Thank God! I can still believe in the Gospel—I can yet be a Christian." The remark that a miracle, divested of all connection with a doctrine, is identical with witchcraft, which in all ages has been regarded with instinctive horror by the human mind, and the reference to our Lord's own declarations concerning miracles, were among the passages that particularly impressed his mind.

I should have sent a corrected copy of the Sibylline Leaves; but for a two-legged little *accident* having torn out two leaves at the beginning, and I will no longer delay this parcel, but will transcribe at another time what I had written in them, and I hope it will not be long before you let us see you. The people

* Though myself opposed to apologetic prefaces or modifications of opinion to suit conventional influences, I give this note as an act of justice to its author.

here are occupied in raising and distributing relief for the poor of the hamlet. On the first day there were seven hundred and fifty applicants to whom small sums were given! It would be most un-christian moroseness not to feel delight in the unwearied zeal with which every mode and direction of charity is supported; and I hope that this is a sunshiny spot in our national character, and that this virtue will suspend the judgments that threaten the land. But it would, on the other hand, be wilful blindness not to see that the lower orders become more and more improvident in consequence, more and more exchange the sentiments of Englishmen for the feelings of Lazzaroni.

God bless you; and, S. T. COLERIDGE.

P.S.—Charles and Mary Lamb dined with us on Sunday.

When I next see you, that excellent brother and sister will supply me with half an hour's interesting conversation. When you know the *whole* of him, you will love him in spite of all oddities and even faults—nay, I had almost said, *for* them—*at least*, admire that under his visitations they were so few and of so little importance. Thank God, his circumstances are comfortable; and so they ought, for he has been in the India House since his fourteenth year.

I have subjoined the MS. addition mentioned above, and should wish you to read it with great care and attention in its proper place; which is, after the word 'vacuum,' in page 263, vol. iii. of the 'Friend.'

If we thoughtfully review the course of argument pursued, we shall rest in the following as our sum and ultimatum. The dialectic intellect, by exertion of its own powers exclusively, may enable us to affirm the reality of an absolute Being, generally. But here it stops. It can command neither insight nor conviction concerning the existence (or even the possibility) of the world as distinct and different from Deity. It finds itself constrained to confound the Creator with the creation; and then, cutting the knot it cannot solve, merges the latter in the former, and denies reality to all finite existence. But here the philosophizer is condemned to meet with his sure confutation in his own secret dissatisfaction, and is forced at length to shelter himself from his own importunate queries in the wretched evasion, that of Nothings no solution can be required. Wretched indeed, and weak as desperate! Nature herself—his own inevitable Nature—through every organ of sense, compels his own abused reason to reiterate the demand: How and whence did this sterile Nothing split or multiply into *plurality*? Whence this portentous transnihilation of Nothing into Nothings? What, above all, is that inward mirror, the human mind, in and for which these Nothings possess at least a relative existence? Or dost thou wait till, with a more bitter irony, Pain and Anguish and Remorse ask thee, Are WE too Nothings?

O youthful reader! (for such The Friend dares anticipate), thou, that in my mind's eye, standest beside me, like my own youth! Fresh and keen as the morning Hunter in the pursuit of Truth, glad and restless in the feeling of mental growth! O learn early, that if the Head be the Light of the Heart, the Heart is the Life of the Head: yea, that Consciousness itself, that Consciousness of which all reasoning is the varied modification, is but the Reflex of the Conscience when most luminous; and too often a fatuous vapour, a warmthless bewildering mockery of Light, exhaled from its corruption or stagnation. Mark the inevitable result of all *consequent* reasoning, when the intellect refuses to acknowledge a higher and deeper ground than itself can supply, and weens to possess within itself the centre of its own system! From Zeno the Eleatrice to Spinoza, and from Spinoza to Schelling, Oken, and the German "*Natur-philosophen*" of the present day, the Result has been, and ever must be, PANTHEISM, under some one or other of its modes or disguises: and it is of awful importance to the speculative Inquirer to be aware, that the seemliest of these modes differs from the most repulsive, not in its consequences, which in all alike are Atheistic, but only as far as it evinces the efforts of the individual to hide these consequences from his own consciousness.

This, then, I again repeat, is our ultimate conclusion. All *speculative* disquisition must begin with *Postulates*, authorised and substantiated by the conscience exclusively. From whatever point the reason may start, whether from the *Things that are seen* to the One Invisible, or from the idea of the ABSOLUTE ONE to the *things that are seen*, it will in either case find a chasm, which the moral being, the *spirit* and the *religion* of man, can alone fill up or overbridge. "THE LIFE IS THE LIGHT OF MAN:" and "WE LIVE BY FAITH."

I may as well state here that the writer, possessing confessedly great and extraordinary powers, has been wholly and entirely misconceived, and by none more so than those who fondly deemed him of *their* belief. *His belief* was so capacious that it contained not only theirs and a hundred others, but also their opposites, and existed in the equipoise or equilibrium. Thus in speaking as was his wont, of Peter, towards whom he felt an especial distaste, he was accustomed to refer to the passage in Matthew, ch. xix. ver. 27, where the Janitor asks, "Behold, we have forsaken all, and followed thee ; what shall we have therefore?" and in a humorous strain of contemptuous remark, exhibit the selfishness of the (in mind) vulgar fisherman who, having left a wretched and precarious calling, seeks to make of this a merit, and to demand a reward for that which could only be a merit, as it did not seek to obtain any earthly reward or advantage. It ought to be known that many men in these latter days, many even from the especial land of cant and *notions*, used to seek to pick up the crumbs from his mental banquets; and, as these were chiefly weak-minded and superstitious men, with a few men of strong heads and minim hearts, which latter class are *not*, however, *self-deceived*, he was led, being then feeble in health, to assent to their conclusions, seeing that between minds like theirs and his giant intellect an impassable chasm existed; in short, for peace' sake he humoured them, and for sympathy, as he used to say of Cromwell, spoke in the language but not in the sense of the canters.

Charles and Mary Lamb! what recollections, pleasant and painful, do these twin names recall. Well do I remember the first time I met this most delightful couple, and the kindness with which I was received and greeted by this twin union in partition; now, alas! for a short time separated. No man that I have ever known was so well fitted to attract and engage the sympathies, the love, the affectionate regards, and the respect of ingenuous natures. To all others his heart was (I will not say closed) unresponsive. To you, my dear children, who from your earliest years have been familiar with his incomings, the impression made by the remarkable appearance of this *model-man*, his kindness, his expressive and pensive face and figure, must, and ever will remain; would that I could even faintly shadow out the more admirable qualities of his mind. Utterly unlike any or all of his contemporaries, having had his lot cast in hard places, he yet by a sweetness, an uncomplainingness the very opposite, however, of torpid sorrow or resignation, had fashioned for himself a happiness, a well-being peculiarly his own. To a sound mind in a sound body, if we take sound to mean robust, my kind and gentle-hearted friend had no claim; but out of his very infirmities had he made delights for himself and for all those who had the unspeakable privilege of his intimacy. When I think of this loved and loveable being, and of all he has been to me, I am almost tempted to repine at that inevitable destiny by which our being is borne onwards; an absurdity than which nothing can be more deplorable, if indeed *that* were not *necessary*. Often as the recollection of that familiar face flits across my memory, and the consciousness that I cannot, as heretofore, meet him in his old haunts, or see him walk in as was his wont frequently, I am tempted to repeat his own lines.

"A month or more hath he been dead,
Yet cannot I by force be led
To think on him and the wormy bed
Together.

"My sprightly neighbour, gone before
To that unknown and silent shore;
Shall we not meet as heretofore
Some summer morning?"

What a beautiful thing is faith, if it would but last for ever.

The following lines from a short poem in the Sibylline Leaves, will more vividly impress you, if you should ever be able to catch the particular, the very peculiar cadence or rhythm, which of right belongs to the poetry of Coleridge in somewhat the same relation as a tune to a song, and without which it would not be a song.

——— "Yes! they wander on
In gladness all; but thou, methinks, most glad,
My gentle hearted Charles! for thou hast pined
And hungered after Nature many a year,
In the great city pent, winning thy way
With sad yet patient soul, through evil and pain
And strange calamity . . . Henceforth I shall know
That Nature ne'er deserts the wise and pure,
No plot so narrow, be but Nature there,
No waste so vacant, but may well employ
Each faculty of sense, and keep the heart
Awake to Love and Beauty! *and sometimes*
'Tis well to be bereft of promised good,
That we may lift the soul and contemplate
With lively joy, the joys we cannot share.
My gentle hearted Charles! when the last rook
Beat its straight path along the dusky air
Homewards, I blest it! deeming, its black wing
(Now a dim speck, now vanishing in light)
Had crossed the mighty orb's dilated glory,
While thou stoodst gazing; or, when all was still,
Flew creaking o'er thy head, *and had a charm*
For thee, my gentle hearted Charles, *to whom*
No sound is dissonant that tells of life."

I have said that I never knew any one who at all approached or resembled our delightful housemate. I am wrong; I once met a man with his smile,—HIS smile. There is nothing like it upon earth; unless, perchance, this man survives. And yet how unlike in every other regard personal and mental; not that the man, who had by some most extraordinary means acquired or appropriated this *sunshine of the face,* was at all deficient in mental qualities. He seemed amiable, thoughtful, and introspective; a man better than his condition, or rather, his calling. He was, I believe, a stock-broker, and had been with his son to traverse the haunts of his childhood, near Lymington; *with his son*, afflicted with a sudden and complete deafness; hence, perchance, these sweet smiles springing from, and compounded of, love and pain. Yet this man had never known Lamb; still his smile was the same—the *self*-same expression on a different face,—if, indeed, whilst that smile passed over it, you could see any difference. I mentioned this strange encounter to Coleridge, and he immediately constructed a most delightful theory of association, and corroborated it with so many instances, that he must have been sceptical that could *at the moment* have refused him credence. To those who wish to see the only thing left on earth, *if it is still left*, of Lamb, his best and most beautiful remain,—his smile, I will indicate its possessor,—Mr. Harman, of Throgmorton Street.

Subjoined is a tribute of love and admiration from one least fitted by genius and intellectual sympathies to appreciate the loved being so much deplored. If, to this disciple of the useful and the prudent, Lamb appeared so worthy of homage, judge you what he was to me, and to a herd, each more worthy than I. If by a Scotchman, with whom as a nation and as individuals he acknowledged no sympathy, he was esteemed and reverenced, think what must be the loss to those better fitted, by position and by sympathy, to *relish* and enter into his opinions and pursuits. Contrast this tribute, forced as it were, from strange lips, with the reminiscences of one on whom all his kindness and self-devotion were lavished, and upon whom his charities both of mind and purse were poured out even to self-sacrifice, and then bear in mind that gratitude is a feeble flame, which needs constantly to be kept alive by a repetition of benefits, or that IN IMPROVIDENT NATURES it gives place to rancorous disparagement, even after death.

"One of the conductors of this journal did justice to a long-cherished and deeply-rooted admiration of this writer, by making a kind of pilgrimage to his house at Edmonton, where a letter from a mutual friend introduced him to the presence of one whom he would willingly have gone ten times farther to see. All stranger as he was, he had the gratification of experiencing a share—and he thought it a large one—of that kindness which Mr. Lamb had in store for all his fellow-creatures; and, after an hour's conversation, parted with the object of his journey near the famed 'Bell,' carrying with him *a profound sense of the excellence of one of the finest model-beings whom it ever was his fortune to meet*."—*Chambers' Journal.*

LETTER VII.

MY DEAR FRIEND, *Highgate, April 10th*, 1820.

May I venture to obtrude on you what I cannot intrust to a messenger, much less to the post. Sackville-street is not I hope more than fifteen or twenty minutes' walk from your house. It is to inquire if Mr. Caldwell is *in town;* if he be, then to leave the letter, and that is all; but if not, to learn whether he is at his living, and if so, then to transfer his present address to the letter, and put it into the nearest General Post Office box. It is of serious importance to Derwent that the inclosed should reach Mr. Caldwell with as little delay as possible, or I need not say that I should not have taxed your time and kindness merely to make a letter-carrier of you.

On Saturday evening I received a note from Mathews, which I have inclosed. I took it very kind of him; but to obtrude myself on Walter Scott, *nolentem volentem*, and within a furlong of my own abode, as he knows (for Mr. Frere told him my address), was a liberty I had no right to take; and though it would have highly gratified me to have conversed with a brother bard, and to have renewed on the mental retina the image of, perhaps, the most extraordinary man, assuredly the most *extraordinary* writer, of his age, yet I dared not purchase the gratification at so high a price as that of risking the respect which I trust has not hitherto been forfeited by,

My dear friend,

Your obliged and very affectionate friend,

T. Allsop, Esq. S. T. COLERIDGE.

P.S. I had not the least expectation, yet I could not suppress a sort of fluttering hope, that my letter might have reached you on Saturday night, and that you might be disengaged and turn your walk Highgate-ward. You will be delighted with the affectionate attachment of the two brothers to each other, the boyish high spirits with manly independence of intellect, and, in one word, with the simplicity which is their nature, and the common *ground* on which the differences of their mind and characters (for no two can be more distinct) shoot and play. When I say that nothing can exceed their fondness for their father, I need not add that they are impatient to be introduced to you. And I can offer no better testimony of the rank you hold in my bosom, my dear Allsop, than the gladness with which I anticipate their becoming your *friends*, in the noblest sense of the word. Would to Heaven their dear sister were with us, the cup of paternal joy would be full to the brim! The rapture with which both Hartley and Derwent talk of her, quite affects Mrs. Gillman, who has always felt with a sort of lofty yet refined enthusiasm respecting the relations of an only sister to her brothers. Of all women I ever knew, Mrs. G. is the woman who seems to have been framed by Nature for a heroine in that rare species of love which subsists in a tri-unity of the heart, the moral sense, and the faculty, corresponding to what Spurzheim calls the organ of *ideality*. What in other women is *refinement* exists in her as by implication, and, *à fortiori*, in a native *fineness* of character. She often represents to my mind the best parts of the Spanish Santa Teresa, ladyhood of nature.

Vexation! and Mrs. Gillman has this moment burnt

Mathews' note. The purport, however, was as follows :—" I have just received a note from Terry, informing me that Sir Walter Scott will call upon me to-morrow morning (*i. e.* Sunday) at half-past eleven. Will you contrive to be here at the same time? Perhaps the promise of your company may induce Sir Walter to appoint a day on which he will dine with me before he returns to the north."

Now as Scott had asked Terry for my address on his first arrival in town, it is not *impossible*, though not very probable, that Terry may have said,—" You will meet Coleridge at Mathews's," though I was not entitled to presume this. The bottom of all this, my dear friend, is neither more nor less than as follows :—I seem to feel that I *ought* to feel more desire to see an extraordinary man than than I really do feel; and I do not wish to appear to two or three persons (as the Mr. Freres, William Rose, &c.), as if I cherished any dislike to Scott respecting the *Christabel*, and generally an increasing dislike to appear out of the common and natural mode of thinking and acting. All this is, I own, sad weakness, but I am weary of *dyspathy*.

In this last sentence may be read the whole secret of the writer's latter days. In thought, action, opinion, he always sought for harmony and agreement, and frequently created a harmony of his own. Hence his dislike of, and distaste for, the new sciences, *so called*, of Political Economy and the Utilitarian Philosophy, in which nothing is proved, nothing settled, and with respect to the very elements of which no two professors are agreed. When one of the self-sufficient of this last class, now so numerous as to infest, beset, and defile all places of public resort where anything is to be obtained, was controverting one of the more profound opinions of Coleridge, upon which he had brought to bear, *but not exhausted*, all the stores of a mind perfectly unequalled, both with respect to the mass of knowledge,—nay more, true wisdom,—and the eloquence with which that knowledge was adorned, and asserting, in opposition to views, to the comprehension of the least of which his mechanical mind was unequal, that the tendency of public opinion and the state of things was in another direction, Coleridge, taking up the down of a thistle which lay by the road side, and holding it up, said, after observing the direction in which it was born by the wind,—"The tendency of that thistle is towards China, but I know with assured certainty that it will never get there; nay, that it is more than probable that, after sundry eddyings and gyrations up and down, backwards and forwards, that it will be found somewhere near the place in which it grew." Then, turning to me,—"I refer to your experience, if you ever knew the probabilities, the suppositions of any man or set of men, realised in their main features, *permanently*. No! no! Hence, such institutions as poor laws have never answered, never can answer, unless the framers could compel society to remain in the same state as when these laws or regulations were made, which is a manifest absurdity. It was not the barbarism of our forefathers, as is so complacently taken for granted, but the flux and change of events which unfit *all laws* for after-times. Bishop Berkely, in his imaginary travels, shows very ingeniously the evil of all laws; and I have no doubt that the time will arrive when all penal laws will be held to be barbarous, and proofs of the barbarism of this and all antecedent ages."

LETTER VIII.

MY DEAR FRIEND, *Highgate, April 8th*, 1820.

It is not the least advantage of friendship, that by communicating our thoughts to another, we render them distinct to ourselves, and reduce the subjects of our sorrow and anxiety to their just magnitude for our own contemplation.

As long as we inly brood over a misfortune (there being no divisions or separate circumscriptions in things of mind, no *proper* beginning nor ending to any thought, on the one hand; and, on the other, the confluence of our recollections being determined far more by sameness or similarity of the feelings that have been produced by them, than by any positive resemblance or connection between the things themselves that are thus recalled to our attention) we establish a centre, as it were, a sort of nucleus in the reservoir of the soul; and toward this, needle shoots after needle, cluster points on cluster points, from all parts of contained fluid, and in all directions, till the mind with its best faculties is locked up in one ungenial frost. I cannot adequately express the state of feeling in which I wrote my last letter; the letter itself, I doubt not, bore evidence of its *nest* and mode of incubation, as certain birds and lizards drag along with them part of the egg-shells from which they had forced their way. Still one good end was answered. I had made a clearance, so far as to have my head in light and my eyes open; and your answer, every way worthy of you, has removed the rest.

But before I enter on this subject, permit me to refer to some points of *comparative* indifference, lest I should forget them altogether. I occasioned you to misconceive me respecting Sir Walter Scott. My purpose was to bring proofs of the energetic or inenergetic state of the minds of men, induced by the excess and unintermitted action of stimulating events and circumstances,—revolutions, battles, *newspapers*, mobs, sedition and treason trials, public harangues, meetings, dinners; the necessity in every individual of ever increasing activity and anxiety in the improvement of his estate, trade, &c., in proportion to the decrease of the actual value of money, to the multiplication of competitors, and to the almost compulsory expedience of expense, and prominence, even as the means of obtaining or retaining competence; the consequent craving after amusement as proper *relaxation*, as *rest* freed from the tedium of vacancy; and, again, after such knowledge and such acquirements as are *ready coin*, that will pass *at once*, unweighed and unassayed; to the unexampled facilities afforded for this end by reviews, magazines, &c., &c. The theatres, to which few go to see *a play*, but to see Master Betty or Mr. Kean, or some one individual in some *one* part: and the single fact that our neighbour, Mathews, has taken more, night after night, than both the regular theatres conjointly, and when the best comedies or whole plays have been acted at each house, and those by excellent comedians, would have yielded a striking instance, and illustration of my position. But I chose an example in literature, as more in point for the subject of my particular remarks, and because every man of genius, who is born for his age, and capable of acting *immediately* and widely on that age, must of necessity *reflect* the age in the first instance, though as far as he is a man of genius, he will doubtless be himself reflected by it reciprocally. Now I selected Scott for the very reason, that I do hold him for a man of *very extraordinary* powers; and when I say that I have read the far greater part of his novels twice, and several three times over, with undiminished pleasure and interest; and that, in my reprobation of the Bride of Lammermoor (with the exception, however, of the almost Shakspearian old witch-wives at the funeral) and of the Ivanhoe, I mean to imply the grounds of my admiration of the others, and the permanent nature of the interest which they excite. In a word, I am far from thinking that Old Mortality or Guy Mannering would have been less admired in the age of Sterne, Fielding, and Richardson, than they are in the present times; but only that Sterne, &c., would not have had the same *immediate* popularity in the present day as in their own less stimulated and, therefore, less languid reading world.

Of Sir Walter Scott's poems I cannot speak so highly, still less of the Poetry in his Poems; though even in these the power of presenting the most numerous figures, and figures with the most complex movements, and under rapid succession, in *true picturesque unity*, attests true and peculiar genius. You cannot imagine with how much pain I used, many years ago, to hear ———'s contemptuous assertions respecting Scott; and if I mistake not, I have yet the fragments of the rough draft of a letter written by me so long ago as my first lectures at the London Philosophical Society, Fetter Lane, and on the backs of the unused admission tickets.

One more remark. My criticism was *confined* to the one point of the higher degree of intellectual activity implied in the reading and admiration of Fielding, Richardson, and Sterne;—in moral, or, if that be too high and inwardly a word, in *mannerly* manliness of taste the present age and its *best* writers have the decided advantage, and I sincerely trust that Walter Scott's readers would be as little disposed to relish the stupid lechery of the courtship of Widow Wadman, as Scott himself would be capable of presenting it. And, that though I cannot pretend to have found in any of these novels a character that even approaches in genius, in truth of conception, or boldness and freshness of execution, to Parson Adams, Blifil, Strap, Lieutenant Bowling, Mr. Shandy, Uncle Toby and Trim, and Lovelace; and though Scott's *female* characters will not, even the very best, bear a comparison with Miss Byron, Clementina Emily, in Sir Charles Grandison; nor the comic ones with Tabitha Bramble, or with Betty (in Mrs. Bennet's Beggar Girl); and though, by the use of the Scotch dialect, by Ossianic mock-highland motley-heroic, and by extracts from the printed sermons, memoirs, &c., of the fanatic preachers, there is a good deal of *false effect* and stage trick: still the number of characters *so good* produced by one man, and in so rapid a succession, must ever remain an illustrious phenomenon in literature, after all the subtractions for those borrowed from English and German sources, or compounded by blending two or three of the old drama into one—*ex. gr.* the Caleb in the Bride of Lammermoor.

Scott's great merit, and, at the same time, his *felicity*, and the true solution of the long-sustained *interest* novel after novel excited, lie in the nature of the subject; not merely, or even chiefly, because the struggle between the Stuarts and the Presbyterians and sectaries, is still in lively memory, and the passions of the adherency to the former, if not the adherency itself, extant in our own fathers' or grandfathers' times; nor yet (though this is of great weight) because the language, manners, &c., introduced are sufficiently different from our own for *poignancy*, and yet sufficiently near and similar for sympathy; nor yet because, for the same reason, the author, speaking, reflecting, and descanting in his own person, remains still (to adopt a painter's phrase) in sufficient *keeping* with his subject matter, while his characters can both talk and feel interesting to *us* as men, without recourse to *antiquarian* interest, and nevertheless without moral anachronism (in all which points the Ivanhoe is so wofully the contrary, for what Englishman cares for Saxon or Norman, both brutal invaders, more than for Chinese and Cochin-Chinese?)—yet great as all these causes are, the essential wisdom and happiness of the subject consists in this,—that the contest between the loyalists and their opponents can never be *obsolete*, for it is the contest between the two great moving principles of social humanity; religious adherence to the past and the ancient, the desire and the admiration of permanence, on the one hand; and the passion for increase of knowledge, for truth, as the offspring of reason—in short, the mighty instincts of *progression* and *free agency*, on the other. In all subjects of deep and lasting interest, you will detect a struggle between two opposites, two polar forces, both of which are alike necessary to our human well-being, and necessary each to the continued existence of the other. Well, therefore, may we contemplate with intense feelings those whirlwinds which are for free agents the appointed means, and the only possible condition of that equilibrium in which our moral Being subsists; while the disturbance of the same constitutes our sense of life. Thus in the ancient Tragedy, the lofty struggle between irresistible fate and unconquerable free will, which finds its equilibrium in the Providence and the future retribution of Christianity. If, instead of a contest between Saxons and Normans, or the Fantees and Ashantees,—a mere contest of indifferents! of minim surges in a boiling fish-kettle,—Walter Scott had taken the struggle between the men of arts and the men of arms in the time of Becket, and made us feel how much to claim our well-wishing there was in the cause and character of the priestly and papal party, no less than in those of Henry and his knights, he would have opened a new mine, instead of translating into Leadenhall Street Minerva Library sentences, a cento of the most common incidents of the stately self-congruous romances of D'Urfe, Scuderi, &c. N.B. I have not read the Monastery, but I suspect that the thought or element of the faery work is from the German. I perceive from that passage in the Old Mortality, where Morton is discovered by old Alice in consequence of calling his dog Elphin, that Walter Scott has been reading Tieck's Phantasies (a collection of faery or witch tales), from which both the incident and name is borrowed.

I forget whether I ever mentioned to you, that some eighteen months ago I had planned and half collected, half manufactured and invented a work, to be entitled *The Weather-*BOUND *Traveller;* or, Histories, Lays, Legends, Incidents, Anecdotes, and Remarks, contributed during a detention in one of the Hebrides, recorded by their Secretary, Lory McHaroldson, Senachy in the Isle of ——.

The principle of the work I had thus expressed in the first chapter:—"Though not *fact*, must it needs be false? These things have a truth of their own, if we but knew how to look for it. There is a *humanity* (meaning by this word whatever contradistinguishes man), there is a humanity common to all periods of life, which each *period* from childhood has its own way of representing. Hence, in whatever laid firm hold of us in early life, there lurks an interest and a charm for our maturest years, but which *he* will never draw forth, who, content with mimicking the unessential, though natural defects of thought and expression, has not the skill to remove the *childish*, yet leave the *childlike* untouched. Let each of us then relate that which has left the deepest impression on his mind, at whatever period of his life he may have seen, heard, or read it; but let him tell it in accordance with the *present state* of his intellect and feelings, even as he has, perhaps (Alnaschar-like), acted it over again by the parlour fire-side of a rustic inn, with the fire and the candles for his only companions."

On the hope of my Lectures answering, I had intended to have done this work out of hand, dedicating the most genial hours to the completion of Christabel, in the belief that in the former I should be rekindling the feeling, and recalling the state of mind, suitable to the latter.—But the Hope was vain.

In stating the names and probable size of my works, I by no means meant any reference to the mode of their publication; I merely wished to communicate to you the amount of my labours. In two moderate volumes it was my intention to comprise all those more prominent and systematic parts of my lucubrations on Shakspeare as should be published (in the first instance at least, in the form of books), and having selected and arranged them, to send the more particular illustrations and analysis to some respectable magazine. In like manner, I proposed to include the philosophical critiques on Dante, Milton, Cervantes, &c., in a series of Letters entitled The Reviewer in Exile, or Critic confined to an Old Library. Provided the truths (which are, I dare affirm, original, and all tending to the same principles, and proving the endless fertility of true principle, and the decision and power of growth which it communicates to all the faculties of the mind) are but in existence, and to be read by such as might wish to read, I have no choice as to the mode; nay, I should prefer that mode which most multiplied the chances.—So too as to the order.—For *many* reasons, it had been my wish to commence with the Theological Letters: one, and not the least, is the strong desire I have to put you and Hartley and Derwent Coleridge in full possession of my whole Christian creed, with the grounds of reason and authority on which it rests; but especially to unfold the true "glorious liberty of the Gospel," by showing the distinction between doctrinal faith and its sources and historical belief, with their reciprocal action on each other; and thus, on the one hand, to do away the servile superstition which makes men *Bibliolators*, and yet hides from them the proper excellences, the one continued revelation of the Bible documents, which they idolise; and, on the other hand, to expose, in its native worthlessness, the so-called evidences of Christianity first brought into *toleration* by Arminius, and into fashion by Grotius and the Socinian divines: for as such I consider all those who preach and teach in the spirit of Socinianism, though even in the outward form of a defence of the thirty-nine articles.

I have been interrupted by the arrival of my sons, Hartley and Derwent, the latter of whom I had not seen for so dreary a time. I promise myself great pleasure in introducing him to you. Hartley you have already met. Indeed, I am so desirous of this, that I will defer what I have to add, that I may put this letter in the post, time enough for you to receive it this evening; saying only, that it was not my purpose to have had any further communication on the subject but with Mr. Frere, and with him only as a counsellor. Let me see you as soon as you can and as often. I shall be better able hereafter to talk with you than to write to you on the contents of your last.

Your very affectionate friend,

T. Allsop, Esq. S. T. Coleridge.

If it had been possible for the writer of *this* letter to have been both oracle and priest (or rather popular expounder), then indeed should we have wanted little (for the present time at least) in the way of aids to knowledge in its highest aim and tendency. But powers like his have never yet existed in conjunction with familiar and popular elucidation. There was nothing shapeless and unmeaning in anything he ever said or wrote. There were no crudities, no *easy* reading in his productions. To follow the train of his reasoning demanded *at first* severe and continued attention; and to this how few of the self-called seekers after that knowledge which is truth are equal. To him, details were of little value, except as far as they illustrated, proved, a principle; whilst to the greater part of those who latterly became his hearers, they constituted the only part of his conversation which was intelligible or of the least interest. Would that it were possible to recall some of those delightful tales which my friend used to relate in his inimitable manner, as forming part of the collection existing in his mind of the "Weather-bound Traveller." Myself a proficient when a youth as a *raconteur*, I was still surprised at the extraordinary ease with which he produced story after story, each more incredible, more mystic, and more abounding with materials for future meditation, than the one preceding. Ardently do I hope that the fragments above alluded to have been saved, and that the worthy and excellent friend to whom they are confided will give them to the world as he finds them.

The allusion to the Socinians may need some explanation. Having for a short time, in early youth, been a convert to what is now called Unitarianism, through the instrumentality of a Mr. Friend, of Cambridge (no friend to him), he had opportunities of free and unrestrained intercourse and intercommunion with the more influential and distinguished of this sect; and the result was a conviction of the insincerity (conscious or otherwise), selfishness, or, as he expressed it, self-centering, and want of moral courage, produced by this faith, or, as he again termed it, this want of faith. That this was the fact at that time, I am willing to admit; but my own experience, my own *knowledge*, of many who delight in, or *endure* this name, leads me to the conclusion, that a change has come over their spirit. To the charge of want of moral courage they appear as obnoxious now as at any previous period: nay, more—for in the earlier period of their history, the very expression of *these* opinions was an act of great moral daring; whilst at this time, when toleration is universal, it would be more in unison with that universal progression which we see in every other sect and party, to find them casting away the small remnant of superstition which they have hitherto retained, out of consideration, as it should seem, to the fouler superstitions and mental degradation by which they are still surrounded.

But my excellent friend had another cause of quarrel with this sect. He saw with what readiness they received and adopted the atrocious, the, *in any*, *in every* sense, hateful opinions and views of Malthus and the so called economists; a sect and a class having about as much title to that name (as first generally given to Turgot and his associates), as a crab to an apple, or a mule to a race-horse. This he attributed to the selfish and cold character of minds in which neither imagination nor love had a place, and to the restlessness superinduced by the absence of those two faculties. To observations as to their being the slaves of the circumstances by which they were surrounded, or to the education which they had received, he opposed the fact, that they were all to a great degree sceptical, and not therefore passive, recipients of any faith.

I have thought it fitting and desirable thus to notice, in passing, his great dislike to this class, that it may lead to a more full and satisfactory elucidation from the pen of his friend and biographer. For myself, opposed as I am both from principle and feeling to the plans and practices which this class encourages and abets,—a system at once petty in its details and mighty in the extent of its application, that tends to a tyranny, compared with which the cruelties of a Nero and a Caligula were mild and beneficent,—I am desirous and anxious to do justice to individuals who adhere from habit to this sect, and who thus share in the odium so justly incurred by the more restless, and unhappy because restless, of this party. To you especially, my dear children, and to the ingenuous youth of this age (if, perchance, this mechanical and utilitarian age should permit of ingenuous youth), there can be no need to teach or preach toleration. If it were necessary to enforce the great truth, that opinion is always the result of previous circumstances and influences, not the consequence of any choice or will of the individual mind, I should be able with ease to prove the *necessity* of charity; but this has been made so manifest, that I shall content myself with giving in this place a short extract from the "Friend" in relation to this *great truth.*

"For a subdued sobriety of temper, a practical faith in the doctrine of philosophical necessity seems the *only* preparative. That vice is the effect of error and the offspring of surrounding circumstances, the object therefore of condolence, not of anger, is a proposition easily understood and as easily demonstrated. But to make it spread from the *understanding* to the *affections*, to call it into action, not only in the great exertions of patriotism, but in the daily and hourly occurrences of social life, requires the most watchful attentions of the most energetic mind.

"It is not enough that we have once swallowed these truths; we must feed on them, as insects on a leaf, till the whole heart be coloured by their qualities, and show its food in every the minutest fibre."

As I have begun to quote, I cannot deny myself the gratification of transcribing an admirable passage, in which the author feelingly denounces and exposes the attempts of the mischievous and heartless meddlers who are now tyrannising alike over poor and rich, who, hating all above, are applying the power extorted from the aristocracy to purposes to which the oligarchy would neither have desired *nor dared* to apply it,—to the coercion and frightful slavery of the poor. But to my quotation :—

"If we hope to instruct others, we should familiarise our own minds to some *fixed* and *determinate* principles of action. The world is a vast labyrinth, in which almost every one is running a different way, and almost every one manifesting hatred to those who do not run the same way. A few, indeed, stand motionless, and, not seeking to lead themselves or others out of the maze, laugh at the failures of their brethren. Yet with little reason; for more grossly than the most bewildered wanderer does *he* err who never aims to go right. It is more honourable to the head, as well as to the heart, to be misled by our eagerness in the pursuit of truth, than to be safe from blundering by contempt of it. The happiness of mankind is the *end* of virtue, and truth is the knowledge of the *means*, which he will never seriously attempt to discover who has not habitually interested himself in the welfare of others. *The searcher after truth must love and be beloved*, for general benevolence is a necessary motive to constancy of pursuit; and this general benevolence is begotten and rendered permanent by social and domestic affections. *Let us beware of that reasoning which affects to inculcate philanthropy, while it denounces* EVERY HOME-BORN FEELING *by which it is produced and nurtured.* The paternal and filial duties discipline the heart and prepare it for the love of mankind. The intensity of private attachments encourages, not prevents, universal benevolence. The nearer we approach to the sun the more intense his heat; yet what corner of the system does he not cheer and vivify?"

Well do I recollect the very last conversation I had with my lamented friend. The projected Poor Law Bill was mentioned as an instance of the tyranny contemplated by the new parliament. He predicted that it would be carried. I remember that in allusion to the system of coercive regulation which formed part of the bill by which all relief was denied at home, he made the affecting remark,—"*It is not bread alone, but the place where you eat it.*" He then, by a felicitous transition, turned to a beautiful tale of Tieck, in which there is an allusion to the question of pauperism, introduced by an affecting story of a beggar in Switzerland, who, being offended by a refusal where he had hitherto met with kindness, said, as he departed,—"Well, you will find I shall not come again, and then you may see if you can get another beggar." The whole is so admirably stated and reasoned, as well as felt, that, for the gratification as well as the profit of the ingenuous and affectionate natures to whom I address myself, I will extract the passage, premising only that the conversation is carried on at the table of an old counsellor, between old and young Eisenschlicht, Erich an old bachelor, Sophia, the daughter of the counsellor, and Edward, her suitor.

In reading this extract the reader will recognise, in the arguments and reasoning of old and young Eisenschlicht, a faint resemblance to the bolder daring of Lord Brougham and Chadwick, whilst in Edward and Sophia may be recognised a noble and high-purposed humanity which, however, has few counterparts in any of our public men.

"'But why,' said Erich to his neighbour, 'are you disgusted with most of the works of the Flemish school here?'

"'Because they represent so many tatterdemalions and beggars,' answered the rich man. 'Nor are these Netherlanders the sole objects of my dislike: I hate particularly that Spaniard Murillo on that account, and even a great number of your Italians. It is melancholy enough that one cannot escape this vermin in the streets and market-places, nay, even in our very houses; but that an artist should require me besides to amuse myself with this noisome crew upon a motley canvass is expecting rather too much from my patience.'*

"'Perhaps then,' said Edward, 'Quintin Matsys would suit you, who so frequently sets before us with such truth and vigour money-changers at their couters, with coins and ledgers.'

"'Not so either, young gentleman,' said the old man: 'that we can see easily and without exertion in reality. If I am to be entertained with a painting, I would have stately royal scenes, abundance of massy silk stuffs, crowns and purple mantles, pages and blackamoors; that combined with a perspective of palaces and great squares, and down broad straight streets, elevates the soul; it often puts me in spirits for a long time, and I am never tired of seeing it over and over again.'

"'Undoubtedly,' said Erich, 'Paul Veronese, and several other Italians, have done many capital things in this department also.'

* This man was an economist of the worst kind, without knowing anything of political economy.

"'What say you to a marriage of Cana in this manner?' asked Edward.

"'All eating,' replied the old man, 'grows tiresome in pictures, because it never stirs from its place; and the roast peacocks and high-built pasties, as well as the cup-bearers half bent double, are in all such representations annoying things. But it is a different case when they are drawing a little Moses out of the water, and the king's daughter is standing by, in her most costly attire, surrounded by richly dressed ladies, who might themselves pass for princesses, men with halberds and armour, and even dwarfs and dogs: I cannot express how delighted I am when I meet with one of these stories, which in my youth I was forced to read in the uneasy confinement of a gloomy school-room, so gloriously dressed up. But you my dear Mr. Walther, have too few things of this sort. Most of your pictures are for the feelings, and I never wish to be affected*, and least of all by works of art. Nor, indeed, am I ever so, but only provoked.'

"'Still worse,' began young Eisenschlicht, 'is the case with our comedies. When we leave an agreeable company, and, after a brilliant entertainment, step into the lighted theatre, how can it be expected that we should interest ourselves in the variety of wretchedness and pitiful distress that is here served up for our amusement? Would it not be possible to adopt the same laudable regulation which is established by the police in most cities, to let me subscribe once for all for the relief of poverty, and then not be incommoded any farther by the tattered and hungry individuals?'

"'It would be convenient, undoubtedly,' said Edward; 'but whether absolutely laudable, either as a regulation of police, or a maxim of art, I am not prepared say. For my own part, I cannot resist a feeling of pity towards the individual unfortunates; and would not wish to do so, though to be sure one is often unseasonably disturbed, impudently importuned, and sometimes even grossly imposed upon.

"'I am of your opinion,' cried Sophia: 'I cannot endure those dumb blind books, in which one is to write one's name, in order placidly to rely upon an invisible board of management, which is to relieve the distress as far as possible. In many places even it is desired that the charitable should engage to give nothing to individuals.† But how is it possible to resist the sight of woe? When I give to him who complains to me of his distress, I at all events see his momentary joy, and may hope to have comforted him.'

---

* Just so.

† Surely H. B. must have read this.

"'This is the very thing,' said the old merchant, 'which in all countries maintains mendicity, that we cannot and will not rid ourselves of this petty feeling of soft-hearted vanity and mawkish philanthropy. This it is, at the same time, that renders the *better* * measures of states abortive and impracticable.'

"'You are of a different way of thinking from those Swiss whom I have heard of,' said Edward. 'It was in a Catholic canton, where an old beggar had long been in the habit of receiving his alms on stated days, and as the rustic solitude did not allow much trade and commerce, was accounted in almost every house one of the family. It happened, however, that once, when he called at a cottage where the inmates were extremely busied in attending a woman in labour, in the confusion and anxiety for the patient he met with a refusal. When, after repeating his request, he really obtained nothing, he turned angrily away, and cried as he departed, 'Well, I promise you, you shall find I do not come again, and then you may see where you can catch another beggar.'

"All laughed, except Sophia, who would have it the beggar's threat was perfectly rational, and concluded with these words:—'Surely if it were put out of our power to perform acts of benevolence, OUR LIFE ITSELF WOULD BECOME POOR ENOUGH. If it were possible that the impulse of pity could die in us, THERE WOULD BE A MELANCHOLY PROSPECT FOR OUR JOY AND OUR PLEASURE. *The man who is fortunate enough to be able to bestow, receives more than the poor taker. Alas! it is the only thing*,' she added with great emotion, '*that can* AT ALL *excuse and mitigate the* HARSHNESS OF PROPERTY, THE CRUELTY OF POSSESSION, that a *part* of what is *disproportionately accumulated* is dropped upon the wretched creatures who are pining below us, THAT IT MAY NOT BE UTTERLY FORGOTTEN THAT WE ARE ALL BRETHREN.†

---

* This is of the very essence of the new blasphemy. This general system will be found to require modification in a small parish of fifty souls. How can it be enforced throughout a whole nation without frightful suffering?—S. T. C.

† I know nothing so ludicrous, and at the same time so affecting, as this little incident and the after remarks of Sophia. The very essence of femineity seems to speak in the few and delicate, yet true and touching words. I am not ashamed to say that when I first read them the tears came into my eyes, and often, as I have read them since to others, I cannot refrain from praying inwardly that the time may be far distant when such sentiments shall be scouted by our women.—S. T. C.

"The father looked at her with a disapproving air, and was on the point of saying something, when Edward, his beaming eyes fixed on the moist eyes of the maid, interposed with vehemence: 'If the majority of mankind were of the same way of thinking, we should live in a different and a better world. We are struck with horror when we read of the distress that awaits the innocent traveller in wildernesses and deserts of foreign climes, or of the terrible fate which wastes a ship's crew on the inhospitable sea, when, in their sorest need, no vessel or no coast will appear on the immeasurable expanse; we are struck with horror when monsters of the deep tear to pieces the unfortunate mariner;—AND YET, *do we not live in great cities, as upon the peak of a promontory, where immediately at our feet all this woe,* THE SAME HORRIBLE SPECTACLE DISPLAYS ITSELF, ONLY MORE SLOWLY, *and* THEREFORE *the more* CRUELLY?* But, from the midst of our concerts and banquets, and from the safe hold of our opulence, we look down into this abyss, where the shapes of misery† are tortured and wasted in a thousand fearful groups, as in Dante's imagery, AND DO NOT VENTURE EVEN TO RAISE THEIR EYES TO US, because *they* KNOW what a cold look they meet, when their cry rouses us at times out of the torpor of our cold apathy.'

"'These,' said the elder Eisenschlicht, 'are youthful exaggerations. I still maintain, the really good citizen, the genuine patriot, ought not to suffer himself to be urged by a momentary emotion to support beggary. Let him bestow on those charitable institutions as much as he can conveniently spare; but let him not waste his slight means, which ought in this respect also to be subservient to the higher views of the state. For, in the opposite case, what is it he does? He promotes by his weakness—nay, I should be inclined to call it a voluptuous itching of the heart—imposture, laziness, and impudence, and withdraws his little contribution from real poverty, which, after all, he cannot always meet with or discern. Should we, however, be willing to acknowledge that overcharged picture of wretchedness to be correct, what good, even in this case, can a single individual effect? Is it in his power to improve the condition of the wretch who is

* Say selfishness, for the opulent have not a monopoly of cruelty.

† Say rather the punishments the selfish seek to inflict upon those by and through whom they have the opportunity of punishing. ALL men might be improvident, and ALL would be better if ALL were lavish, profuse, generous. It would not be possible for ALL to be selfish and grasping.—S. T. C.

driven to despair? What does it avail to give relief for a single day or hour? The unfortunate being will only feel his misery the more deeply, if he cannot change his state into a happy one; he will grow still more dissatisfied, still more wretched, and I injure instead of benefiting him.'

"'Oh! do not say so,' exclaimed Edward, 'if you would not have me think harshly of you, for it sounds to me like blasphemy. *What the poor man gains in such a moment of sunshine! Oh! sir, he who is accustomed to be thrust out of the society of men; he*, for whom there is *no holiday, no market-place, no society*, AND SCARCELY A CHURCH; for whom ceremony, *courtesy*, and all the attentions which every man usually pays to his neighbour, are extinct; this wretched creature, for whom, *in public walks and vernal nature*, there shoots and blossoms *nothing but contempt*, often turns his dry eye to heaven and the stars above him, and sees there *even*, nothing but vacancy and doubts; *but in such an hour as that which unexpectedly bestows on him a more liberal boon*, and enables him to return to his gloomy hovel, to cheer his pining family with more than momentary comfort, faith in God, in his father, again rises in his heart, *he becomes once more a man, he feels again the neighbourhood of a brother, and can again love him and himself. Happy the rich man, who can promote this faith, who can bestow with the visible the invisible gift; and woe to the prodigal, who, through his criminal thoughtlessness, deprives himself of those means of being a man among men; for most severely will his feelings punish him, for having poured out in streams in the wilderness, like a heartless barbarian, the refreshing draught, of which a* SINGLE DROP *might have cheered his brother, who lay drooping under the load of his wearisome existence.*' He could not utter the last words without a tear; he covered his face, and did not observe that the strangers and Erich had taken leave of their host. Sophia too wept; but she roused herself and recovered her composure as her father returned."

LETTER IX.

MY VERY DEAR FRIEND, 31*st July*, 1820.

Before I opened your letter, or rather before I gave it to my best sister, and, under God, best comforter, to open, a heavy, a very heavy affliction came upon me with all the aggravations of surprise, sudden as a peal of thunder from a cloudless sky.*

* * * * *

* * * *

* * * * *

* * * *

* * * * *

Alas! both Mr. and Mrs. Gillman had spoken to him with all the earnestness of the fondest parents; his cousins had warned him, and I (long ago) had written to him, conjuring him to reflect with what a poisoned dagger it would arm my enemies: yea, and the phantoms that, half-*counterfeiting*, half-expounding the conscience, would persecute my sleep. My conscience indeed bears me witness, that from the time I quitted Cambridge, no human being was more indifferent to the pleasures of the table than myself, or less needed any stimulation to my spirits; and that by a most unhappy quackery, after having been almost bedrid for six months with swollen knees and other distressing symptoms of disordered digestive functions, and through that most pernicious form of ignorance, medical half-knowledge, I was *seduced* into the use of narcotics, not secretly, but (such was my ignorance) openly and exultingly, as one who had discovered, and was never weary of recommendiug, a grand panacea, and saw not the truth till my *body* had contracted a habit and a necessity; and that, even to the latest, my responsibility is for cowardice and defect of fortitude, not for the least craving after gratification or pleasurable sensation of any sort, but for yielding to pain, terror, and haunting bewilderment. But this I say to *man* only, who knows only what has been yielded not what has been

---

* Here follows a detail of charges brought against one very near, and deservedly dear, to the writer, originating with, or adopted by the present Bishop of Llandaff. These charges were afterwards, I believe, withdrawn; at all events compensation was tendered to the party implicated.

resisted; before God I have but one voice—"Mercy! mercy! woe is me."—This was the sin of his nature, and this has been fostered by the culpable indulgence, at least non-interference, on my part; while, in a different quarter, contempt of the self-*interest* he saw seduced him unconsciously into *selfishness.*

Pray for me, my dear friend, that I may not pass such another night as the last. While I am awake and retain my reasoning powers, the pang is gnawing, but I am, except for a fitful moment or two, tranquil; it is the howling wilderness of sleep that I dread.

I am most reluctant thus to transplant the thorns from my own pillow to yours, but sooner or later you must know it, and how else could I explain to you the incapability I am under of answering your letter? For the present (my late visitation and sorrow out of the question) my anxiety is respecting your health. Mr. Gillman feels satisfied that there is nothing in your case symptomatic of aught more dangerous than irritable, and at present disordered, organs of digestion, requiring indeed great care, but by no means incompatible with comfortable health on the whole. Would to God! that your uncle lived near Highgate, or that we were settled near Clapham. Most anxious am I—(for I am sure I do not *over*rate Gillman's medical skill and sound medical good sense, and I have had every possible opportunity of satisfying myself on this head, *comparatively* as well as positively, from my intimate acquaintance with so many medical men in the course of my life)—I am most anxious that you should not apply to any medical practitioner at Clapham, till you have consulted some physician recommended by Gillman, and with whom our friend might have some confidential conversation.—The next earnest petition I make to you,—for should I lose *you* from this world, I fear that religious terrors would shake my strength of mind, and to how many are you, must you be, very dear,—is that you would stay in the country as long as is *morally* practicable. Let nothing but *coercive* motives have weight with you; a month's tranquillity in pure air (O! that I could spend that month with you, with no greater efforts of mental or bodily exercise than would exhilarate both body and mind) might save you many months' interrupted and half-effective labour.

If any thoughts occur to you at Clapham on which it would amuse or gratify you to have my notions, write to me, and I shall be served by having something to think and write about not connected with myself. But, at all events, write as often as you can, and as much as (but not a syllable more than) you ought. Need I say how unspeakably dear you are to your, you must not refuse me to say in heart,

S. T. Coleridge.

T. Allsop, Esq.

This letter, interesting as it is to me from the recollections and associations of those delightful days, when its writer was to me a guide, philosopher, and, above and before all, a dear, very dear, and valued friend, has an interest and a value from the clear and simple account of his first using laudanum. If any other testimony were or could be needed, I have received ample confirmation from subsequent communications. From this *bodily* slavery (*for it was bodily*) to a baneful drug, he was never *entirely* free, though the quantity was so greatly reduced as not materially to affect his health or spirits. For this alleviation he was indebted to the skill and attention of the medical friend of whom mention is made above, who, in a calling which, as at *present* pursued, tends more than perhaps any other *trade*, to degrade the moral being, has preserved a simplicity and singleness of purpose, united to a manly frankness, and combined with, or rather springing out of, a kindness and disinterestedness, which, as far as I have seen, has few equals. This excellent man seems to realise, in suburban practice, the example given in the following extract from the conversations of Coleridge:—

"The functions of a simple, earnest, and skilful country

surgeon, living in a small town or village, and circulating in a radius of ten miles, are, and might *always* be made, superior in real, urgent, instant, and fitting relief, to the Lady Bountiful, and even to that of the Parson of the parish. I often think with pleasure of the active *practical* benevolence of Salter.* His rides were often sixty, averaging more than thirty miles, every day, over bad roads and in dark nights; yet not once has he been known to refuse a summons, though quite sure that he would receive no remuneration, nay, not sure that it would not be necessary to supply wine or cordials, which, in the absence of the landlord of his village, must be at his own expense. This man was generally pitied by the affluent and the idle, on the score of his constant labours, and the drudgery which he almost seemed to court. Yet with little reason: for never knew I the man more to be envied, one more cheerful, more *invariably* kind, or more patient: always kind from real kindness and delicacy of feeling; never, even for a moment, angry. The present system of money-making, and, what is worse, sleight of hand, and other tricks for ostentation and stage effect, leave little hope of future Salters."

As I have extracted a part, I will even give the remainder of the conversation of the day; one of those—alas! too few—which I have preserved at great length. Bitterly do I *now* regret, both for my own sake, and still more for yours, my dear children and youthful readers (for such chiefly do I wish), that a contempt for the character and pursuits of Boswell deterred me from making constant memorandums of conversations, which spread over a period of seventeen years, and, for a part of that time, almost daily, would now to me have been a treasure and a consolation unspeakable, in the dear and delightful recollections which they would have contained. These recollections, which are now so misty, so shadowy, and so

---

* Salter, if I recollect right, lived in Devonshire; but whether at Ottery or in its neighbourhood, I am ignorant.

unsubstantial, as to present little that is tangible, little that can be recalled bodily, would not be the less delightful to me as harmonising with the general character of my mind, if they did not also include regret the most poignant at the opportunities that I suffered to pass unimproved.

It may seem a contradiction, but I am never more grateful, never more thankful for the communion vouchsafed, never more revere the memory of the illustrious departed, than when I am compelled to come to conclusions directly opposed to those of the great teacher himself.

I have not observed the transitions from one subject to another; indeed, this was not possible without giving the whole conversation, with the remarks and observations of others—a course quite out of the question, seeing that each conversation would make a small volume; a volume, I may add, of great and most delightful interest throughout.

"I believe that processes of thought might be carried on independent and apart from spoken or written language. I do not in the least doubt, that if language had been denied or withheld from man, or that he had not discovered and improved that mode of intercommunication, thought, as thought would have been a process more simple, more easy, and more perfect than at present, and would both have included and evolved other and better means for its own manifestations, than any that exist now."

"A clergyman has even more influence with the women than the handsome captain. The captain will captivate the fancy, whilst the young parson seizes upon the imagination, and subdues it to his service. The captain is *conscious* of his advantages, and sees the impression he has made long before his victim suspects the reality of any preference. The parson, unless he be the vain fop, for which, however, his education essentially unfits him, has often secured to himself the imagination, and, through the imagination, the best affections of those amongst whom he lives, before he is seriously attached himself."

"Hark yet again to that sweet strain! See how calm, how beauteous that prospect toward my garden! (thus he used sportively to call the demesne of Caen Wood, and its honest, though unreasoning owner, his head gardener). Would to God I could give out my being amidst flowers, and the sight of meadowy fields, and the chaunt of birds. Death without pain at such a time, in such a place as this, would be a reward for life. If I fear at all, I fear dying—I do not fear death."

"No, no; Lamb's scepticism has not come lightly, nor is he a sceptic. The harsh reproof to Godwin for his contemptuous allusion to Christ before a well-trained child, proves that he is not a sceptic. His mind, never prone to analysis, seems to have been disgusted with the hollow pretences, the false reasonings, and absurdities of the rogues and fools with which all establishments, and all creeds seeking to become established, abound. I look upon Lamb as one hovering between earth and heaven; neither hoping much nor fearing anything.

"It is curious that he should retain many usages which he learnt or adopted in the fervour of his early religious feelings, now that his faith is in a state of suspended animation. Believe me, who know him well, that Lamb, say what he will, has more of the *essentials* of Christianity than ninety-nine out of a hundred professing Christians. He has all that would still have been Christian had Christ never lived or been made manifest upon earth."*

---

* It will be interesting to compare Lamb's estimate of the belief of Coleridge—half serious, half sportive—with this defence of Lamb from the charge of scepticism. After a visit to Coleridge, during

"I deprecate a literal still more than an ideal religion. The miracles may be fairly illustrated by the familiar example of a lecture with experiments at the institution. A man ignorant of the law whence these *conjurations* proceeded would be acted upon in a very different manner, when compared with the philosopher who, familiar with the law, or the principle whence they emanate, and with which they are congruous, sees in them only the natural results, hardly the confirmation of that which had previously been known. Compare this with the no-results obtained from meteorology, a science so misnamed, which so far from being in its infancy is not yet in its fetal state. The meteorological journals are as little to be relied upon, as would be the account of a ploughman, taken to an experimental lecture at the institution. Ignorant of the law and the principle, he would give an account of the *results*, so different from the actual *facts*, that no one could conjecture a law from *his* evidence. So with the miracles. They are supererogatory. The law of God and the great principles of the Christian religion would have been the same had Christ never assumed humanity. It is for these things, and for such as these, for telling unwelcome truths, that I have been termed an atheist. It is for these opinions that William Smith assured the Archbishop of Canterbury that I was (what half the clergy are in *their lives*) an atheist. Little do these men know what atheism is. Not one man in a thousand has either strength of mind or goodness of heart to be an atheist. I repeat it. Not one man in ten thousand has goodness of heart or strength of mind to be an atheist.

---

which the conversation had taken a religious turn, Leigh Hunt, after having walked a little distance, expressed his surprise that such a man as Coleridge should, when speaking of Christ, always call him our Saviour. Lamb, who had been exhilarated by one glass of that gooseberry or raisin cordial which he has so often anathematised, stammered out, "ne—ne—never mind what Coleridge says; he is full of fun."

"And, were I not a Christian, *and that only in the sense in which I am a Christian*, I should be an atheist with Spinosa; rejecting all in which I found insuperable difficulties, and resting my only hope in the *gradual, and certain because gradual, progression of the species.*"

"This, it is true, is negative atheism; and this is, next to Christianity, the purest spirit of humanity!"

"Disliking the whole course and conduct of Carlile, I yet hold with him as against his judges and persecutors. I hold the assertion, that Christianity is part and parcel of the law of the land, to be an absurdity. It might as well be said because there is, or might be, a law to protect carpenters in the exercise of their trade, that architecture is part and parcel of the law. The government, or rather the party administering the functions of government, have never had the courage to place the question in its true light, and bring the action for a crime against society, not against *a creed.* When a man gives up the right of self-defence to a state, it is tacitly understood that the state undertakes to protect him equally against* *bodies* of

* To explain this allusion it will be necessary to state that the prosecution against Carlile was carried on by a loyal and constitutional association; better known, at that time, as the Bridge Street Gang. I have preserved an impromptu of Coleridge's, (which I wrote down at the time,) upon this body; the allusions in, and the application of, which, will be readily made by all interested.

Jack Stripe
Eats tripe,
It is therefore credible
That tripe is edible.
And therefore, perforce,
It follows, of course,
That the devil will gripe
All who do not eat tripe.

And as Nick is too slow
To fetch 'em below,

men as against individuals. Carlile *may be wrong; his persecutors undoubtedly are so.*"

"How I loathed the horrid speeches of the Attorney-General and of Mr. Justice Bayley, at the trial of that wretched man (Carlile). They said in so many words, 'The Unitarian who differs with you in nine points out of ten is sacred, but in the one point where he agrees with you, you condemn the deist.' Certainly the repeal of the act against Unitarianism was entirely and unequivocally an acknowledgment that those points were not of moment. Carlile, if he had not been blinded by the steams arising from that hell, his own mind, might have taken advantage of this. Judge Abbot acted very well; he put the question on the ground of incivism, and not on the religious ground. No doubt the early Christians, who in the second century threw down altars, attacked with uproar, railing and abuse, the existing religion, are not to be considered as martyrs, but as justly punished on the ground of incivism; their conduct was contrary to the injunction of their Great Master."

"The vulgar notion that a deist neither believes in a future state nor in the existence of spirits is false, according to the evidence of Christ himself; who expressly says, when questioned on this point, 'Believe ye not this; neither would ye believe if one were to rise from the dead.' And again, 'No man who believes not in this, is worthy to be received.'"

And Gifford, the attorney,
Won't quicken the journey;
The Bridge-Street Committee
That colleague without pity,
To imprison and hang
Carlile and his gang,
Is the pride of the city:
And 'tis association
That, alone, saves the nation
From death and damnation.

"The paradox that the greater the truth the greater the libel, has done much mischief. I had once intended to have written a treatise on Phrases and their Consequences, and this would have been at the head. Certainly, if extended, it has some truth; a man may state the truth in words, and yet tell a lie in spirit, and as such deserve punishment for calumny."

"All men in power are jealous of the pre-eminence of men of letters; they feel, as towards them, conscious of inferior power, and a sort of misgiving that they are, *indirectly, and against their own will, mere instruments and agents of higher intellects.*

Men in power, for instance Lord Castlereagh, are conscious of inferiority, and are yet ashamed to own, even to themselves, the fact, which is only the more evident by their neglect of men of letters. So entirely was Mr. Pitt aware of this, that he would never allow of any intercourse with literary men of eminence; fearing, doubtless, that the charm which spell-bound his political adherents would, at least for *the time*, fail of its effect."

"There is a great, a general want of intellect at this time, so much so that when any convulsion occurs, *it will tell fatally.* The fabric of our society resembles a house of cards built by children, which so long as the squares support a roof, and that roof an angle, and the inter-dependence is sufficient, all seems well; but the moment the fabric is shaken, and when the component parts can no longer form an angle, it will assuredly fall to the ground. See First Lay Sermon. The Second Lay Sermon, and the Letters to Judge Fletcher are, in truth, wonderful prophecies."

"If I should finish 'Christabel,' I shall certainly extend it and give new characters, and a greater number of incidents.

This the 'reading public' require, and this is the reason that Sir Walter Scott's Poems, though so loosely written, are pleasing, and interest us by their picturesqueness.

"If a genial recurrence of the ray divine should occur for a few weeks, I shall certainly attempt it. I had the whole of the two cantos in my mind before I began it; certainly the first canto is more perfect, has more of the true wild weird spirit than the last. I laughed heartily at the continuation in Blackwood, which I have been told is by Maginn: it is in appearance, and in appearance *only*, a good imitation; I do not doubt but that it gave more pleasure, and to a greater number, than a continuation by myself in the *spirit* of the two first cantos.

"The 'Ancient Mariner' cannot be imitated, nor the poem, 'Love.' *They may be excelled; they are not imitable.*"

"Peter's Letters to his Kinsfolk * seem to have originated in a sort of familiar conversation between two clever men, who have said, 'Let us write a book that will sell; you write this, and I will write that,' and in a sort of laughing humour set to work. This was the way that Southey and myself wrote many things together."

"I am glad you are now to see the Wallenstein for the first time, as you will then see a specimen of my happiest attempt, during the prime manhood of my intellect, before I had been buffetted by adversity or crossed by fatality. The 'Remorse' is certainly a great favourite of mine, the more so as certain pet abstract notions of mine are therein expounded."

---

* I have extracted from the above work the following tribute to the genius of Coleridge by Professor Wilson, *clarum et venerabile nomen*.

"If there be any man of grand and original genius alive at this moment, in Europe, it is Coleridge; nothing can surpass the melodious richness of words which he heaps around his images—images which

"Mr. Green is indeed a worthy man, at least so all my friends say. Bred up from the age of twelve in a hospital, he has yet not failed to shun their horrid materialism. He has come to a very different conclusion to that at which most other operators, most psychologists have arrived. He has been able to believe in a spiritual first cause and in a presiding free will. This you will see in his preface.*

"I deplore in my inmost heart the present mental degradation of E., who, not contented with denying the primal truths of religion and the divine nature of man, holds opinions which were *ever* considered as base, hateful, and to be abhorred; opinions which degrade man below the beast. Quoted that passage of Cicero, wherein he says,—"Concerning these things there are (or may be) different opinions; but those who disbelieve the existence of goodness, not only from the want of it themselves but after much consideration, are to be held as out of the pale of society."

---

are not glaring in themselves, but which are always affecting to the very verge of tears, because they have all been formed and nourished in the recesses of one of the most deeply musing spirits that ever breathed forth its inspirations in the majestic language of England. Who that ever read 'Genevieve' can doubt this? That poem is known to all readers of poetry, although comparatively few of them are aware that it is the work of Coleridge. His love-poetry is, throughout, the finest that has been produced in England since the days of Shakspeare and the old dramatists. The old dramatists, and Coleridge, regard women with far higher reverence—far deeper insight into the true grandeur of their gentleness. I do not think there is any poet in the world who ever touched so truly the mystery of the passion as he has done in 'Genevieve,' and in that other exquisite poem where he speaks of

Her voice—
Her voice, that, even in its mirthful mood,
Hath made me wish to steal away and weep."

* It is to be hoped that Mr. Green will favour the world with the process by which he has arrived at these conclusions.

"Tobin came one morning with a face of much interest to inform me that Davy had made a wonderful discovery. 'I doubt it not; I think he will make many discoveries.' 'Yes, yes; but I mean in philosophy. He tells me he has discovered that it is *possible* there may be a God!'"

"I once asked Tom Clarkson whether he ever thought of his probable fate in the next world, to which he replied, 'How can I? I think only of the slaves in Barbadoes!' Does Mr. Wilberforce care a farthing for the slaves in the West Indies, or if they were all at the devil, so that *his soul were saved?*

"As there is a worldliness or the *too-much* of this life, so there is *another-worldliness*, or rather *other worldliness*, equally hateful and selfish with *this worldliness.*"

"Lord Erskine, speaking of animals, hesitating to call them brutes, hit upon that happy phrase—'the mute creation.'"

"Lord Kenyon, on the trial of a bookseller, for publishing Paine's 'Age of Reason,' in his charge to the jury, enumerated many celebrated men who had been sincere Christians; and, after having enforced the example of Locke and Newton,—both of whom were Unitarians, and therefore not Christians,—proceeded:—'Nor, gentlemen, is this belief confined to men of comparative seclusion, since men, the greatest and most distinguished both as philosophers and as monarchs, have enforced this belief, and shown its influence by their conduct, Above all, gentlemen, need I name to you the Emperor Julian, who was so celebrated for the practice of every Christian virtue that he was called Julian the Apostle.'"*

---

* This most extraordinary blunder must have arisen from the judge's reading having been more select than various. It is probable that all the knowledge he had of Julian was picked out of Fielding's "Journey to the Next World," which, however, he seems not to have understood.

"It is indisputable that nervous excitation is contagious. The greater part of ghost stories may be traced to this source."

"Forms exist before the substance out of which they are shaped."

"One thought includes all thought, in the sense that a grain of sand includes the universe.

"I hold with St. Paul that charity is the greatest of the virtues. Original sin is best explained by depravation of the will. Calvinism, or the belief in election, is not simply blasphemy, but superfetation of blasphemy."

"For one person who has remarked or praised a beautiful passage in Walter Scott's works, a hundred have said, 'How many volumes he has written!' So of Mathews: it is not 'How admirable such and such parts are!' but, 'It is wonderful that one man can do *all this!*'"

LETTER X.

MY VERY DEAR FRIEND, *August 8th*, 1820.

Neither indolence nor procrastination have had any place among the causes of my silence, least of all either yourself, or the subject of your letter, or the purpose of answering it, having been absent from my thoughts. You may with almost literal truth attribute it to want of time, from the number, quantity, and quality of my engagements, the necessity of several journeys *to* and (still worse) *in* town being the largest waster of time and spirits. At length I have settled J. for the next six or eight weeks with Mr. Montague, where he is engaged on an Essay on the Principles of Taste in relation to Metre and Rhythm, containing, first, a new scheme of prosody, as applied to the choral and lyrical stanzas of the Greek drama; secondly, the possibility of improving and enriching our English versification by digging in the original mines, viz.—the tunes of nature and impassioned conversation, both of which may be illustrated from Mr. Frere's* Aristophanic Poems. I have

* As these poems, the precursors of "Beppo" and "Don Juan," are not now in general circulation, I subjoin two short extracts—one a sketch of a gallant knight; the second showing the advantage of being well victualled.

On every point, in earnest and in jest,
His judgment, and his prudence, and his wit
Were deemed the very touchstone and the text
Of what was proper, graceful, just, and fit.
A word from him set everything at rest,
His short decisions never failed to hit;
His silence, his reserve, his inattention,
Were felt as the severest reprehension.
His memory was the magazine and hoard
Where claims and grievances, from year to year,
And confidences and complaints were stored,
From dame and knight, from damsel, boor and peer;
Loved by his friends, and trusted by his lord,
A generous courtier, secret and sincere,
Adviser-general to the whole community,
He served his friend, but watched his opportunity.

For, in the garrison where he presided,
Neither distress, nor famine, nor disease
Were felt, nor accident nor harm betided
The happy monk; but plenteous, and with ease,
All needful monkish viands were provided;
Bacon and pickled herring, pork and peas;
And, when the table-beer began to fail,
They found resources in the bottled ale.

Dinner and supper kept their usual hours,
Breakfast and luncheon never were delayed,
While to the sentries on the walls and towers,
Between two hot plates, messes were conveyed.
At the departure of the invading power,
It was a boast the noble abbot made,
None of his monks were weaker, paler, thinner,
Or, during all the siege, had lost a dinner.

been working hard to bring together for him the notes, &c., that I had prepared on this subject. E. has been ill, and even now is far from well. There are some persons—I have known several—who, when they find themselves uncomfortable, take up the pen and transfer as much discomfort as they can to their absent friends. But I know only one of this sort, who, as soon as they take up the pen, instantly become *dolorous*, however smug, snug, and cheerful the minute before and the minute after.

Now just such is Mrs. D., God bless her! and she has been writing letter after letter to E. about J., and every discomfortable recollection and anticipation that she could conjure up, that she has completely overset him. *This must not be.* Mr. Gillman, too, has been *out* of *sorts*, but at this present we are all better. I at least am as well as I ever am, and my regular employment, in which Mr. Green is weekly my amanuensis, the work on the books of the Old and New Testaments, introduced by the assumptions and postulates required as the preconditions of a fair examination of Christianity as a scheme of doctrines, precepts, and histories, drawn or at least deducible from these books. And now, in the narrative line, I have only to add that Mrs. Gillman desires to be affectionately remembered to you, and bids me entreat you to stay *away as long* as you possibly can, provided it be from *London* as well as from Highgate.

Would to heaven I were with you! In a few days you should see that the spirit of the mountaineer is not yet utterly extinct in me. Wordsworth has remarked (in the Brothers, I believe),

> "The thought of death sits light upon the man
> That has been bred, and dies among the mountains."

But I fear that this, like some other few of Wordsworth's *many* striking passages, means less than it seems, or rather promises, to mean. Poets (especially if philosophers too) are apt to represent the effect made upon themselves as general;

the geese of Phœbus are all swans; and Wordsworth's shepherds and estates men are Wordsworth's, even (as in old Michael) in the unpoetic traits of character. Whether mountains have any particular effect on the native inhabitants by virtue of being mountains exclusively, and what that effect is, would be a difficult problem. If independent tribes, mountaineers are robbers of the lowlanders; brave, active, and with all the usual warlike good and bad qualities that result from habits of adventurous robbery. Add clanship and the superstitions that are the surviving *precipitate* of an established religion, both which are common to the uncivilised Celtic tribes, in plain no less than in mountain, and you have the Scottish Highlanders. But where the inhabitants exist as states, or civilised parts of civilised states, they appear to be in mind and character just what their condition and employments would render them in level plain, the same as amid Alpine heights. At least the influence acts indirectly only, as far as the mountains are the *causa causæ* or occasion of a *pastoral* life instead of an agricultural; thus combining a lax and common property, possessed by a whole district, with small hereditary estates sacred to each, while the properties in sheep seem to partake of both characters. And truly, to this circumstance, aided by the favourable action of a necessarily scanty population (for *man* is an oak that wants room, not a *plantation tree*), we must attribute whatever superiority the mountaineers of Cumberland and Westmoreland and of the Swiss and Tyrolese Alps possess, as the shocking contrast of the Welsh mountaineers too clearly evinces. But this subject I have discussed, and (if I do not flatter myself) satisfactorily, in the Literary Life, and I will not conceal from *you* that this inferred dependency of the human soul on accidents of birth-place and abode, together with the vague, misty, rather than mystic, confusion of God with the world, and the accompanying nature-worship, of which the asserted dependence forms a part, is the trait in

Wordsworth's poetic works that I most dislike as unhealthful, and denounce as contagious; while the odd introduction of the popular, almost the vulgar, religion in his later publications (the popping in, as Hartley says, of the old man with a beard), suggests the painful suspicion of worldly prudence—at best a justification of masking truth (which, in fact, is a falsehood substituted for a truth withheld) on plea of expediency—carried into religion. At least it conjures up to my fancy a sort of *Janus* head of Spinosa and Dr. Watts, or "I and my brother the dean."

Permit me, then, in the place of the two lines,

> "The thought of death sits easy on the man,
> Who hath been bred, and dies among the mountains,"

to say,

> "The thought of death sits easy on the man,
> Whose earnest *will* hath lived among the deathless."

And I can perhaps build upon this foundation an answer to the question, which would deeply interest me, by whomever put, and pained me only because it was put by *you; i.e.* because I feared it might be the inspiration of ill health, and am jealous of any *consenting* of that inward will which, with some mysterious germination, moves in the Bethesda pool of our animal life, to withdraw its resistance. For the soul, among its other regalia, has an energetic veto against all undermining of the constitution, and among these, as not the least insidious, I consider the thoughts and hauntings that tamper with the love of life.

Do not so! you *would not*, if I could transfer into you, in all its depth and liveliness, the sense what a hope, promise, impulse, you are to me in my present efforts to realise my past labours; and by building up the temple,—the shaped stones, beams, pillars, yea, the graven ornaments and the connecting clamps of which have been piled up by me, only in too great abundance,—to enable you and my two (may I not say other) sons to affirm,—*Vivit, quia non frustra vixit.*

In reading an extract in the German Encyclopœdia from Dobrizhoffer's most interesting account of the Abiponenses, a savage tribe in Paraguay, houseless, yet in person and in morals the noblest of savage tribes; who, when first known by Europeans, amounted to 100,000 warriors, yet have a tradition that they were but the relic of a far more numerous community, and who by wars with other savage tribes, and by intestine feuds among themselves, are now dwindled to a thousand (men, women, and children do not exceed five thousand), it struck me with distinct remembrance—first, that this is the history of *all* savage tribes; and, second, that all tribes *are* savage that have not a positive religion defecated from witchcraft, and an established priesthood contra-distinguished from individual conjurers. Nay, the islands of the Pacific (the Polynesia, which sooner or later the swift and silent masonry of the coral worms will compact into a rival continent, into a *fifth quarter* of the world), blest with all the plenties of nature, and enjoying an immunity from all the ordinary dangers of savage life, were many of them utterly dispeopled since their first discovery, and wholly by their own feuds and vices; nay, that their bread-fruit tree and their delicious and healthful climate had only made the process of mutual destruction and self-destruction more hateful, more basely sensual. This, therefore, I assume as an undoubted fact of history; and from this, as a portion of the history of *men*, I draw a new (to my knowledge, at least, a new) series of proofs of several, I *might* say of *all*, the positions of pre-eminent importance and interest more than vital; a series which, taken in harmonious counterpart to a prior series drawn from *interior* history (the history of *man*), the documents of which are to be found only in the archives of each individual's own consciousness, will form a complete *whole*—a system of evidence, consisting of two correspondent worlds, as it were, correlative and mutually potentiating, yet each integral and self-subsistent—having the same correlation, as the geometry and the observations, or the metaphysics and the physics, of astronomy. If I can thus demonstrate the truth of the doctrine of existence after the present life, it is not improbable that some rays of light may fall on the question, what *state* of existence it may be reasonably supposed to be? At all events, we shall, I trust, be enabled to determine negatively, what it can *not* be for *any;* and *for whom* this or that, which does not appear universally precluded, is yet *for them* precluded. In plainer words, what can *not* be, universally speaking; second, what may be; third, what the differences may be for different individuals, within the limits prescribed in No. 2; fourth, what scheme of embodied representation of the future state (our *reason* not forbidding the same) is recommended by the truest analogies; and, fifth, what scheme it is best to combine with our belief of a hereafter, as most conducive to the growth and cultivation of our collective faculties in this life, or of each in the order of its comparative worth, value, and permanence. This I must defer to another letter, for I cannot let another post pass by, without your knowing that we are all thinking of and loving you.

T. Allsop, Esq. S. T. Coleridge.

To the preceding letter, pregnant as it is with materials for thinking, your attention will be attracted, both by the great variety of subjects brought forward and illustrated, and by the expressions of earnest and affectionate attachment which it contains.

Certainly no man that I ever knew united in so great a degree, *so entirely,* "fondeur" with the most extreme simplicity, and the most artless and confiding affection. The whole craving of his moral being was for love. Who is not affected, what man does not grieve, when he hears him exclaim—

"*To be* BELOVED *is* ALL *I need,*
"*To be* BELOVED *is I* LOVE *indeed.*"

"Why was I made for love, and love denied to me?"

Alas! my dear children, how can I hope to convey to you (except your own minds are consenting) all that this glorious being was to me in the days when his *vast* intellect was in its most gorgeous manhood, and I was yet in the first singleness, and, I will add, purity, of mind.

"Few, and far between," are the moments when I can recall that other self, which, in days past, sat at the feet of the greatest of moderns—that seemed to unite energy, variety, a mind eminently suggestive, with an affection and a reverence, without any assignable limits, for whatever was beautiful and loveable in man or in external nature,

"Who was retired as noon-tide dew
Or fountain in a noon-day grove;
And you must love him, ere to you
He will seem worthy of your love.

"The outward shows of sky and earth,
Of hill and valley he has viewed;
And impulses of deeper birth
Have come to him in solitude.

"In common things that round us lie,
Some random truths he can impart,
The harvest of a quiet eye,
That broods and sleeps on his own heart.

"But he is shy, both man and boy
Hath been an idler in the land;
Contented, if he might enjoy
The things that others understand."

The next letter which contained the farther development of the very interesting matters opened in the preceding letter, I have mislaid, or, I much fear, lost.

LETTER XI.

MY DEAR FRIEND, *Highgate, Oct. 11th*, 1820.

You will think it childish in me, and more savouring of a jealous boarding-school miss than a friend and a philosopher, when I confess that the "with great respect, your obliged and grateful...," gave me pain. But I did not return from Mr. Cooper's, at whose house we all dined, till near midnight, and did not open the packet till this morning after getting out of bed; and this you know is the hour in which the cat-organ of an irritable viscerage is substituted for the brain as the mind's instrument.

The Cobbett is assuredly a strong and battering production throughout, and in the best bad style of this political rhinoceros, with his coat armour of dry and wet mud, and his one horn of brutal strength on the nose of scorn and hate; not to forget the flaying rasp of his tongue! There is one article of his invective, however, from which I cannot withhold my vote of consent: that I mean which respects Mr. Brougham's hollow complimentary phrases to the ministry and the House of Lords. On expressing my regret that his poor hoaxed and hunted client had been lured or terrified into the nets of the revolutionists, and had taken the topmost perch, as the flaring, screaming *maccaw*, in the clamorous aviary of faction, Sheriff Williams, who dined with us, premising that his *wishes* accorded with mine, declared himself, however, fully and deeply convinced, that, without this alliance, the Queen must have been overwhelmed, not wholly or even chiefly from the strength of the party itself, but because, without the activity, enthusiasm, and combination, peculiar to the reformists, her case, in all its detail and with all its appendages, would never have had that notoriety so beyond example universal; which (to translate Sheriff Williams into Poet Coleridge), with kettle-drum reveillée, had echoed through the mine and the coal-pit, which had lifted the latch of every cottage, and thundered with no run-away knock at Carlton Palace. I could only reply, that I had never yet seen, heard, or read of any advantage in the long run, occurring to a good cause from an unholy alliance with evil passions and incongruous or alien purposes. It was ever heavy on my heart, that the people, alike high and low, do perish for lack of knowledge; that both sheep and shepherd, the Flocks and the Pastors, go astray among swamps and in desolate places, for want of the *Truth*, the *whole* Truth, and nothing but the Truth; and that the sacred motto, which I had adopted for my first political publication ("The Watchman"), would be the aspiration of my death-bed—THAT ALL MAY KNOW THE TRUTH; AND THAT THE TRUTH MAY MAKE US FREE.

I observed farther, that in bodies of men, not accidentally collected nor promiscuously, but such as our House of Lords, the usual effect of terror was, first, self-justification as to the worst of their past violent and unconstitutional measures; and, next, a desperate belief that their safety would be still more endangered by giving way than by plunging onward; that, if they must fall, they would fall in that way in which they might take vengeance on the occasion of the mischief. If the proposition be either . . . or . . . , and the latter blank is to be filled up by *a Civil War*, what shall we put for the former, to make our duty to submit to it deniable or even doubtful? A Legislature permitted by us to stand in the eye of the whole civilised World as the representative of our country, corruptly and ruthlessly pandering to an Individual's Lust and Hate! Open Hostility to Innocence, and the subversion of justice, a shameless trampling under foot of the Laws of God and the Principles of the Constitution, in the name and against the known will of the Nation! Well! if anything, it must be this! It is a decision, compared with which the sentence of the elder Brutus were a grief for which an onion might supply the tears. A dreadful decision! But be it so!—How much more then are we bound to be careful, that no conduct of our own, no assent or countenance given by us to the violence of others, no want of courage and alertness in denouncing the same, should have the least tendency to bring about an act or event, dire enough to justify a civil war for its preventive? I produced, as you may suppose, but small effect; and yet your very note enforces the truth of my reply—for these very answers of the Queen's conjointly with her plebicolar (or plebicolous) Clap-Trapperies in the live puppet-show of wicked Punch and his wife, that has come back again, and the devil on all sides, make it impossible for me to ask you, as I otherwise should have done,—What proof, proveably independent of the calumny plot, have we of any want of delicacy in the Queen? What act or form of demeanour can be adduced on competent testimony, from which we are forced or entitled to infer innate Coarseness, if not Grossness? The dire disclosure of the extent and extremes to which Calumny may be carried—and perhaps the recent persecution of poor dear . . . . . mixes its workings—makes me credulous in incredulity; so that I am almost prepared to reverse the proverb, and think that "what every one says must be a lie!" They put a body up to the nostrils in the dunghill of reeking slander, and then exclaim: There is no smoke without some fire!

It is my purpose, God willing! to leave this place on Friday, so as to take an afternoon coach, if any such there be, or the Oxford mail, as the dernier resource—and so to be in Oxford by Saturday morning, while my letter, which is unfortunately a very long one (and I could not make it otherwise), will reach Dr. Copplestone, if arrived, on Friday morning; thus giving him a day's preparation for the personal interview. How long my absence from Highgate may be, I cannot of course predetermine; certainly not an hour beyond what . . . . .'s interest requires.

God bless you, my dear friend, and your truly affectionate, and—if it did not look like a *retort*, how truly might I not add— Your obliged and grateful friend,

T. Allsop, Esq. S. T. Coleridge.

P.S.—Sheriff Williams is apparently a very worthy, and assuredly a very entertaining man. He gave us accounts, on his own evidence, of wonderful things respecting Miss M'Evoy and a Mr. De Vains of Liverpool; so wonderful as to threaten the stoppage even of my Bank of Faith.

I have just heard from Derwent, who is well; but I have not had time to decipher his villainous scrawl.

I wish it was possible for me to give even a faint notion of the splendid eloquence of my friend on this topic. The interest he took in this great question on all occasions, induced me to entreat *repeatedly* that he would embody his views and opinions in a pamphlet, to be called "Thoughts on the Present Persecution;" but better, certainly more prudent, counsels prevailed.

On the conduct of Mr. Brougham in this case, he was accustomed to animadvert with great severity. His great and constant indiscretions, and, above all, an insincerity, which then seemed to have an object, but which greater experience has shown to arise from want of Ballast, in short (why should I not say it?) from mental unsoundness, were at that time matters of deep regret to all right-minded men.

It is painful thus to speak of a man variously gifted, and possessed unquestionably of great talents; but it is needful to bear in mind, that though men of restless natures and irritable temperaments have frequently been the instruments of functional improvements, they are totally unsuited to times which require organic changes. If this be the case with regard to men who are restless from enthusiasm, or whose fermentation arises from the crude state of their minds, and respecting whom there is yet hope when experience shall have mellowed their convictions, what shall we say of those, to whom time brings no improvement—age, no mental repose? It is the duty of all men, who have calmly observed, meditated, and reflected, who are sufficiently near to be interested, and remote enough for quiet contemplation, to put their testimony on record; which, though it may not avail in the present times, will yet serve as a time-mark for the future.

Yet I can never believe but that a man so variously gifted must, at some time or other, have had aspirations of a higher and purer nature than should seem possible, judging of the turmoil and turbulence of his latter career. Hear what is thought of this man by an accomplished foreigner. In a letter of Jacquemont's, written from the Himalaya, are the following reflections, which are but too just:—"I have just read the sixteen immense columns of Lord Brougham's speech on 7th Oct., 1831. What talents! but what a perverted use of talent. What a disagreeable kind of talent is that, which disgusts the hearer instead of conciliating him. If I were a public man, I would study Brougham, *not* to resemble him. What is the *use* of that cutting irony, that bitter sarcasm, that supercilious pride? What is the *use* of those Greek and Latin verses?"

I must also protest against the terms employed, in speaking of the very extraordinary man lately lost to that country he so dearly loved, and for the welfare of which country, and those who lived upon it and by it, his last words were uttered.

A man more kind-hearted, *more kindly*, I never knew. That he was intolerant, turbulent, and domineering, I admit freely, but towards whom? To those only who were self-seekers, proud, narrow in their views, and, above all, to those who sought to oppress and degrade that great class from which he sprung, and with which he gloried to identify himself.

To the concluding portion of this letter it will be needless to point attention. Like every thing my friend wrote, it is for all time, and would be equally applicable in its spirit under any conceivable form of society.

The American coachman, who, to the great surprise of Mr. Stewart, told him more of the practice and mode of teaching at the High School of Edinburgh than he knew himself, although educated* at that school, justly observed that the two great principles which have divided and still divide mankind, are eternal, and not dependent upon the names with which they are associated. Substituting only the words "true Reformer" for "Whig" (for *here* the Whigs are not *true* Reformers), I know not a more just observation. "In truth, the parties of Whig and Tory are those of Nature. They exist in all countries, whether called by those names or by those of aristocrats and democrats, *côté droite* and *côté gauche*, ultras and radicals, serviles and liberals. The sickly, weakly, timid man fears the people, and is a Tory by nature; the healthy, strong, and bold man cherishes them, and is a Whig by nature." It is well that the people of England are not educated to any knowledge of their political rights, or the scandalous frauds of the past year would have met their fitting punishments. How long will the manly and mature intellect of this great mother, *this great hive*, of nations submit to the guidance of *litterateurs* and lordlings, who, by virtue of pretension and prescription alone, are held to be fit to govern *nations*, though there are *few men* in the present cabinet to whom a merchant would intrust a ship, a farmer employ as a bailiff, or a draper engage as an assistant, even were their services offered gratuitously.

---

* When Lord Stanley was in America, it was necessary to speak of the General Post Office: he did not know where it was; whilst a judge who was at the table pointed out its exact situation in Lombard-street, and evinced so much local knowledge, that Lord Stanley said—"You must have been a long time in London, ——?" "I was never there in my life," was the reply.

See here the difference. The American had informed himself of that which he was not expected to know, which it was excusable in him not to know; whilst the aristocrat was ignorant of that which it was incumbent upon him to have known.

LETTER XII.

MY DEAR FRIEND, *Oct. 20th*, 1820.

Doubtless nothing can be more delightful to me, independent of Mrs. Gillman's kind but unnecessary anxieties, than to go to Oxford with you. Nay, though it will be but a flight to and fro, with a sojourn but of two days, if so much, yet I should even ask it of you if I were quite sure, absolutely sure, that it would not inconvenience you.

But in the fear of this, I could not ask or receive your companionship without some selfishness which would completely baffle itself.

I have not yet received an answer from Oxford respecting Dr. Coplestone's return to Oriel.

God bless you, my ever dear friend,

T. Allsop, Esq. S. T. COLERIDGE.

Of this journey to Oxford I have a very painful recollection; perhaps the most painful recollection (one excepted) connected with the memory of Coleridge. Still I think that the journey was beneficial to his health, and that he was better for some weeks after his return.

" A single thought is that which it is from other thoughts, as a wave of the sea takes its form and shape from the waves which precede and follow it."

" In the system of gravity, Newton only developed the idea of Kepler. He advanced a step, and there he fixed his followers. Kepler would have progressed, or have been stationary in act at least."

LETTER XIII.

MY DEAREST FRIEND, *Oct. 25th*, 1820.

It will please you, though I scarcely know whether the pleasure is worth the carriage, to know that my own feelings and convictions were, from the very commencement of this unhappy affair, viz.—the terms proposed to the Queen by Lord Hutchinson, in coincidence with your present suggestion, and that I actually began an essay, and proposed a sort of *diary*, *i. e.* remarks moral and political, according as the events of the day suggested them. But Mr. Gillman dissuaded me. Again, about five weeks ago I had written a letter to Conder, the editor of the "Eclectic Review" and *ci-devant* bookseller, offering, and offering to *execute*, a scheme of publication, "the Queen's case stated *morally;* 2, judicially; 3, politically." But *again* Mr. G. earnestly persuaded me to suppress it. His reasons were, first, that my mind was not sufficiently tranquil, in consequence of I.'s affair, to enable me to rely upon going through with the publication; secondly, that it would probably involve me with certain of my connexions in high life, and be injurious to Hartley and Derwent, especially the latter; with thirdly, the small chance of doing any good, people are so guided by their first notions. To tell you the truth, Mr. G.'s *own dislike* to it was of more weight than all his three reasons.

However, we will talk of the publication, if *it be not too late*, and at all events I will compose the statement.

I pray you make no apologies for doing that which cannot but add to the esteem and affection with which I am most truly your *friend*, fraternally and paternally,

We shall soon see you? S. T. COLERIDGE.

T. Allsop, Esq.

Shortly after this I find the following heads of conversation:—

"I recollect meeting Mr. Brougham well. I met him at

Mr. Sharp's with Mr. Horner. They were then aspirants for political adventures. Mr. Horner bore in his conversation and demeanour evidence of that straight-forward and generous frankness which characterised him through life. You saw, or rather you felt, that you could rely upon *his* integrity. His mind was better fitted to reconcile discrepancies than to discover analogies. He had fine, nay, even high, talent rather than genius. Mr. Brougham, on the contrary, had an apparent restlessness, a consciousness, not of superior powers, but of superior activity, a man whose heart was placed in what should have been his head: you were never sure of him—you always doubted his sincerity. He was at that time a hanger-on upon Lord Holland, Mr. Horner being under the auspices of Lord Lansdowne.

"From that time I lost sight of Mr. Brougham for some time. When we next met, the subject of the parliamentary debates was alluded to, previously to which Mr. Brougham had expressed opinions which were in unison with my own upon a matter at that time of great public interest.

"I said 'I could never rely upon what was given for the future in the newspapers, as they had made him say directly the contrary; I was glad to be undeceived.'

"'Oh,' said Brougham, in a tone of voice half confidential and half jocular, 'Oh, it was very true I said so in Parliament, where there is a party, but *we* know better.'

"*I said nothing; but I did not forget it.*"

"The question of the atonement and of the sacrament being introduced, he insisted on the divine origin of the sacrament, and that it was to be understood in a mystical sense, not, however, as a real presence. It has very clearly relation to the sixth chapter of John; nay, Clement expressly affirms it to be a solemn mysterious ceremony, in which he is sustained by Justin Martyr. With respect to free will, in the ordinary acceptation, he affirmed it to be incompatible with omnipotence, with the attributes of that God who is omniscient and omnipresent, who is in all things, and in whom all things are, to whom time past and time to come ever *is*. Man is not to be saved without *his* saving grace."

"Speaking of the term 'Son of Man,' taken literally by the Socinians, he said,—'The Son of Man! What is it but mockery if he were really a man, the man Jesus Christ. He was incarnate in Trinity or tri-unity; first, he was incarnate as the Logos, or Word; next, he was incarnate with the Holy Spirit unto all things, that he might remain in the spirit; and, lastly, he was incarnate in his humanity.'"

"Compared to the Jewish law, given as it was in thunders and in terrible convulsions of the elements, the miracles of the Christian dispensation were devoid of interest.

"There can be no doubt that a religion like that of the Jews, a religion of punishments and threatenings only, was incomplete; it must, *therefore*, be false, or it required to be perfected."

"Speaking of Baxter, he affirmed that he was a century before his time, that he was a logician, and first applied the tri-fold or tri-une demonstration. Heretofore, the two-fold method only was known as the arguing from a positive to a negative, the reality *ergo* the visionary. He also first introduced the method of argument, that the thing or reason given contains a positive and its opposite; *e. g.*, reality contains the actual and the potential, as, I sit, the actual, but I have the power, the potentiality, of walking. Baxter tried to reconcile the almost irreconcilable tenets of Calvinism and Arminianism. He more than any other man was the cause of the restoration, and more than any other sectarian was he persecuted by Charles II.

"He is borne out in all his statements by Mrs. Lucy

Hutchinson, that most delightful of women and of regicidesses. No doubt the Commons had a right to punish the weak and perfidious king, inasmuch as he first appealed to the God of Battles."

"The present ministry (the Liverpool-Castlereagh cabinet), although it contains some men of ability, is supported chiefly by its own weakness, which in every instance leads or rather compels it to a mean and abject prostration of the prerogative to the House of Commons, and by the unpopularity of the opposition, arising from their having opposed themselves to the French war and to the grant of assistance to Spain. The grand mistake of Mr. Fox was, that he did not separate the causes of the war from the consequences, but acted as though, having espoused the cause of the French revolution, he must in every instance advocate its measures. This lost him his party, and swelled the ranks of Mr. Pitt, a man utterly unfitted for the conduct of a war, all his plans being based upon, so called, expediency, and pernicious short-sightedness, which would never allow him to take into his calculation the future."

"Even the very successes of our naval power contributed, and that in a most influential degree, to form and render extreme the military spirit in France; for, utterly and entirely weaning men from commerce and maritime concerns, they necessarily gave exclusive attention to military affairs, for on the sea, hope, even, did not exist for France."

"It is not uncommon for 100,000 *operatives* (mark this word, for words *in this sense* are things) to be out of employment at once in the cotton districts (this was in 1820), and, thrown upon parochial relief, are dependent upon hard-hearted task-masters for food. The Malthusian doctrine would indeed afford a certain means of relief if this were not a two-fold question.

If, when you say to a man,—'You have no claim upon me; you have your allotted part to perform in the world, so have I. In a state of nature, indeed, had I food, I should offer you a share from sympathy, from humanity; but in this advanced and artificial state of society, I cannot afford you relief; *you must starve.* You came into the world when it could not sustain you.' What would be this man's answer? He would say,—'You disclaim all connexion with me; I have no claims upon you? *I can then have no duties towards you,* and this pistol shall put me in possession of your wealth. You may leave a law behind you which shall hang me, but what man who saw assured starvation before him, ever feared hanging.' It is this accursed practice of ever considering *only* what seems *expedient* for the occasion, disjoined from all principle or enlarged systems of action, of never listening to the true and unerring impulses of our better nature, which has led the colder-hearted men to the study of political economy, which has turned our Parliament into a real committee of public safety. In it is all power vested; and in a few years we shall either be governed by an aristocracy, or, what is still more likely, by a contemptible democratical oligarchy of glib economists, compared to which the worst form of aristocracy would be a blessing."

"Commerce has enriched thousands, it has been the cause of the spread of knowledge and of science, but has it added one particle of happiness or of moral improvement? Has it given us a truer insight into our duties, or tended to revive and sustain in us the better feelings of our nature? No! no! when I consider what the consequences have been, when I consider that whole districts of men, who would otherwise have slumbered on in comparatively happy ignorance, are now little less than brutes in their lives, and something worse than brutes in their instincts, I could almost wish that the manufacturing districts were swallowed up as Sodom and Gomorrah."

"Some men—Jeffrey is one—refer taste to palate."

"Absurd terms, when compared, as 'conclusion of a war,' 'conclusion of a peace.' In the one case it means the end, in the other the beginning."

"I am unable to account for Mr. Locke's popularity; in some degree it may be owing to his having exposed and confuted the absurdities, or rather the absurd part, of the schoolmen. Hume has carried his premises to their natural and inevitable conclusion."

"The idea of the mind forming images of itself, is as absurd as the belief of Descartes with respect to the external world. There is nothing in the mind which was not previously in the senses, except the mind itself. Philosophy, properly so called, began with Pythagoras. He saw that the mind, in the common sense of the word, was itself a fact, that there was something in the mind not individual; this was the pure reason, *something in which we are, not which is in us.*"

"Socrates seems to have been continually oscillating between the good and the useful."

"To most men, experience is like the stern lights of a ship, which illumine only the track it has passed."

"On William Smith, of Norwich, asking me what I thought of the Monthly Review or Magazine, and of Dr. Aikin, its editor, I was provoked, by his evident wish that I should say something in its favour, to reply,—'That all men of science or literature could attest that the one was a void Aikin, and the other an aching void.'"

LETTER XIV.

MY VERY DEAR FRIEND, *Nov.* 27, 1820.

I have been more than usually unwell, with great depression of spirits, loss of appetite, frequent sickness, and a harassing pain in my left knee; and at the same time anxious to preclude, as much as I can, the ill effects of poor J.'s procrastination—indolence it is not, for he is busy enough in his own way, and rapidly bringing together materials for his future credit as a man of letters and a poet, but shrinking from all things connected with painful associations, and of that morbid temperament, which I too well understand, that renders what would be motives for men in general, narcotics for him, in exact proportion to their strength; and this I could only do by taking on myself as much of the document writing as was contrivable. Besides this, I have latterly felt increasingly anxious to avail myself of every moment that ill health left me, to get forward with my Logic and with my "Assertion of Religion."

Nay, foolish though it be, I cannot prevent my mind from being affected by the alarming state of public affairs, and, as it appears to me, the want of stable principle even in the chiefs of the party that seem to feel aright, yet chirrup like crickets in warmth without light.

The consequence of all this is, that I not only have deferred writing to you, but have played the procrastinator with myself, even in giving attention to your very interesting letter. For minor things your kindness and kind remembrances are so habitual, that my acknowledgments you cannot but take for granted. Mr. Gillman has been ill; Mrs. Gillman—and this leads me to the particular object of this letter—expresses aloud and earnestly what I feel no less, her uneasiness that three weeks have passed, and we have not had the comfort of seeing you. Do come up when you can, with justice to yourself and other connections, for it is a *great* comfort to me; something, I trust, I shall have to show you. A note of warning from one who has been a true but unheard prophet to my countrymen for five-and-twenty years.

May God bless you, my dear friend,

T. Allsop, Esq. S. T. Coleridge.

As I do not intend that these brief notices shall form any consecutive narrative of the events in the life of the writer, any farther than the letters may contain allusions to them, the life itself being, I hope, soon to make its appearance from the pen of his best friend, I shall content myself with the insertion of the following sonnet; it is well worthy a place in future editions. The second sonnet I have found on a detached piece of paper, without note or observation. How it came into my possession I have now forgotten, though I have some faint impression that I wrote it down from dictation, and that it was the transcript of an early, a *very early* sonnet, written probably at the time when the author's heart, as well as his head, was with Spinosa.

FAREWELL TO LOVE.

Farewell, sweet Love! yet blame you not my truth;
  More fondly ne'er did mother eye her child
Than I your form: *yours* were my hopes of youth
  And as *you* shaped my thoughts I sighed or smiled.
While most were wooing wealth, or gaily swerving
  To pleasure's secret haunt, and some apart
Stood strong in pride, self-conscious of deserving,
  To you I gave my whole weak wishing heart.
And when I met the maid that realised
  Your fair creations, and had won her kindness,
Say, but for her if aught in earth I prized!
  Your dreams alone I dreamt, and caught your blindness.
O grief!—but farewell, Love! I will go play me
  With thoughts that please me less, and less betray me.

TO NATURE.

It may indeed be phantasy, when I
Essay to draw from all created things
Deep, heartfelt, inward joy that closely clings;
And trace, in leaves and flowers that round me lie,

Lessons of love and earnest piety.
So let it be; and if the wide world rings
In mock of this belief, it brings
Nor fear, nor grief, nor vain perplexity.
So will I build my altar in the fields,
And the blue sky my fretted dome shall be,
And the sweet fragrance that the wild flower yields,
Shall be the incense I will yield to Thee,
Thee only God! and thou shalt not despise
Even me, the priest of this poor sacrifice.

LETTER XV.

MY DEAR YOUNG FRIEND, *January*, 1821.

The only impression left by you on my mind is an increased desire to see you again, and at shorter intervals. Were you my son by nature, I could not hold you dearer, or more earnestly desire to retain you the adopted of whatever within me will remain, when the dross and alloy of infirmity shall have been purged away. I feel the most entire confidence that no prosperous change of my outward circumstances would add to your *faith* in the sincerity of this assurance; still, however, the average of men being what it is, and it being neither possible nor desirable to be fully conscious in our understanding of the habits of thinking and judging in the world around us, and yet to be wholly impassive and unaffected by them in our feelings, it would endear and give a new value to an honourable competence, that I should be able to evince the true nature and degree of my esteem and attachment beyond the suspicion even of the sordid, and separate from all that is accidental or adventitious. But yet the friendship I feel for you is so genial a warmth, and blends so undistinguishably with my affections, is so perfectly one of the family in the household of love, that I would not be otherwise than obliged to you: and God is my witness, that my wish for an easier and less embarrassed lot is *chiefly*

(I thing I might have said *exclusively*) grounded on the deep conviction, that exposed to a less bleak aspect I should bring forth flowers and fruits both more abundant and more worthy of the unexampled kindness of your *faith* in me. Interpreting the "wine" and the "ivy garland" as figures of poetry signifying competence, and the removal of the petty needs of the body that plug up the pipes of the playing fountain (and such it is too well known was the intent and meaning of the hardly used poet), and oh! how often, when my heart has begun to swell from the genial warmth of thought, as our northern lakes from the (so called) bottom winds, when all above and around is stillness and sunshine—how often have I repeated in my own name the sweet stanza of Edmund Spenser:—

"Thou kenst not, Percie, how the rhyme should rage,
O! if my temples were bedewed with wine,
And girt in garlands of wild ivy twine;
How I could rear the muse on stately stage,
And teach her tread aloft in buskin fine
With queint Bellona in her equipage."

Read what follows as you would a note at the bottom of a page.

"But ah! Mecænas is ywrapt in clay, and great Augustus long ago is dead."

(This is a natural sigh, and natural too is the reflection that follows.)

"And if that any buds of poesy
Yet of the old stock 'gin to shoot again,
'Tis or *self*-lost the worldling's meed to gain,
And with the rest to breathe its ribauldry,
Or as it sprung it wither must again;
Tom Piper makes them better melody."

But though natural, the complaint is not equally philosophical, were it only on this account,—that I know of no age in which the same has not been advanced, and with the same grounds. Nay, I retract; there never was a time in which the *complaint* would be so little wise, though perhaps none in which the *fact* is more prominent. Neither philosophy nor poetry ever did, nor as long as they are terms of comparative excellence and contradistinction, ever can be *popular*, nor honoured with the praise and favour of contemporaries. But, on the other hand, there never was a time in which either books, that were *held* for excellent as poetic or philosophic, had so extensive and rapid a sale, or men reputed poets and philosophers of a high rank were so much *looked up* to in society, or so munificently, almost profusely, rewarded. Walter Scott's poems and novels (except only the two wretched abortions, Ivanhoe and the Bride of Ravensmuir, or whatever its name may be) supply both instance and solution of the *present* conditions and components of popularity, viz. to amuse without requiring any effort of thought, and without exciting any deep emotion. The age seems *sore* from excess of stimulation, just as, a day or two after a thorough debauch and long sustained drinking match, a man feels all over like a bruise. Even to admire otherwise than *on the whole*, and where "I admire" is but a synonym for "I remember I *liked* it very much *when I was reading it*," is too much an effort, would be too disquieting an emotion. Compare Waverley, Guy Mannering, and Co., with works that had an *immediate run* in the last generation, Tristram Shandy, Roderick Random, Sir Charles Grandison, Clarissa Harlowe, and Tom Jones (all which became popular as soon as published, and therefore instances fairly in point), and you will be convinced that the difference of taste is real, and not any fancy or croaking of my own.

But enough of these generals. It was my purpose to open myself out to you in detail. My health, I have reason to believe, is so intimately connected with the state of my spirits, and these again so dependent on my thoughts, prospective and retrospective, that I should not doubt the being favoured with a sufficiency for my noblest undertaking, had I the ease of heart requisite for the necessary abstraction of the thoughts, and such a reprieve from the goading of the immediate exigencies as might make tranquillity possible. But, alas! I know by experience (and the knowledge is not the less because the regret is not unmixed with self-blame, and the consciousness of want of exertion and fortitude), that my health will continue to decline, as long as the pain from reviewing the barrenness of the past is great in an inverse proportion to any rational anticipations of the future. As I now am, however, from five to six hours devoted to actual writing and composition in the day is the utmost that my strength, not to speak of my nervous system, will permit; and the invasions on this portion of my time from applications, often of the most senseless kind, are such and so many as to be almost as ludicrous even to myself as they are vexatious. In less than a week I have not seldom received half-a-dozen packets or parcels, of works printed or manuscript, urgently requesting my candid *judgment*, or my correcting hand. Add to these, letters from lords and ladies, urging me to write reviews or puffs of heaven-born geniuses, whose whole merit consists in being ploughmen or shoemakers. Ditto from actors; entreaties for money, or recommendations to publishers, from ushers out of place, &c. &c.; and to *me*, who have neither interest, influence, nor money, and, what is still more *àpropos*, can neither bring myself to tell smooth falsehoods nor harsh truths, and, in the struggle, too often do both in the anxiety to do neither.—I have already the *written* materials and contents, requiring only to be put together, from the loose papers and commonplace or memorandum books, and needing no other change, whether of omission, addition, or correction, than the mere act of arranging, and the opportunity of seeing the whole collectively bring with them of course,—I. Characteristics of Shakspeare's Dramatic Works, with a Critical Review of each Play; together with a relative and comparative Critique on the kind and degree of the Merits and Demerits of the Dramatic Works of Ben Jonson, Beaumont and Fletcher, and Massinger. The History of the English Drama; the accidental advantages it afforded to Shakspeare, without in the least detracting from the perfect originality or proper creation of the Shakspearian Drama; the contradistinction of the latter from the Greek Drama, and its still remaining *uniqueness*, with the causes of this, from the combined influences of Shakspeare himself, as man, poet, philosopher, and finally, by conjunction of all these, dramatic poet; and of the age, events, manners, and state of the English language. This work, with every art of compression, amounts to three volumes of about five hundred pages each.—II. Philosophical Analysis of the Genius and Works of Dante, Spenser, Milton, Cervantes, and Calderon, with similar, but more compressed Criticisms on Chaucer, Ariosto, Donne, Rabelais, and others, during the predominance of the Romantic Poetry. In one large volume.—These two works will, I flatter myself, form a complete code of the principles of judgment and feeling applied to Works of Taste; and not of *Poetry* only, but of Poesy in all its forms, Painting, Statuary, Music, &c. &c.—III. The History of Philosophy considered as a Tendency of the Human Mind to exhibit the Powers of the Human Reason, to discover by its own Strength the Origin and Laws of Man and the World from Pythagoras to Locke and Condillac. Two volumes.—IV. Letters on the Old and New Testament, and on the Doctrine and Principles held in common by the Fathers and Founders of the Reformation, addressed to a Candidate for Holy Orders; including Advice on the Plan and Subjects of Preaching, proper to a Minister of the Established Church.

To the completion of these four works I have literally nothing more to do than *to transcribe;* but, as I before hinted, from so many scraps and *Sibylline* leaves, including margins of books and blank pages, that, unfortunately, I must be my own scribe, and not done by myself, they will be all but lost; or perhaps (as has been too often the case already) furnish feathers for the caps of others; some for this purpose, and some to plume

6

the arrows of detraction, to be let fly against the luckless bird from whom they had been plucked or moulted.

In addition to these—of my GREAT WORK, to the preparation of which more than twenty years of my life have been devoted, and on which my hopes of extensive and permanent utility, of fame, in the noblest * sense of the word, mainly rest—that, by which I might,

> " As now by thee, by all the good be known,
> When this weak frame lies moulder'd in the grave,
> Which self-surviving I might call my own,
> Which Folly cannot mar, nor Hate deprave—
> The incense of those powers, which, risen in flame,
> Might make me dear to Him from whom they came."

---

* Turn to Milton's Lycidas, sixth stanza—

> " Alas ! what boots it with incessant care
> To tend the homely slighted shepherd's trade,
> And strictly meditate the thankless Muse ?
> Were it not better done as others use,
> To sport with Amaryllis in the shade,
> Or with the tangles of Neæra's hair ?
> Fame is the spur that the clear spirit doth raise
> (That last infirmity of noble mind)
> To scorn delights and live laborious days ;
> But the fair guerdon when we hope to find,
> And think to burst out into sudden blaze,
> Comes the blind Fury with the abhorred shears,
> And slits the thin-spun life. But not the praise,
> Phœbus replied, and touched my trembling ears ;
> Fame is no plant that grows on mortal soil,
> Nor on the glistering foil
> Set off to the world, nor in broad Rumour lies,
> But lives and spreads aloft by those pure eyes,
> And perfect witness of all-judging Jove ;
> As he pronounces lastly in each deed,
> Of so much fame in heav'n expect thy meed."

The sweetest music does not fall sweeter on my ear than this stanza on both mind and ear, as often as I repeat it aloud.

Of this work, to which all my other writings (unless I except my Poems, and these I can exclude in part only) are introductory and preparative; and the result of which (if the premises be, as I with the most tranquil assurance, am convinced they are—insubvertible, the deductions legitimate, and the conclusions commensurate, and only commensurate, with both), must finally be a revolution of all that has been called *Philosophy* or Metaphysics in England and France since the era of the commencing predominance of the mechanical system at the restoration of our second Charles, and with this the present fashionable views, not only of religion, morals, and politics, but even of the modern physics and physiology. You will not blame the earnestness of my expressions, nor the high importance which I attach to this work; for how, with less noble objects, and less faith in their attainment, could I stand acquitted of folly, and abuse of time, talents, and learning, in a labour of three-fourths of my *intellectual* life? Of this work, something more than a volume has been dictated by me, so as to exist fit for the press, to my friend and enlightened pupil, Mr. Green; and more than as much again would have been evolved and delivered to paper, but that, for the last six or eight months, I have been compelled to break off our weekly meeting, from the necessity of writing (alas! alas! of *attempting* to write) for purposes, and on the subjects of the passing day.—Of my poetic works, I would fain finish the Christabel. Alas! for the proud time when I planned, when I had present to my mind, the materials, as well as the scheme, of the Hymns entitled Spirit, Sun, Earth, Air, Water, Fire, and Man: and the Epic Poem on—what still appears to me the one only fit subject remaining for an Epic Poem—Jerusalem besieged and destroyed by Titus.

And here comes, my dear friend—here comes my sorrow and my weakness, my grievance and my confession. Anxious to perform the duties of the day arising out of the wants of the day, these wants, too, presenting themselves in the most painful of all forms,—that of a debt owing to those who will not exact it, and yet need its payment, and the delay, the long (not live-long but *death*-long) behind-hand of my accounts to friends, whose utmost care and frugality on the one side, and industry on the other, the wife's management and the husband's assiduity are put in requisition to make both ends meet, I am at once forbidden to attempt, and too perplexed earnestly to pursue, the *accomplishment* of the works worthy of me, those I mean above enumerated,—even if, savagely as I have been injured by one of the two influensive Reviews, and with more effective enmity undermined by the utter silence or occasional detractive compliments of the other,* I had the probable chance of disposing of them to the booksellers, so as even to liquidate my mere boarding accounts during the time expended in the transcription, arrangement, and proof correction. And yet, on the other hand, my heart and mind are for ever recurring to them. Yes, my conscience forces me to plead guilty, I have only by fits and starts even prayed. I have not prevailed on myself to pray to God in sincerity and entireness for the fortitude that might enable me to resign myself to the abandonment of all my life's best hopes, to say boldly to myself,—"Gifted with powers confessedly above mediocrity, aided by an education, of which, no less from almost unexampled hardships and sufferings than from manifold and peculiar advantages, I have never yet found a parallel, I have devoted myself to a life of unintermitted reading, thinking, meditating, and observing. I have not only sacrificed all worldly prospects of wealth and advancement, but have in my inmost soul stood aloof from temporary reputation. In consequence of these toils and this self-dedication, I possess a

* Neither my Literary Life (2 vols.), nor Sibylline Leaves (1 vol.), nor Friend (3 vols.), nor Lay Sermons, nor Zapolya, nor Christabel, have ever been noticed by the Quarterly Review, of which Southey is yet the main support.

calm and clear consciousness, that in many and most important departments of truth and beauty I have outstrode my contemporaries—those at least of highest name; that the number of my printed works bears witness that I have not been idle, and the seldom acknowledged, but strictly *proveable*, effects of my labours appropriated to the immediate welfare of my age in the *Morning Post* before and during the peace of Amiens, in the *Courier* afterwards, and in the series and various subjects of my lectures at Bristol and at the Royal and Surrey Institutions, in Fetter-lane, at Willis's Rooms, and at the Crown and Anchor (add to which the unlimited freedom of my communications in colloquial life), may surely be allowed as evidence that I have not been useless in my generation. But, from circumstances, the *main* portion of my harvest is still on the ground, ripe indeed, and only waiting, a few for the sickle, but a large part only for the *sheaving*, and carting, and housing; but from all this I must turn away, must let them rot as they lie, and be as though they never had been, for I must go and gather blackberries and earth-nuts, or pick mushrooms and gild oak-apples for the palates and fancies of chance customers. I must abrogate the name of philosopher and poet, and scribble as fast as I can, and with as little thought as I can, for Blackwood's Magazine, or as I have been employed for the last days, in writing MS. sermons for lazy clergymen, who stipulate that the composition must not be more than respectable, for fear they should be desired to publish the visitation sermon!" This I have not yet had courage to do. My soul sickens and my heart sinks; and thus, oscillating between both, I do neither, neither as it ought to be done, or to any profitable end. If I were to detail only the various, I might say capricious, interruptions that have prevented the finishing of this very scrawl, begun on the very day I received your last kind letter, you would need no other illustrations.

Now I see but one possible plan of rescuing my permanent utility. It is briefly this and plainly. For what we struggle with inwardly, we find at least easiest to *bolt out*, namely—that of engaging from the circle of those who think respectfully and hope highly of my powers and attainments a yearly sum, for three or four years, adequate to my actual support, with such comforts and decencies of appearance as my health and habits have made necessaries, so that my mind may be unanxious as far as the present time is concerned; that thus I should stand both enabled and pledged to begin with some one work of these above mentioned, and for two-thirds of my whole time to devote myself to this exclusively till finished, to take the chance of its success by the best mode of publication that would involve me in no risk, then to proceed with the next, and so on till the works above mentioned as already in full material existence should be reduced into formal and actual being; while in the remaining third of my time I might go on maturing and completing my great work, and (for if but easy in mind, I have no doubt either of the re-awakening power or of the kindling inclination), and my Christabel, and what else the happier hour might inspire—and without inspiration a barrel-organ may be played right deftly; but

> "All otherwise the state of *poet* stands;
> For lordly want is such a tyrant fell,
> That where he rules all power he doth expel.
> The vaunted verse a vacant head demands,
> Ne wont with crabbed Care the muses dwell:
> *Unwisely weaves who takes two webs* IN HAND!"

Now Mr. Green has offered to contribute from £30 to £40 yearly, for three or four years; my young friend and pupil, the son of one of my dearest old friends, £50; and I think that from £10 to £20 I could rely upon from another. The sum required would be about £200, to be repaid, of course, should the disposal or sale, and as far as the disposal and sale, of my writings produce the means.

I have thus placed before you at large, wanderingly, as well as diffusely, the statement which I am inclined to send in a compressed form to a few of those of whose kind dispositions towards me I have received assurances,—and to their interest and influence I must leave it—anxious, however, before I do this, to learn from you your very, very inmost feeling and judgment as to the previous questions. Am I entitled, have I earned *a right* to do this? Can I do it without moral degradation? and, lastly, can it be done without loss of character in the eyes of my acquaintance, and of my friends' acquaintance, who may have been informed of the circumstances? That, if attempted at all, it will be attempted in such a way, and that such persons only will be spoken to, as will not expose me to indelicate rebuffs to be afterwards matter of gossip, I know those, to whom I shall entrust the statement, too well to be much alarmed about.

Pray let me either see or hear from you as soon as possible; for, indeed and indeed, it is no inconsiderable accession to the pleasure I anticipate from disembarrassment, that *you* would have to contemplate in a more gracious form, and in a more ebullient play of the inward fountain, the mind and manners of,

My dear friend,

Your obliged and very affectionate friend,

S. T. Coleridge.

T. Allsop, Esq.

This is one of the most beautiful, the most interesting and, in many respects, the most affecting letter I have preserved; it is a letter which no one but my lamented friend could have written.

I am precluded by the determination with which I set out (not to attach blame to persons farther than blame is attributed by the writer, or to be clearly inferred from the letters or conversations themselves,) from sundry explanations and strictures which constantly occur to me as often as I peruse and re-peruse this letter. The condition here so fully laid open has been in all ages that of the seekers after truth for its own sake; and *exclusively* and NECESSARILY arises from those conditions of mind which render such a course possible. Viewing man, as far as the facts established as *truths*, and the truths which result from antecedent truth, enable us to speak on this matter, as subject in all his actions, or rather in the will in which they originate, to external and internal influences which exist antecedent to, and independent of, his will, I cannot hesitate to declare my calm and settled opinion that it is unjust to blame or to praise, or if it *could* be just, only so as applied to the cause, not to the necessary effect. Acting upon these views, it would ill accord with my fixed purpose, if I should blame individuals or systems, or waste time in seeking for proximate or remote causes. All that I have permitted myself is, to narrate, and sometimes to regret results; regrets which to me, and for me, are as *necessary* as the results themselves.

No blame, therefore, do I attach to the parties who permitted such an appeal, from such a man, to strangers. Unworthy as the motives have been termed, by which sundry persons were considered to be influenced, I am *conscious that for them* no other course was *possible*. I cannot call either their motives or their actions evil; it would be untrue if I, with the settled convictions at which I have arrived, were so to characterise them. It will be sufficient for the future that we see what physical suffering and what mental pain were the results. It is only when we apply the experience of the past to the similar or like events of the present, that we add to the sum and amount of permanent pleasurable existence. If a thousandth part of the time consumed in regulating *actions* had been devoted to creating good *motives*, if but a millionth part of the time devoted to the punishment of crime had been bestowed in a right direction, crime, in the form at least in which it now exists, would have been impossible. If the less ccupied, instead of busying themselves with spiritual responsibility, respecting which nothing *is or can certainly be* known, had applied themselves to the question of moral and physical responsibility, the lamentable ignorance now prevailing, an ignorance which is synonymous with moral and physical degradation, could not have continued to this hour. If, instead of blaming men for what they are, and are *made to be*, we occupied and interested ourselves with earnest inquiries into the causes of the evils we deplore, with a view to their removal, it cannot be doubted that this real labour of love, if carried on with and through the spirit of love, would in its *very endeavour* include much of the good sought to be obtained. To me it seems that the greatest amount of benefit will result from the labours or the exertions of those, who unite the good to others with that which is—has been made—pleasurable to themselves; from those who seek to make what is genial and joyous to themselves more genial and more joyous to others. This is a labour in which not merely some favourite crochet, some abstract opinion, or even sincere and honest *convictions* are engaged; it is one in which the best, the purest, the highest sympathies of our nature are enlisted in the service, and in the promotion of those enjoyments, and of those practical occupations from which our own well-being has resulted, or with which it has been associated.*

---

* As examples of the success attending the removal of the exciting causes of vice or crime, instead of seeking a cure by punishment, I should wish to direct all unprejudiced minds to the results of the system successfully practised by the celebrated Robert Owen, at New Lanark, founded upon the eternal truth, that men, and, much more, children take their character from the surrounding influences. The result of Mr. Owen's benevolent exertions has proved what can be done with a vicious *population*. The quotation which follows, though not so well known as it deserves, will show what can be effected by a benevolent and decided man with a vicious *adult* population.

To M. Victor de Tracy.

"*Malwa*, 29*th March*, 1832.

"During a short stay in Adjmeer, I contrived to visit the Mhairwanah, the former Abruzzi of Rajpootana. It was well worth riding eighty-four miles. I saw a country whose inhabitants, since an im-

Much that is now sought to be attained is very pleasant, nay, very desirable, but the means by which it is sought are not practicable, the harmonious combinations, to any adequate extent, are not yet possible; and all endeavours to force the

---

memorial time, had never had any other means of existence but plunder in the adjacent plains, a people of murderers; now changed into a *quiet, industrious, and happy* people of shepherds and cultivators. No Rajpoot chiefs, no Mogul emperors, had ever been able to subdue them; fourteen years ago everything was to be done with them, and in seven years the change was effected. I will add, that Major Hall has accomplished this admirable social experiment without taking a single life.

"The very worst characters were secured, confined, or put in irons to work on the roads. Those who had lived long by the sword, without however becoming notorious for their cruelty, were made soldiers; in that capacity they became the keepers of their former associates, and often of their chiefs; and the rest of the population was gained to the plough. Female infanticide was a prevalent practice with the Mhairs, and generally throughout Rajpootana; and now female casualties do not exceed male casualties; a proof that the bloody practice has been abandoned; and scarcely has a man been punished. Major Hall did not punish the offenders; he removed the cause of the crime, and made the crime useless, even injurious to the offender, and it was never more committed.

"Major Hall has shown me the corps he raised from these former savages, and I have seen none in India in a higher state of discipline. He was justly proud of his good work, and spared no trouble that I might see it thoroughly. Upwards of a hundred villagers were summoned from the neighbouring hamlets; I conversed with them on their former mode of life, and of their present avocations. Most of these men had shed blood. They told me they knew not any other mode of life: it was a most miserable one by their account; they were naked and starving.

"Now, poor as is the soil of their small valleys, and barren their hills, *every hand being set at work, there is plenty of clothes, of food;* and so sensible are they of the immense benefit conferred by the British government, that willingly they pay to it already 500,000 francs, which they increase every year as the national wealth admits of it.

"Often I had thought that gentle means would prove inadequate

time of action have hitherto failed, owing to the time being unpropitious, or to the means being unsuitable; or, still more, from the great, the fatal mistake, a mistake to which benevolent natures are too liable, that of mistaking the changed convictions of the mind for an equally decided and simultaneous change in the habits or actions. From those men the highest good is to be hoped "who have encouraged the sympathetic passions until they have become irresistible habits, and made their duty a necessary part of their self-interest; who derive their most exquisite pleasures from the contemplation of possible perfection, and proportionate pain from the perception of existing *depravation*. Accustomed to regard all the affairs of man as a process, they never hurry and they never pause. Theirs is not that *twilight* of political knowledge which gives us just light enough to place one foot before the other; as they advance, the scene still opens upon them, and they press right onward with a vast and various landscape of existence around them. Internal calmness and energy mark all their actions. Convinced that vice originates not in the man, but in the surrounding circumstances; not in the heart, but in the understanding, they are hopeless concerning no one—to correct a vice or generate a virtuous conduct they pollute not their hands with the scourge of coercion; but by endeavouring to alter the circumstances would remove, or by strengthening the intellect disarm, temptation. These soul-ennobling views bestow the virtues they anticipate.

"That general illumination should precede revolution is a

---

to the task of breaking-in populations addicted for ages to a most savage life, such as the Greeks, for instance. Yet the Klephts were but lambs compared to the Mhairs, and the Mhairs in a few years have become an industrious, a laborious, and well-behaved people.

"I see M. Capo d'Istria has been murdered. I wish Major Hall were his successor, for now I have the greatest confidence in the efficacy of gentle means."

Jaquemont's Letters.

truth as obvious as that the vessel should be cleansed before we fill it with a pure liquor. But the mode of diffusing it is not discoverable with equal facility. We certainly should never attempt to make proselytes by appeals to the *selfish* feeling, and consequently should plead *for* the oppressed, not* *to* them. Godwin considers private societies as the sphere of real utility; that (each one illuminating those immediately below him) truth by a gradual descent may at last reach the lowest order. But this is rather plausible than just or practicable. Society, as at present constituted, does not resemble a chain that ascends in a continuity of links; alas! between the parlour and the kitchen, the tap and the coffee-room, there is a gulf that may not be passed. He would appear to me to have adopted the best as well as the most benevolent mode of diffusing truth, who, uniting the zeal of the methodist with the views of the philosopher, should be *personally* among the poor, and teach them their *duties* in order that he may render them susceptible of their rights."

The present tendencies are, I believe, adverse to the attainment of any high, pure, or lasting advantage, unless it be from the necessary re-action or recoil. I can conceive of no blasphemy more vile or self-degrading, than that which contemplates the degradation of the moral being into a political or social subjection to combinations, which, if they were as perfect and as practical as they are crude and impossible, would end in solving, by proving, the depravity of human nature.

What is to be said of a science (so called), which tends to the destruction of all that has hitherto been associated with the pure in thought and act, and which has declared, through

---

* I consider *both* necessary, nay, desirable. Would pleading for rights withheld have procured their restoration, if also the people had not been aroused by direct appeals to their sense of wrong? Pleading to the oppressed alone would be of terrific danger, did not a sense of justice aided by personal fears create advocates, who end in becoming mediators.

one of the most favoured and influential of its organs, that it would be of the *highest possible advantage* to Great Britain, if its *country* were wholly destroyed by a volcano, so that its *factories* and *towns* might be compelled to have recourse to other lands for food, and thus sell sundry additional bales of cotton or pigs of iron ?*

Well might Frederic of Prussia say, if it were wished effectually to ruin a province or a kingdom, the surest and swiftest way would be to appoint an economist the administrator. To believe that this most pernicious of all systems can long exist; to think that this faith in mechanics, mental and distributive, could long continue, except as a preparative to something higher or better, or as a condition of a quick and complete re-action, would for me sadden the earth around, and wither the very grass in the fields.

> "Toy-bewitched,
> Made blind by lusts, disherited of soul,
> No common centre Man, no common sire
> Knoweth ! A sordid solitary thing,
> 'Mid countless brethren with a lonely heart
> Through courts and cities the smooth savage roams
> Feeling himself, his own low Self, the whole ;
> When he by sacred sympathy might make

---

* This writer has, in the very article referred to, strangely verified the passage in the preceding letter, in which my excellent friend states that his MS. suggestions have been made, some to furnish feathers for the caps of others, and some for the purpose of defaming him from whom they were stolen. This writer has done both. He has most grossly defamed the admirable man whom he was incapable of estimating or appreciating, and in the last number of his work has appropriated some of the most striking of Coleridge's views, even to his very illustrations. This writer, formerly a butcher, a man-butcher (I say this *illustratively*, not disparagingly), would be more innocently employed in destroying life than in attempting to mutilate the reputation of the great dead.

The whole ONE SELF! SELF, that no alien knows!
SELF, far diffused as Fancy's wing can travel!
Self, spreading still! Oblivious of its own,
Yet all of all possessing!"

Religious Musings, p. 90-1.

To you, my dearest children, and to those not less dear, because equally docile and ingenuous, whom only, or chiefly, I desire as readers, I would as the result of my experience say,—cultivate all the social relations, all the recognised modes of kindly intercourse and intercommunication; yet always preserving, even in moments of the most entire interfusion of mind and the affections, a consciousness and presence of identity, which alone gives value to this sympathy and sympathetic union. So also I would have you to consider this self as cultivable, as deriving its chiefest and highest value from its relation to and dependence upon congenial natures, which by a natural attraction and harmony are drawn together, and respond to each other.

To be conscious of existence only, as its sorrows are shared or its pleasures enhanced by affection and love in its *nobler* sense, appears the highest condition of humanity, and this I hold to be attainable. To this I seek to approximate; and this, my dearest friends, every one may to some considerable extent arrive at, who, yearning after the pure and unearthly,

"Shall, when brought
Among the tasks of real life, have wrought
Upon the plan that pleased his *child-like* thought;
Abides by this resolve, and stops not there,
But makes his moral being his prime care,
And therefore does not stoop, nor lie in wait
For wealth or honours, or for worldly state;
Whom they must follow, on whose head must fall,
Like showers of manna, if they come at all.
His is a soul, whose master-bias leans
To home-felt pleasures and to gentle scenes;
Sweet images! which, wheresoe'er he be,
Are at his heart; and such fidelity

It is his darling passion to approve,
More brave for this—that he has much to love.
'Tis, finally, the man who, lifted high,
Conspicuous o'ject in a nation's eye,
Or left unthought on in obscurity,
Who with a toward or untoward lot,
Prosperous or adverse, *to his wish or not,*
Plays in the many games of life *that one*
Where what he most doth value must be won."

LETTER XVI.

MY DEAREST FRIEND, *Blandford-place, March 1st,* 1821.

God bless you, and all who are dear and near to you! but as to your pens, they seem to have been plucked from the *devil's* pinions, and slit and shaped by the blunt edge of the broad sprays of his antlers. Of the ink (*i.e.* your inkstand), it would be base to complain. I hate abusing folks in their *absence*. Do you know, my dear friend, that having sundry little snug superstitions of my own, I shrewdly suspect that whimsical ware of that sort is connected with the state and garniture of your paper-staining machinery.—Is it so? Well, I have seen Murray, and he has been civil, I may say kind, in his manners. Is this your knock?—Is it you on the stairs?—No. I explained my full purpose to him, namely,—that he should take me and my concerns, past and future, for print and reprint, under his umbrageous foliage, though the original name of his great predecessor in the patronage of genius, who gave the name of Augustan to all happy epochs—Octavius would be more appropriate—and he promises,—*cætera desunt.*

It was about this time that I met with an odd volume of the Tatler, during a forced stay at a remote and obscure inn* in the wilds of Kinder Scout.

* Those who have been kept at a cheerless inn in a dreary country by continued rain in late autumn, without external resource or the

The book opened at a paper (one of Steele's) giving an account of the writer's meeting with an old friend, recalling to his memory their early intimacy, and the services he had rendered him in his courtship, the delightful pictures which he calls up of the youthful, animated, and happy lovers, which, with a felicity peculiar to Steele, such was the fineness, the pure gold of *his* nature, he associates, rather than contrasts, with the quiet happiness, the full content and the still devotion (the heart-love), which makes an *Elysium of a home* in other respects only *home*-ly.

This picture, yet I think one of the most pure and most delightful of that age, for it belongs in its manners and some of its accessories to the past century, I mentioned to Coleridge on my return, and had, as I expected, my pleasure repeated, deepened, and extended. It was a joy and ever new delight to listen to him on any congenial theme, on one congenial to *you* as well as to *him*. I was especially pleased to find that he

---

means of communication, without books, and even without writing materials, — that is, without paper upon which to write, — need not be told *how delightful*, what an event, it is to meet with a book, such as by a special providence is always discovered in these places when the powers are propitious, such as a stray volume of Sir Charles Grandison, which you will find at the Swan at Brecon ; an odd volume of the Tatler at the inn on Kinder Scout ; the fifth volume of Clarissa Harlowe at the inn at Lyndhurst ; the Abelard and Heloise, an undomestic translation (which I hasten to recommend to my excellent friend, Charles Cowden Clark, to be immediately expurgated and made *decent*, and *fit for introduction* into seminaries, and into demure and orderly families), at the Crab and Lobster, Bonchurch ; to Bell's Luther's Table Talk, full of odd things, at Camps Inn, Ilfracombe ; the Athenian Oracle, containing many unnoticed contributions by Swift, at the Pelican, Speenhamland ; and last, because the most ungenial and most unseemly, Pamela, in one large volume, at the little inn at Bembridge Ledge or Point. To enjoy these you must be without any other resource, and the book, discovered after a long, and, as you begin to think, hopeless, search, must be one that you have read *very* early in youth, and of which you only retain very faint recollections.

valued Steele, always my prime favourite, so much above Addison and the other essayists of that day; he denied that Steele was, as he himself said in a pleasantry, "like a distressed prince who calls in a powerful neighbour to his aid, and who, once in possession, became sovereign." Addison was necessary to give variety to the papers, but in no other sense did he give value. Steele's papers are easily distinguished to this day by their pure humanity springing from the gentleness, the *kindness* of his heart. He dwelt with much *unction* on the curious and instructive letters of Steele to his wife; and with much approval on the manliness with which, in the first letters, he addressed the lady to whom he was afterwards united. He quoted the following as models of their kind, and worthy of especial admiration:—

"As I know no reason why difference of sex should make our language to each other differ from the ordinary rules of right reason, I shall use plainness and sincerity in my discourse to you, as much as other lovers do perplexity and rapture. Instead of saying, 'I shall die for you,' I profess I should be glad to lead my life with you. You are as beautiful, as witty, as prudent, and as good-humoured as any woman breathing; but I regard all these excellences as you will please to direct them for my happiness or misery. With me, Madam, the only lasting motive to love is the hope of its becoming mutual. . . All great passion makes us dumb; and the highest happiness, as well as the greatest grief, seizes us too violently to be expressed by words. . . . To know so much pleasure with so much innocence is, methinks, a satisfaction beyond the present condition of human life; but the union of minds in pure affection is renewing the first state of man. . . . This is an unusual language to ladies; but you have a mind above the giddy notions of a sex ensnared by flattery, and misled by a false and short adoration, into a solid and long contempt. Beauty palls in the possession; but I love also your mind; your soul is as dear to me as my own; and if the advantage of a liberal education, some knowledge, and as much contempt of the world, joined with endeavours towards a life of strict virtue and religion, can qualify me to raise new ideas in a breast so well disposed as yours is, our days will pass away with joy, and instead of introducing melancholy prospects of decay, give us hope of eternal youth in a better life. . . . Let us go on to make our regards to each other mutual and unchangeable; that while the world around us is enchanted with the false satisfactions of vagrant desire, our persons may be shrines to each other, sacred to conjugal faith, unreserved confidence, and heavenly society."

Even when the extreme thrift of his wife—the necessary result or reaction from the husband's improvidence—caused him uneasiness, his replies show the true gentleness of his nature:—

"I assure you, any disturbance between us is the greatest affliction to me imaginable. You talk of the judgment of the world; I shall never govern my actions by it, but by the rules of morality and right reason. I love you better than the light of my eyes or the life-blood in my heart; but you are also to understand, that neither my sight shall be so far enchanted, nor my affection so much master of me, as to make me forget our common interest. To attend my business as I ought, and improve my fortune, it is necessary that my time and my will should be under no direction but my own. . . . We must take our portion of life as it runs without repining. I consider that good nature, added to that beautiful form God has given you, would make a happiness too great for human life. . . . You may think what you please, but I know you have the best husband in the world in your affectionate

"RICHARD STEELE."

This letter, written about a year after their marriage, seems to me calculated to appease any woman who was not both a shrew and a niggard. Careful attention to fortune, even if it exceeds its fit and just proportion, may, perhaps, be excusable in a man; in a woman, this most unfeminine and ungentle property of niggardliness is most unseemly, even when redeemed, as it was not in this case, by an upheaped love and devotion to her admirable husband.

"There are not words to express the tenderness I have for you. Love is too harsh a term for it; but if you knew how my heart aches when you speak an unkind word to me, and springs with joy when you smile upon me, I am sure you would place your glory rather in preserving my happiness, like a good wife, than tormenting me, like a peevish beauty. Good Prue, write me word you shall be overjoyed at my return to you, and pity the figure I make when I pretend to resist you, by complying with my reasonable demands. . . . It is in no one's power but Prue's to make me constant in a regular course; therefore will not doubt but you will be very good-humoured and a constant feast to your affectionate husband. . . . I send you seven pennyworths of walnuts at five a penny, which is the greatest proof I can give you at present of my being, with my whole heart, yours,

"RICHARD STEELE.

"P.S.—There are but twenty-nine walnuts."

"DEAR, DEAR PRUE,

"Your pretty letter, and so much good nature and kindness, which I received yesterday, is a perfect pleasure to me. . . . I am, dear Prue, a little in drink, but at all times

"Your faithful husband,

"RICHARD STEELE."

"DEAR PRUE,

"If you do not hear from me before three to-morrow afternoon, believe I am too fuddled to observe your orders; but, however, know me to be

"Your most faithful and affectionate

"RICHARD STEELE.

"I am very sick with too much wine last night."

The last passage would, at the present time, be considered evidence of a vicious, degraded course of life, and therefore not confessed to a wife of whom the writer was somewhat in awe. *At that time* drinking was held a mark of good fellowship, and was considered, as indeed it is, far more venial than the vices which at present have usurped its place; vices which partake of the intense selfishness of this age of mechanical activity.

With how sweet a grace does he address Lady Steele, after seven years' intimate communion; and with how much true delicacy does he dwell upon her homely virtues: virtues which, when they attain the great and highest aim of every right-minded woman, to make home cheerful and happy to her husband, are, beyond all others, pure and ennobling; but in this case, that result was neither sought nor obtained.

"Madam,

"To have either wealth, wit or beauty, is generally a temptation to a woman to put an unreasonable value upon herself; but with all these, in a degree which drew upon you the addresses of men of the amplest fortunes, you bestowed your person where you could have no expectations but from the gratitude of the receiver, though you knew he could exert that gratitude in no other returns but esteem and love. For which must I first thank you? for what you have denied yourself, or for what you have bestowed on me?

"I owe to you, that for my sake you have overlooked the prospect of living in pomp and plenty, and I have not been circumspect enough to preserve you from care and sorrow. I will not dwell upon this particular; you are so good a wife, that I know you think I rob you of more than I can give, when I say anything in your favour to my own disadvantage.

"Whoever should see or hear you, would think it were worth leaving all the world for you; while I, habitually possessed of that happiness, have been throwing away impotent endeavours for the rest of mankind, to the neglect of her for whom any other man, in his senses, would be apt to sacrifice everything else.

"I know not by what unreasonable prepossession it is, but methinks there must be something austere to give authority to wisdom; and I cannot account for having rallied many seasonable sentiments of yours, but that you are too beautiful to appear judicious.

"One may grow fond, but not wise, from what is said by so lovely a counsellor. Hard fate! that you have been lessened by your perfections, and lost power by your charms!

"That ingenuous spirit in all your behaviour, that familiar grace in your words and actions, has for this seven years only inspired admiration and love; but experience has taught me, the best counsel I ever have received has been pronounced by the fairest and softest lips, and convinced me that I am in you blest with a wise friend, as well as a charming mistress.

"Your mind shall no longer suffer by your person; nor shall your eyes, for the future, dazzle me into a blindness towards your understanding. I rejoice to show my esteem for you; and must do you the justice to say, that there can be no virtue represented in the female world, which I have not known you exert, as far as the opportunities of your fortune have given you leave. Forgive me, that my heart overflows with love and gratitude for daily instances of your prudent economy, the just disposition you make of your little affairs, your cheerfulness in dispatch of them, your prudent forbearance of any reflections, that they might have needed less vigilance had you disposed of your fortune suitably; in short, for all the arguments you every day give me of a generous and sincere affection.

"It is impossible for me to look back on many evils and pains which I have suffered since we came together, without a pleasure which is not to be expressed, from the proofs I have had, in those circumstances, of your unwearied goodness. How often has your tenderness removed pain from my sick head! how often anguish from my afflicted heart! With how skilful patience have I known you comply with the vain projects *which pain has suggested, to have an aching limb removed by journeying from one side of a room to another! how often, the next instant, travelled the same ground again,* WITHOUT TELLING *your patient it was to no purpose to change his situation!* If there are such beings as guardian angels, thus are they employed. I will no more believe one of them more good in its inclinations, than I can conceive it more charming in its form, than my wife.

"I will end this without so much as mentioning your little flock, or your own amiable figure at the head of it. That I think them preferable to all other children, I know is the effect of passion and instinct; that I believe you the best of wives, I know proceeds from experience and reason.

"I am, Madam, your most obliged husband, and most obedient humble servant,

"RICHARD STEELE."

"I sometimes compare my own life with that of Steele (yet oh! how unlike!) led to this from having myself also for a brief time *borne arms*, and written 'private' after my name, or rather another name; for being at a loss when suddenly asked my name, I answered *Cumberback*, and verily my habits were so little equestrian, that my horse, I doubt not, was of that opinion. Of Steele, also, it might in one sense, at least, have been said,

'Lingering he raised his latch at eve,
Though tired in heart and limb!
He loved no other place, and yet
Home was no home to him.'

Oh! the sorrow, the bitterness of that grief which springs from love not participated, or not returned in the spirit in which it is bestowed. Fearful and enduring is that canker-worm of the soul, that

> 'Grief without a pang, void, dark, and drear,
> A stifled, drowsy, unimpassioned grief,
> Which finds no natural outlet, no relief
> In word, or sigh, or tear.'

"I sometimes think I shall write a book on the duties of women, more especially to their husbands. If such a book were *well written*, I cannot doubt but that its results would be most salutary. I am inclined to think that both men and women err in their conduct and demeanour towards each other, quite as much from ignorance and unconsciousness of what is displeasing, as from selfishness or disregard. But to the execution of such a work, or rather such works (for 'A New Duty of Man' is quite as much required, and this must be written by an affectionate and right-minded woman), the present sickly delicacy, the over-delicacy (and therefore essential indelicacy) of the present taste would be opposed. To be of any use it should be a plain treatise, the results of experience, and should be given to all newly married couples by their parents, not in the form of admonition, but rather as containing much important information which *they* can no where else obtain."

LETTER XVII.

MY DEAR FRIEND, *May 4th*, 1821.

Mr. and Mrs. Gillman's kind love, and we beg that the good lady's late remembering that (as often the very fullness and vividness of the purpose and intention to do a thing imposes on the mind a sort of counterfeit feeling of quiet, similar to the satisfaction which the having done it would produce) you had not been written to, will not prejudice the present attempt at "better late than never." We have a party *to-morrow*, in which, because we believed it would interest you, you stood included. In addition to a neighbour, Robert Sutton, and ourselves, and Mrs. Gillman's most un-Mrs. Gillmanly sister (but *n. b.* this is a secret to all who are both blind and deaf), there will be the Mathews (Mr. and Mrs.) *at home*, Mathews I mean, and Charles and Mary Lamb.

Of myself the best thing that I can say is that, in the belief of those well qualified to judge, I am not so ill as I fancy myself. Be this as it may,

I am always, my dearest friend,
With highest esteem and regard,
Your affectionate friend,

T. Allsop, Esq. S. T. Coleridge.

Of this day and the one following I have a few notes, which appear to me of interest. It must be borne constantly in mind, that much of what is preserved has relation to positions enforced by others, and which Coleridge held to be untenable on the particular grounds urged, not as being untrue in themselves.

"Had Lord Byron possessed perseverance enough to undergo the drudgery of research, and had his theological studies and attainments been at all like mine, he would have been able to unsettle all the evidences of Christianity, upheld as it is at present by simple confutation. Is it possible to assent to the doctrine of redemption as at present promulgated, that the moral death of an *unoffending* being should be a consequence of the transgression of humanity* *and its atonement!*"

---

* Let it always be borne in mind, that this and other expressions in these pages were the opinions which he ever expressed *to me*, and are not to be taken as evidences of doubt generally, but of disbelief in the corruptions of the vulgar Christianity in vogue.

"Walter Scott's novels are chargeable with the same faults as Bertram, *et id omne genus*, viz., that of ministering to the depraved appetite for excitement, and, though in a far less degree, creating sympathy for the vicious and infamous, solely because the fiend is *daring*. Not twenty lines of Scott's poetry will ever reach posterity; it has relation to nothing."

"When I wrote a letter upon the scarcity, it was generally said that it was the production of an immense cornfactor, and a letter was addressed to me under that persuasion, beginning 'Crafty Monopolist.'"

"It is very singular that no *true poet* should have arisen from the lower classes, when it is considered that every peasant who can read knows more of books now than did Æschylus, Sophocles, or Homer; yet if we except Burns, none* such have been."

"Crashaw seems in his poems to have given the first ebullience of his imagination, unshapen into form, or much of, what we now term, sweetness. In the poem, Hope, by way of question and answer, his superiority to Cowley is self-evident. In that on the name of Jesus equally so; but his lines on St. Theresa are the finest.

"Where he does combine richness of thought and diction nothing can excel, as in the lines you so much admire—

> Since 'tis not to be had at home,
> She'l travel to a matyrdome.
> No home for her confesses she,
> But where she may a martyr be.
> She'l to the Moores, and trade with them
> For this invalued diadem,

---

* In after years he excepted Elliot, the smith, though he held his [illegible] in [illegible] estimation.

She offers them her dearest breath
With Christ's name in't, in change for death.
She'l bargain with them, and will give
Them God, and teach them how to live
In Him, or if they this deny,
For Him she'l teach them how to die.
So shall she leave amongst them sown,
The Lord's blood, or, at least, her own.
Farewell then, all the world—adieu,
Teresa is no more for you:
Farewell all pleasures, sports and joys,
Never till now esteemed toys—
Farewell whatever dear'st may be,
Mother's arms or father's knee;
Farewell house, and farewell home,
She's for the Moores and martyrdom.'

"These verses were ever present to my mind whilst writing the second part of Christabel; if, indeed, by some subtle process of the mind they did not suggest the first thought of the whole poem.—Poetry, as regards small poets, may be said to be, in a certain sense, conventional in its accidents and in its illustrations; thus Crashaw uses an image:—

'As sugar melts in tea away,'

which, although *proper then*, and *true now*, was in bad taste at that time equally with the present. In Shakspeare, in Chaucer there was nothing of this.

"The wonderful faculty which Shakspeare above all other men possessed, or rather the power which possessed him in the highest degree, of anticipating everything, evidently is the result—at least partakes—of meditation, or that mental process which consists in the submitting to the operation of thought every object of feeling, or impulse, or passion observed *out* of it. I would be willing to live only as long as Shakspeare were the mirror to nature."

"What can be finer in any poet than that beautiful passage in Milton—

'—— Onward he moved
And thousands of his saints around.'

This is grandeur, but it is grandeur without completeness: but he adds—

'Far off their coming shone;'

which is the highest sublime. There is *total* completeness.

"So I would say that the Saviour praying on the Mountain, the Desert on one hand, the Sea on the other, the city at an immense distance below, was sublime. But I should say of the Saviour looking towards the City, his countenance full of pity, that he was majestic, and of the situation that it was grand.

"When the whole and the parts are seen at once, as mutually producing and explaining each other, as unity in multiety, there results shapeliness—*forma formosa.* Where the perfection of *form* is combined with pleasurableness in the sensations, excited by the matters or substances so formed, there results the beautiful.

"*Corollary.*—Hence colour is eminently subservient to beauty, because it is susceptible of forms, *i.e.* outline, and yet is a sensation. But a rich mass of scarlet clouds, seen without any attention to the *form* of the mass or of the parts, may be a *delightful* but not a beautiful object or colour.

"When there is a deficiency of unity in the line forming the whole (as angularity, for instance), and of number in the plurality or the parts, there arises the formal.

"When the parts are numerous, and impressive, and predominate, so as to prevent or greatly lessen the attention to the whole, there results the grand.

"Where the impression of the whole, *i.e.* the sense of unity predominates, so as to abstract the mind from the parts—the majestic.

"Where the parts by their harmony produce an effect of a

whole, but there is no seen form of a whole producing or explaining the parts, *i.e.* when the parts only are seen and distinguished, but the whole is felt—the picturesque.

"Where neither whole nor parts, but unity, as boundless or endless *allness*—the sublime."

"It often amuses me to hear men impute all their misfortunes to fate, luck, or destiny, whilst their successes or good fortune they ascribe to their own sagacity, cleverness, or penetration. It never occurs to such minds that light and darkness are one and the same, emanating from, and being part of, the same nature."

"The word Nature, from its extreme familiarity, and in some instances, fitness, as well as from the want of a term, or *other* name for God, has caused very much confusion in the thoughts and language of men. Hence a Nature-God, or God-Nature, not God in Nature; just as others, with as little reason, have constructed a natural and sole religion."

"Is it then true, that reason to man is the ultimate faculty and that, to convince a *reasonable* man, it is sufficient to adduce adequate reasons or arguments? How, if this be so, does it happen that we reject as insufficient the *reasoning* of a friend in our affliction for this or that *cause or reason*, yet are comforted, soothed, and reassured, by similar or far less sufficient *reasons*, when urged by a friendly and affectionate woman? It is no answer to say that women were made *comforters;* that it is the tone, and, in the instance of man's chief, best comforter, the wife of his youth, the mother of his children, the oneness with himself, which gives value to the consolation; the *reasons* are the same, whether urged by man, woman, or child. It must be, therefore, that there is something in the will itself, above and beyond, if not higher than, reason. Besides, is reason or the reasoning always the same, even when free from passion, film, or fever? I speak of the same person. Does he hold the doctrine of temperance in equal reverence when hungry as after he is sated? Does he at forty retain the same *reason*, only extended and developed, as he possessed at four and twenty? Does he not love the meat in his youth which he cannot endure in his old age? But these are appetites, and therefore no part of him. Is not a man one to-day and another to-morrow? Do not the very ablest and wisest of men attach greater weight at one moment to an argument or a *reason* than they do at another? Is this a want of sound and stable judgment? If so, what then is this perfect reason? for we have shown what it is not."

"It is prettily feigned, that when Plutus is sent from Jupiter, he limps and gets on very slowly at first; but when he comes from Pluto, he runs and is swift of foot. This, rightly taken, is a great sweetener of slow gains. Bacon (alas! the day) seems to have had this in mind when he says, 'seek not proud gains, but such as thou mayst get justly, use soberly, distribute cheerfully, and leave contentedly.' He that is covetous makes too much haste; and the wise man saith of him, 'he cannot be innocent.'"

"I have often been pained by observing in others, and was fully conscious in myself, of a *sympathy* with those of rank and condition in preference to their inferiors, and never discovered the source of this sympathy until one day at Keswick I heard a thatcher's wife crying her heart out for the death of her little child. It was given me all at once to feel, that I sympathised equally with the poor and the rich in all that related to the best part of humanity—the affections; but that, in what relates to fortune, to *mental* misery, struggles, and conflicts, we reserve consolation and sympathy for those who can appreciate its force and value."

"There are many men, especially at the outset of life, who, in their too eager desire for the end, overlook the difficulties in the way; there is another class, who see nothing else. The first class *may* sometimes fail; the latter rarely succeed."

Having been for nearly sixteen years a constant guest, and, for part of that time, the housemate of Charles Lamb—the gentle, the pensive Elia—and his admirable, his every way delightful sister—it becomes a duty, sacred though painful, to place on record all that I can convey in a brief space of the dearest, best loved, and earliest associate of Coleridge.—Is it too much to hope that the friend whom he so loved and cherished when young, of whose splendid talents and their fit application he always augured so highly, may yet be induced to furnish what recollections he retains of those days when Lamb was in the height and vigour of his genius, relished, and appreciated by troops of friends, by whom he was loved even more than he was admired? What names, and what recollections are there not in those names! Mrs. Inchbald, Mrs. Barbauld (the two Bald women, as he used to call them), Lloyd, Hazlitt, Coleridge, Irving, Colonel Phillips, Admiral Burney, William Godwin, Monkhouse—all dead: Wordsworth, Southey, Sergeant Talfourd, Basil Montagu, Martin Burney, Mr. Carey, Barry Cornwall, Robert Jameson, Leigh Hunt, Manning, Crabb, Robinson, Charles Cowden Clark, Hood, Novello, Liston, Miss Kelly, Mr. Moxon, William Godwin, Mrs. Shelley, Ned Phillips, &c. &c. &c.

I am quite aware that I can convey no notion of what Charles Lamb *was*, hardly even of what he said, as far the greatest part of its value depended upon the manner in which it was said. Even the best of his jokes—and *how good* they were you can never know—depended upon the circumstances, which to narrate would be to overlay and weary the attention.

The following lines of Lloyd will convey some idea, though very imperfect, of this model-man :—

LAMB.

"The child of impulse ever to appear,
And yet through duty's path strictly to steer!

"Oh Lamb, thou art a mystery to me!
Thou art so prudent and so mad with wildness,
Thou art a source of everlasting glee!
Yet desolation of the very childless
Has been thy lot! Never in one like thee
Did I see worth majestic from its wildness;
So far in thee from being an annoyance,
E'en to the vicious 'tis a source of joyance."

The first night I ever spent with Lamb was after a day with Coleridge, when we returned by the same stage; and from something I had said or done of an unusual kind, I was asked to pass the night with him and his sister. Thus commenced an intimacy which never knew an hour's interruption to the day of his death.

He asked me what I thought of Coleridge. I spoke as I thought. "You should have seen him twenty years ago," said he, with one of his sweet smiles, "when he was with me at the Cat and Salutation in Newgate Market. *Those were* days (or nights), but they were marked with a white stone. Such were his extraordinary powers, that when it was time for him to go and be married, the landlord entreated his stay, and offered him free quarters if he would only talk."

"I once wrote to Wordsworth to inquire if he was really a Christian. He replied, 'When I am a good man, *then* I am a Christian.'"

"I advised Coleridge to alter the lines in Christabel—

"Sir Leoline, the Baron rich,
Had a toothless mastiff bitch,"

into—

"Sir Leoline, the Baron round,
Had a toothless mastiff hound;"

but Coleridge, who has no alacrity in altering, changed this first termination to which, but still left in the other, bitch."

"Irving once came back to ask me if I could ever get in a word with Coleridge. 'No!' said I, 'I never want.'

"'Why, perhaps it is better not,' said the parson, and went away, determined how to behave in future."

"I made that joke first (the *Scotch* corner in hell, *fire without brimstone*), though Coleridge somewhat licked it into shape."

"Wordsworth, the *greatest* poet of these times. Still he is not, nor yet is any man, an Ancient Mariner."

"Proctor is Jealous of his own fame, which he cannot now claim.

"Somerset House, Whitehall Chapel (the old Banqueting Hall), the church at Limehouse and the new church at Chelsea, with the Bell house at Chelsea College, which always reminded him of Trinity College, Cambridge, were the objects most interesting to him in London. He did not altogether agree with Wordsworth, who thought the view from Harewood-place one of the finest in *old* London; admired more the houses at the Bond-street corner of George-street, which Manning said were built of bricks resembling in colour the great wall of China."

Martin Burney, whilst earnestly explaining the three kinds of acid, was stopped by Lamb's saying,—"The best of all kinds of acid, however, as you know, Martin, is uity—assiduity."

---

well until midnight, when George Frederick, getting very drunk, his host began to be tired of his company. George took the hint, and his host lighted him down stairs into the hall, when Cooke, laying hold of both his ears, shouted—"Have I, George Frederick Cooke, degraded myself by dining with bricklayers to meet boxkeepers?"—tripped up his heels and left him sprawling in darkness.

I retain a very vivid recollection of Manning, though so imperfect in my memory of persons that I should not recollect him at this time. I think few persons had so great a share of Lamb's admiration, for to few did he vouchsafe manifestations of his *very* extraordinary powers. Once, and once only, did I witness an outburst of his *unembodied* spirit, when such was the effect of his more than magnetic, his magic power (learnt was it in Chaldea, or in that sealed continent to which the superhuman knowledge of Zoroaster was conveyed by Confucius, into which he was the first to penetrate with impunity), that we were all rapt and carried aloft into the seventh heaven. He seemed to see and to convey to us clearly (I had almost said adequately), what was passing in the presence of the Great Disembodied ONE, rather by an intuition or the creation of a new sense than by words. Verily there are *more things on earth* than are dreamt of in our philosophy. I am unwilling to admit the influence this wonderful man had over his auditors, as I cannot at all convey an adequate notion or even image of his extraordinary and very peculiar powers. Passing from a state which was only not of the highest excitement, because the power was *felt*, not shown, he, by an easy, a graceful, and, as it seemed at the time, a natural transition, entered upon the discussion, or, as it rather seemed, the solution of some of the most interesting questions connected with the early pursuits of men. Amongst other matters, the origin of cooking, which it seems was deemed of sufficient importance by older, and *therefore* wiser, nations to form part of their archives. How this transcript was obtained, whether from that intuitive knowledge to which allusion has been made, or whether application was had to the keeper of the state paper office of the Celestial Empire, I cannot now say. I can only vouch for the truth of what follows, which, with the reply to a letter of acknowledgment from Coleridge, who, having received a roast pig, and not knowing whence it came, fixed upon Lamb as the donor, were afterwards fused into an essay, perhaps the most delightful in our language.

"A child, in the early ages, was left alone by its mother in a house in which was a pig. A fire took place; the child escaped, the pig was burned. The child scratched and pottered amongst the ashes for its pig, which at last it found. All the provisions being burnt, the child was very hungry, and not yet having any artificial aids, such as golden ewers and damask napkins, began to lick or suck its fingers to free them from the ashes. A piece of fat adhered to one of his thumbs, which, being very savoury alike in taste and odour, he rightly judged to belong to the pig. Liking it much, he took it to his mother, just then appearing, who also tasted it, and both agreed that it was better than fruit or vegetables.

"They rebuilt the house, and the woman, after the fashion of good wives, who, says the chronicle, are now very scarce, put a pig into it, and was about to set it on fire, when an old man, one whom observation and reflection had made a philosopher, suggested that a pile of wood would do as well. (This must have been the father of economists.) The next pig was killed before it was roasted, and thus

"From low beginnings,
We date our winnings."

Met T. at Lamb's. He seemed to tend towards the negative sensualism. Mentioned Coleridge as one possessed of transcendental benevolence and most exquisite eloquence, as one to whom nations might listen and be proud. He spoke of himself as seared and hopeless, and of Austin, who had, by the force, the clearness, and the originality of his views and arguments, won him over to the creed of the veritable sceptics, the sneerers, as "the cold-blooded ruffian." Spoke of Macauley, of Moultrie, of Praed. Of Macauley as the most eloquent, of Moultrie as the most pure and highminded, and of Praed as the most insincere.

Spent a very delightful day at Highgate with Lamb and one or two other congenial spirits. Anster, I think, was one. Had a long stroll over Hampstead Heath; Lamb, with his fine face, taking all the reflective, and the vast volume of the other all the younger and older of the passers-by. It seemed to me—then in my youth and spring of hope and joyance—to realise the olden time; the deep attention with which we all listened, each striving to get nearest to our great teacher, fearing to lose a word, attracted all eyes; many followed us, and still more looked earnestly, as wishing to partake of the intellectual banquet thus open as it were to all comers.

Never will that particular evening be effaced from my recollection. The talk was on duelling, on Kenilworth, and on Peveril of the Peak (which I knew assuredly to have been written by Scott, having myself furnished the first suggestion in a rambling and somewhat excited letter, written amidst the ruins of Castleton, the stronghold of the Peverils), of Sir Thomas Brown, and of old Mandeville. We read old poetry and new; but it was worthy to have been old.—Lamb observed when we got home,—"HE sets his mark upon whatever he reads; it is henceforth sacred. HIS spirit seems to have breathed upon it; and, if not for its author, yet for HIS sake we admire it." Coleridge accused Lamb of having caused the Sonnet to Lord Stanhope to be re-inserted in the joint volume published at Bristol. He declared it was written in ridicule of the exaggerated praises then bestowed upon the French revolution.

"Not, Stanhope! with the patriot's doubtful name
I mock thy worth—FRIEND OF THE HUMAN RACE!
Since scorning faction's low and partial aim,
Aloof thou wendest in thy stately pace,

Thyself redeeming from that leprous stain,
NOBILITY; and aye unterrified,
Pourest thy Abdiel warnings on the train,
That sit complotting with rebellious pride
'Gainst* her, who from the Almighty's bosom leapt
With whirlwind arm, fierce minister of love!
Wherefore, ere virtue o'er thy tomb hath wept,
Angels shall lead thee to the throne above,
And thou from forth its clouds shalt hear the voice,
Champion of freedom and her God! rejoice!"

Sunday.—Dined with Lamb alone. A most delightful day of reminiscences. Spoke of Mrs. Inchbald as the only endurable clever woman he had ever known; called them impudent, forward, unfeminine, and unhealthy in their minds. Instanced, amongst many others, Mrs. Barbauld, who was a torment and curse to her husband. "Yet," said Lamb, "Letitia was only just tinted; she was not what the she-dogs now call an intellectual woman." Spoke of Southey most handsomely; indeed he never would allow any one but himself to speak disparagingly of either Coleridge, Wordsworth, or Southey, and with a sort of misgiving of Hazlitt as a wild, mad being. Attributed his secession, to pique that he had not been asked to meet Wordsworth. He had also accused Lamb of not seeing him when with Wordsworth in Holborn. Lamb was much pleased with Wordsworth's attentions, saying, "He gave me more than half the time he was in London, when he is supposed to be with the Lowthers;" and after supper spoke with great feeling of Coleridge, and with a grateful sense of what he had been to him, adding after a recapitulation of the friends he admired or loved, "But Coleridge is a glorious person," and, with a smile of that peculiar sweetness so entirely his own, "He teaches what is best."

* Gallic liberty.

" Miss Lamb, in her very pleasant manner, said, 'Charles, who is Mr. Pitman?'

" 'Why, he is a clerk in our office.'

" 'But why do you not ask Mr. White and Mr. Field? I do not like to give up old friends for new ones.'

" 'Pitman has been very civil to me, always asking me to go and see him; and when the smoking club at Don Saltero's was broken up, he offered me all the ornaments and apparatus, which I declined, and *therefore* I asked him here this night. I could never bear to give pain; have I not been called th'-th'-th'-the gentle-hearted Charles when I was young, and shall I now derogate?' "

" Lamb one night wanted to demonstrate, after the manner of Swift, that the Man-t-chou Tartars were cannibals, and that the Chinese were identical with the Celtes (Sell Teas)."

" He said that he could never impress a Scotchman with any new truth; that they all required it to be spelled and explained away in old equivalent and familiar words or images. Had spoken to a Scotchman, who sat next to him at a dinner the day before, of a healthy book.

" 'Healthy, sir, healthy did you say?'

" 'Yes.'

" 'I dinna comprehend. I have heard of a healthy man and of a healthy morning, but never of a healthy book."

" Told a story of John Ballantyne, who going in a chair, the two caddies jostled him a good deal, upon which John remonstrated. The two caddies set him down, and told him that he being very little and light, was very wrong to choose that mode of conveyance, and argued the matter with him at great length, he being in the chair and unable to release himself."

" One night, when Mathews was going to the theatre at

Edinburgh, and was almost too late, he took a coach and ordered the coachman to drive to the theatre. In going up the hill, the horses being tired, the coach made no progress, upon which Mathews remonstrated, saying that he should be too late—he should lose his time. The coachman very coolly said, 'Your honour should reflact that I am losing time as weel's yersel.'"

"On another occasion, when Mathews was returning very late, or, by'r lady, it might be early in the morning, to Edinburgh, his friend, who was somewhat fou, refused to pay the toll, stating that he had paid it before that day. The little girl locked the toll, and he loaded her with abuse, to which she made little reply. After much altercation her mother opened a casement above, and in a sleepy, feeble tone, inquired what the gentleman said. "Na, mither," said the child, "it's no the gentleman, it's the wine speaking."

"The best pun ever made is that of Swift, who called after a man carrying a hare over his shoulders, "Is that your own hare or a wig?"

Met Mr. and Mrs. Wordsworth, with Mr. Talfourd, Monkhouse, and Robinson. A very delightful evening. Wordsworth almost as good a reader as Coleridge; to a stranger I think he would seem to carry even more authority both in what he read and said. He spoke of Southey and Coleridge with measured respect, and, as I thought, just appreciation. Pointed out some passages in the Curse of Kehama which he admired, and repeated some portions of the Ancient Mariner; also from the River Duddon and the Excursion. Repeated the Highland Girl. He seemed to me to present the idea of a poet in whom the repressive faculty was predominant. Taken altogether, he impressed me very favourably, and I regret deeply that I did not avail myself of subsequent opportunities, not seldom proffered by Lamb and Coleridge, of meeting him more frequently. But I then laboured under the impression that he had not acted kindly to that dear and loved being, whom I loved living, and honour dead. Even now, when myself almost indifferent to new associations, I regret this enforced denial of what at that period would have enhanced the value of existence,—communion with that glorious and effulgent mind; but I do not regret the impulses which led to this self-denial.

Met Mrs Shelley and Mrs. Williams at Lamb's cottage, in Colebrook Row. Was much interested by these two young and lovely women. *Interesting* in every view. Knew Mrs. Shelley from her likeness to a picture by Titian in the Louvre, which is a far greater resemblance to Mrs. Shelley in the beautiful and very peculiar expression of her countenance than would be any portrait taken now. Hers seemed a face, as Hazlitt remarked when he pointed it out to me, that should be kept to acquire likeness. Mrs. Shelley at first sight appeared deficient in feeling; but this cannot be real. She spoke of Shelley without apparent emotion, without regard or a feeling approaching to regret, without pain as without interest, and seemed to contemplate him, as everything else, through the same passionless medium.

Mrs. Shelley expressed much admiration of the personal manner and conversation of Lord Byron, but at the same time admitted that the account in the London Magazine for September was faithful. She censured his conduct towards Leigh Hunt as paltry and unfeeling; spoke very slightly of his studies or reading; thought him very superficial in his opinions; owed everything to his memory, which was almost preternatural. Said that he felt a supreme contempt for all his contemporaries, with the exception of Wordsworth and Coleridge, and he ridiculed and derided even them, and was altogether proud, selfish, and frequently puerile. Mrs. Williams, I think, gave the account of his determining to have a plum pudding on his birth-day, and after giving minute directions so as to prevent the chance of mishap, it was, to the eternal dishonour of the Italian cucina, brought up in a tureen of the substance of soup. Upon this failure in the production he was frequently quizzed, and betrayed all the petulance of a child, and more than a child's curiosity to learn who had reported the circumstance.

"Wordsworth one day said to me, when I had been speaking of Coleridge, praising him in my way, 'Yes, the Coleridges are a clever family.' I replied, 'I know* one that is.'"

LETTER XVIII.

MY DEAREST FRIEND, *June* 23, 1821.

Be assured that nothing bearing a nearer resemblance to offence, whether felt or perceived, than a syllogism bears to the

---

* My amiable and kind-hearted friend said here less than the truth, at least as I understand it. Cleverness was not at all a characteristic of Coleridge, whilst it happily suits those to whom Wordsworth alluded, who are or have been clever enough to appropriate their uncle's great reputation to their own advancement, and then to allow him to need assistance from strangers. No one who knows the character or calibre of mind, whether of the Bishop or the Judge, can doubt, *cæteris paribus*, that the one would still have been a curate and the other a barrister, with but little practice, had they borne the name of Smith —had they wanted the passport of *his* name. It is not always wise to scan too deeply the source of human actions, but I am irresistibly led to the conclusion, that a sort of half-consciousness of "that same" entered into this almost (in one sense *more* than) parricidal neglect. *I blame them not.* I but narrate this as a curious and painful instance how fearfully we are made; how often we prefer our self-will (so termed), nay, even the most sordid injustice, to our duties.

colour of the man in the moon's whiskers, ever crossed my brain: not even with that brisk diagonal traverse which Ghosts and apparitions always choose to surprise us in. I have *indeed* observed *or* fancied, that, for some time past, you have been anxious about something, have had something pressing upon your mind, which I wished *out of you*, though not particularly *to have* it out of you. I must explain myself. Say that X. were my dearest Friend, to whom I would be as it were transparent, and have him so to me in all respects that concerned our permanent Being, and likewise in all circumstantial accidents in which we could be of service to each other. Yet there are many things that will press upon us which are our *individualities*, which one man does not feel any tendency in himself to speak of to a man, however dear or valued. X. does not think or wish to think of it when with Y., nor Y. in his turn when with X., and yet still the great law holds good—whatever vexes or depresses ought if possible to be *out* of us. Now I say that I should rejoice if you had a female Friend—a Sister, an Aunt, or a Beloved to whom you could lay yourself open. I should further exult if your *confidante* were *my* Friend too, my Sister or my Wife.

God bless you.

T. Allsop, Esq. S. T. Coleridge.

This letter relates to a domestic, not to say family perplexity, peculiarly and sacredly my own; one to which no counsel could apply, no consolation mitigate or assuage. Under the circumstances in which I was at that time placed, I could not, I felt it would be premature, to avail myself of the invitation contained in the above letter: and this will, to a great extent, explain much that is contained in the following letters. I had a still farther reason. The individual to whom allusion is made above, was at that time the *ne plus ultra* of my friend's love and fraternal admiration; yet with qualities of head and heart worthy of all acceptance, was partly (almost I had nearly said) on that very account disqualified in my innermost convictions, certainly according to the *judgment* of my then *feelings*, for the office indicated.

LETTER XIX.

MY DEAR FRIEND,

We are quite sure that you would not allow yourself to fancy any rightful ground, cause, or occasion for not coming here, but the wish, the duty, or the propriety of going elsewhere or staying at home. When the Needle of your Thoughts begins to be magnetic, you may be certain that my *Pole* is at that moment attracting you by the spiritual magic of strong wishing for your arrival. N.B. My *Pole* includes in this instance *both the Poles* of Mr. and eke of Mrs. Gillman, *i.e.*, the head and the heart.

But seriously—I am a little anxious—so give my blest sisterly Friend a few lines by return of post—just to let us know that you are and have been well, and that nothing of a painful nature has deprived us of the expected pleasure; a pleasure which, believe me, stands a good many degrees above *moderate* in the cordi or hedonometer of,

Yours most *cordi*ally,

T. Allsop, Esq. S. T. COLERIDGE.

It must always be borne in mind, that the fragments, letters, and conversations which are here perused at *one* time, were written or spoken at different times, and under the influence of varied feelings and convictions, and the *apparent* discrepancies, or even contradictions, are such as you must be conscious of yourselves as reflective, and *therefore* progressive, beings.

"In the *sense* in which I then spoke and thought, I would again repeat the note to the word PRIEST, originally prefixed to my Juvenile Poems, though perhaps I should somewhat extend it.

"I deem that the teaching the Gospel for hire is wrong, because it gives the teacher an improper bias in favour of particular opinions, on a subject where it is of the last importance that the mind should be perfectly unbiassed. Such is my private opinion :—but I mean not to censure all hired teachers, many among whom I know, and venerate as the best and wisest of men. God forbid that I should think of these when I use the word PRIEST; a name after which any other term of abhorrence would appear an anti-climax. By a PRIEST I mean a man, who, holding the scourge of power in his right hand, and a Bible translated *by authority* in his left, doth necessarily cause the Bible and the scourge to be associated ideas, and so produces that temper of mind that leads to infidelity; infidelity which, judging of Revelation by the doctrines and practices of Established Churches, *honours God by rejecting Christ.*"

"I have been reading Judge Barrington's Sketches. It is the most pleasant book about Ireland I ever read. I was especially amused by the following :—

DIALOGUE BETWEEN TOM FLINTER AND HIS MAN.

" *Tom Flinter.* Dick! said he;
" *Dick.* What? said he.
" *Tom Flinter.* Fetch me my hat, says he,
For I will go, says he,
To Timahoe, says he;
To the fair, says he;
And buy all that's there, says he,
" *Dick* *Pay what you owe*, says he;
And then you may go, says he,
To Timahoe, says he;
To the fair, says he;
And buy all that's there, says he;
" *Tom Flinter.* Well, by this and by that, said he,
Dick! *hang up my hat!* says he."

"Whenever philosophy has taken into its plan religion, it has ended in scepticism; and whenever religion excludes philosophy, or the spirit of free inquiry, it leads to wilful blindness and superstition. Scotus, the first of the schoolmen, held that religion might be above, but could not be adverse to, true philosophy."

"To say that life is the result of organisation, is to say that the builders of a house are its results."

"The 'Friend' is a secret which I have entrusted to the public; and, unlike most secrets, it hath been well kept."

"Interestingness, the best test and characteristic of loveliness."

"Humour is consistent with pathos, whilst wit is not."

"All that is good is in the reason, not in the understanding; which is proved by the malignity of those who lose their reason. When a man is said to be out of his wits, we do not mean that he has lost his reason, but only his understanding, or the power of choosing his means or perceiving their fitness to the end. Don Quixote (and in a less degree, the Pilgrim's Progress) is an excellent example of a man who had lost his wits or understanding, but not his reason."

LETTER XX.

My dear Friend, *Sept.* 15*th*, 1821.

I cannot rest until I have answered your last letter. I have contemplated your character, affectionately indeed, but through a clear medium. No film of passion, no glittering mist of outward advantages, has arisen between the sight and the object: I had no other prepossession than the esteem which my knowledge of your sentiments and conduct could not but secure for you. I soon learnt to esteem you; and in esteeming, became attached to you. I began by loving the man on account of his conduct, but I ended in valuing the actions chiefly as so many looks and attitudes of the same person. "*Hast* thou any thing? Share it with me, and I will pay thee an equivalent. *Art* thou any thing? O then we will exchange souls."

We can none of us, not the wisest of us, brood over any source of affliction inwardly, keeping it back, and as it were pressing it in on ourselves; but we must MAGNIFY it. We cannot see it clearly, much less distinctly; and as the object enlarges beyond its real proportions, so it becomes vivid; and the feelings that blend with it assume a proportionate undue intensity. So the one acts on the other, and what at first was effect, in its turn becomes a cause; and when at length we have taken heart, and given the whole thing, with all its several parts, the proper distance from our mind's eye, by confiding it to a true friend, we are ourselves surprised to find what a dwarf the giant shrinks into, as soon as it steps out of the mist into clear sunlight.

I am aware that these are truths of which you do not need to be informed; but they will not be the less impressive on this account in your judgment, knowing, as you must know, that nothing short of my deep and anxious convictions of their importance in all cases of hidden distress, and of their *unspeakable* importance in yours, could impel me to *seek* and *entreat* your *entire* confidence, to beg you, so fervently as I here am doing, to open out to me the cause of your anxiety, that I may offer you the best advice in my power,—advice that will not be the less dispassionate from its being dictated by zealous friendship, and blended with the truest love.

I fear that in any decision to which you may come in any matter affecting yourself alone, you may, from a culpable delicacy of honour, which, forbidden by wisdom and the universal experience of others, cannot but be in contradiction to the genuine dictates of duty, want fortitude to choose the lesser evil, at whatever cost to your immediate feelings, and to put that choice into immediate and peremptory act. But I must finish. I trust that the warmth and earnestness of my language are not warranted by the occasion; but they are barely proportionate to the present solicitude of,

Your faithful and affectionate friend,

T. Allsop, Esq. S. T. Coleridge.

"The German writers have acquired a style and an elegance of thought and of mind, just as we have attained a style and smartness of composition (thus in my notes), so that if you were to read an ordinary German author as an English one, you would say,—'This man *has something in him*, this man thinks;' whereas it is *merely* a method acquired by them, as we have acquired a style."

"Dr. Young one day was speaking of John Hunter as being greatly over-rated, upon which I replied,—'Yes, to minds which, like birds entangled in the lime, scoff and sneer at those pinions of power that have emancipated themselves from the thrall which bound them, but are nevertheless impeded in their upward progress by the shackles they have broken, but from the slime of which they are not freed.'

"The Doctor noticed my assimilating weight and gravity, *civilly* informing me that those who *understood* these matters considered them as different as fire and heat.

"I said, 'Yes, in that philosophy which, together with a great quantity of old clothes, I discarded thirty years ago, and which, by identifying cause and effect, destroys both.'"

A copy of the Lyrical Ballads was sent to Mr. Fox, who

dissented from the conclusions of Mr. Wordsworth as to Ruth and the Brothers, but expressed his admiration of "We are Seven," and "The Linnet," and conveyed his regret that he knew not to whom he was to refer the most beautiful poem in the language, "Love," adding,—"I learn we are indebted to Mr. Coleridge for that exquisite poem, "The Nightingale."

It is right that I should here observe, that the conversations, of which this is a *very small part*, possessed little that could be abstracted, and that, in preserving these personal traits, I was gratifying myself by retaining more vivid and distinct knowlege of the most prominent of my contemporaries. This will apply equally to many other recollections and memorandums, both before and after.

"Longmans offered me the copyright of the Lyrical Ballads, at the same time saying that, if I would write a few more, they would publish my contributions. When I expressed a hope that 3,000 might be circulated, Wordsworth spurned at the idea, and said that twenty times that number must be sold. I was told by Longmans that the greater part of the Lyrical Ballads had been sold to seafaring men, who having heard of the Ancient Mariner, concluded that it was a naval song-book, or, at all events, that it had some relation to nautical matters."*

---

* It is somewhat singular that the name of another and larger book of Mr. Wordsworth's should also owe its circulation to a misconception of the title. It has been my fortune to have met with the EXCURSION at a great number of inns and boarding-houses in picturesque scenes—in places where parties go for *excursions;* and upon inquiring how it happened that so expensive a book was purchased when an old Universal Magazine, an Athenian Oracle, or, at best, one of the Bridgewater Treatises, would do as well to send the guest to sleep, I was given to understand in three several places that they were left by parties who had finished their *material* excursion, but, alas! for their taste, had left their poetic excursion untouched; uncut, even, beyond the story of Margaret.

Spoke with interest of Irving. Regretted that he should have expressed his inability to preserve his original simplicity when addressing an audience of the highest classes. Thought this the feeling of a third or fourth-rate mind; that he might have been *perplexed* would not have derogated from his character, but to allow an audience to influence him further than the fitness of his discourse to his hearers was not to his advantage.

"The most happy marriage I can picture or image to myself would be the union of a deaf man to a blind* woman."

LETTER XXI.

MY DEAREST FRIEND, *Sept.* 24*th*, 1821.

I will begin with the beginning of your (to me most affecting) letter. Not exactly *obligation*, my entirely beloved and relied-on friend! The soiling hand of the world has dyed and sunk into the sense and import of the term too inseparably, for it to convey the kind and degree of what I feel towards you, on the one scale. I love you so truly, that in the first glance, as it were, and *welcome* of your anxious affection, it delights me for the very act's sake. I think only of it and you, or rather both are one and the same, and I live in you. Nor does the complacency suffer any abatement, but becomes more intense and lively. As a mother would talk of the soothing attentions, the sacrifices and devotion of a son, eager to supply every want and anticipate every wish, so I talk to myself concerning you; and I am proud of you, and proud to be the object of what cannot but appear lovely to my judgment, and which the hard contrast in so many heart-

* Whilst these pages are passing through the press, this most extraordinary conjunction has taken place at Barming, near Maldstone.

withering instances forced on me by the experience of my last twenty years, compels me to feel and value with an additional glow. Lastly, it is a source of strength and comfort to know, that the labours and aspirations and sympathies of the genuine and invisible Humanity exist in a social world of their own; that its attractions and assimilations are no Platonic fable, no dancing flames or luminous bubbles on the magic cauldron of my wishes; but that there are, even in this unkind life, spiritual parentages and filiations of the soul. Can there be a counterpoise to these? Not a counterpoise—but as weights in the counter-scale there will come the self-reproach, that spite of all inauspicious obstacles, not in my power to remove without loss of self-respect, I have not done all I could and might have done to prevent my present state of dependence. I am now able to hope that I shall be capable of setting apart such a portion of my *useable* time to my greater work (in assertion of the ideal truths and *à priori* probability, and *à posteriori* internal and external evidence of the historic truth of the Christian religion), as to leave a sufficient portion for a not unprofitable series of articles for pecuniary supply. I entertain some hope, too, that my Logic, which I could begin printing immediately if I could find a publisher willing to undertake it on equitable terms, might prove an exception to the general fate of my publications. It is a long lane that has no turning, and while my own heart bears witness to the genial delight you would feel in assisting me, I know that you would have a more satisfactory gladness in my not needing it.

And now a few, a very few, words on the latter portion of your letter. You know, my dearest Friend, how I acted myself, and that my example cannot be urged in confirmation of my judgment. I certainly strive hard to divest my mind of every prejudice, to look at the question sternly through the principle of Right separated from all mere Expedience, nay, from the question of earthly happiness *for its own sake*. But I cannot answer to myself that the image of any serious obstacle to your peace of heart, that the Thought of your full development of soul being put a stop to, of a secret anxiety blighting your *utility* by cankering your happiness, I cannot be sure—I cannot be sure that this may not have made me *weigh* with a trembling and unsteady hand, and less than half the presumption of error, afforded by the shrinking and recoil of your moral sense or even feeling, would render it my duty and my impulse to bring my conclusion anew to the ordeal of my Reason and Conscience. But on your side, my dear Friend! try with me to contemplate the question as a problem in the *science* of Morals, in the first instance, and to recollect that there are false or intrusive weights possible in the other scale; that our very virtues may become, or be transformed into temptations to, or occasions of, *partial* judgment; that we may judge partially *against* ourselves from the very fear, perhaps contempt, of the contrary; that self may be moodily gratified by *self*-sacrifice, and that the Heart itself, in its perplexity, may acquiesce for a time in the decision as a more safe way; and, lastly, that the question can only be fully answered, when Self and Neighbour, as equi-distant $_{S}\overset{G}{\Delta}_{N}$ from the conscience or God, are blended in the common term, a *Human Being:* that we are *commanded* to love ourselves as our Neighbour in the Law that requires a Christian to love his Neighbour as himself.

But indeed I persuade myself that this dissonance is not real between us, and that it would not have seemed to exist, had I continued the subject into the possible particular cases; *e. g.*, suppose a case in which the misery, and so far the moral incapacitation, of both parties were certainly foreseen as the immediate consequence. A morality of Consequences I, you well know, reprobate; but to exclude the necessary *effect* of an action is to take away all meaning from the word action—*to strike Duty with blindness.* I repeat it, that I do not, cannot find it in myself to believe, that *on any one* case, made out in all its limbs, features, and circumstances, your heart and mine would prompt different verdicts.

But the thought of you personally and individually is at present too strong and stirring to permit me to reason on any points. If the weather is at all plausible, we propose to set off on Saturday. I do most earnestly wish that you could accompany us; a steam-vessel would give us three-fourths of the whole day to *tête-à-tête* conversation. God bless you,

And your affectionate and faithful friend,

T. Allsop, Esq. S. T. Coleridge.

The affectionate interest expressed in this and the preceding letters was at the time to me a solace and support, placed as I was with relation to my immediate worldly prospects in a position of much perplexity. There were many circumstances which, as they affected others, I could not communicate so fully,—convey so entirely as I desired to my respected friend; hence he altogether misapprehended the particular cause of my anxiety, or, as I doubt not, considered it irresolution and misgiving. In pursuance of the determination with which I set out, I have not hesitated thus to place on record, opinions, views, and suggestions, which, had I considered myself at liberty to make a selection, I might have omitted, for a twofold reason; one, that they concerned myself alone; the other, that I do not imagine they will interest general readers. I have adopted the plan of saying just what occurs to me at the time of writing and of giving the memorandums exactly as I find them, when I have no recollection of the circumstances; and the letters exactly as they are written (unless they contain repetitions or expressions of attachment common to all) with few omissions, and those of no importance.

I should consider it a misfortune for any one to have suggested alterations or omissions in this work, as such suggestions would have disturbed or have interfered with my original determination; a determination to let my dear friend be known in all his strength and all his weakness, as far as these letters and recollections convey any clear idea of either. I might have made this work better with some aids and with longer preparation, but then it would not *so well* have expressed what I sought to convey. It would not have so entirely expressed my own or my late friend's opinions and convictions; and in *this sense*, though another might have made it *better*, no one but myself could have done it so well. In this view Charles Lamb coincided, though he, it seems, from the force of an early impression, never kept any letters, and therefore did not attach the importance which appears to me to belong to this department of autobiography.

When asked to accompany a recent deputation to remonstrate with the present ministers, I assented, stating to my friends that I should go to read their faces, for that nature never lies. So it proved in this case; their conduct being in harmony with the conclusions I drew and expressed at the time, but in strange discrepancy with *what they said*. So I hold that letters, which are the transcript of the writer's mind, give more of interest and more insight into character than volumes of disquisition or surmises.

"Read the Troilus and Cressida; dwelt much upon the fine distinction made by Shakspeare between the *affection* of Troilus and the passion of Cressida. This does not escape the notice of Ulysses, who thus depicts her on her first arrival in the Trojan camp:—

> ——— Fie! fie upon her!
> There's language in her eye, her cheek, her lip,
> Nay, her foot speaks. Her wanton spirits look out
> At every joint of her body. Set such down
> For sluttish spoils of opportunity
> And daughters of the game.'

"The profound affection of Troilus alone deserves the name of love."

"Certainly the highest good is to live happily, and not through a life of mortification to expect a happy death. Should we attain felicity in life, death will be easy, as it will be natural and in due season. Whereas by the present system of *religious teaching*, men are enjoined to value chiefly happiness at the end of life; which, if they were implicitly to follow, they would, by neglecting the first great duty, that of innocent enjoyment during existence, effectually preclude themselves from attaining.

"There is no condition (evil as it may be in the eye of reason), which does not include, or seem to include when it has become familiar, some good, some redeeming or reconciling qualities. I agree, however, that marriage is not one of these. Marriage has, as you say, no *natural* relation to love. Marriage belongs to society; it is a social contract. It should not merely include the conditions of esteem and friendship, it should be the ratification of their manifestation. Still I do not know how it can be replaced; *that* belongs to the future, and it is a question which the future only can solve. I however quite agree that we can now, better than at any former time, say what *will not*, what *cannot* be."

"Truly, when I think of what has entered into ethics, what has been considered moral in the early ages of the world, and even now by civilised nations in the east, I incline to believe that morality *is* conventional; but when I see the doctrines propounded under the name of political economy, I earnestly *hope* that it is so.—As illustrations of the opinions held by philosophers, which to us appear abominable or indecent, I refer to some of the rules of Zeno, some parts of the philosophy of Plato, the whole conduct of Phædon, and the practice of Cato the Censor."

"The Essenians for several ages subsisted by adoption: we shall see if the Shakers continue so long."

"We shun a birth, and make a public exhibition of an execution. The mystery observed at birth is a type of other mysteries. It is a matter of silence and secrecy, and wholly withheld from all but the customary officials.

"Pythagoras first asserted that the earth was a globe, and that there were antipodes. He also seems to have been acquainted with the properties of the atmosphere, at least its weight and pressure. He was the most wonderful of those men whom Greece, that treasure-house of intellect, produced to show her treasures, and to be the ornament and gaze of our nature during all time. In his doctrines, the Copernican system may clearly be traced.

"Pythagoras used the mysteries as one of the means to retain the doctrine of an unity while the multitude sunk into Polytheism.

"It is quite certain most of the ancient philosophers were adverse to the popular worship, as tending to degrade the idea of the Divine Being, and to defile the national manners. Idol worship always demoralises a people who adopt it.

"Witness the Jews, whose idolatry was followed by universal chastisement. Witness Rome, Greece, and Egypt where idol worship led to immorality and vice of the most frightful kind."

The following I find on the back of a letter.

"—— is one of those clergymen who find it more easy to hide their thoughts than to suppress thinking, and who treat the Thirty Nine Articles as the whale did Jonah, *i. e.* swallowed, but could not digest him."

"Quarrels of anger ending in tears are favourable to love in its *spring tide, as plants are found to grow very rapidly after a thunderstorm with rain.*"

"The heart in its physical sense is not sufficient for a kite's dinner; yet the whole world is not sufficient for it."

"God hath from the beginning promised forgiveness to the penitent, but hath nowhere promised penitence to the sinner."

"So Mr. Baker heart did pluck,
And did a courting go!
And Mr. Baker is a buck;
For why?—he needs the *doe.*"

"Oh! there are some natures which, under the most cheerless, all-threatening, nothing-promising circumstances, can draw hope from the invisible; as the tropical trees, that in the sandy desolation produce their own lidded vessels full of water from air and dew. Alas! to my root not a drop trickles down but from the water-pot of immediate friends; and even so it seems much more a sympathy with their feeling rather than hope of my own, even as I should feel sorrow if Allsop's mother, whom I have never seen, were to die."

LETTER XXII.

MY DEAR FRIEND, *Oct.* 20, 1821.

Not a day has passed since we left Highgate in which I have not been tracing you in spirit up and down the Glens and Dells of Derbyshire, while my feet only have been in commune with the sandy beach here at Ramsgate. Once when I had stopped and stood stone still for some minutes, Mrs. Gillman's call snatched me away from a spot opposite to a house, to the second-floor window of which I had been gazing, as if I had feared, yet expected, to see you passing to and fro by it. These, however, were visions to which I had myself given the commencing act—fabrics of which the "I wonder where Allsop is now" had laid the foundation stone. But for the last three days your image, alone or lonely in an unconcerning crowd of human figures, has forced itself on my sleep in dreams of the rememberable kind, accompanied with the feeling of being afraid to go up to you—and now of letting you pass by unnoticed, from want of courage to ask you, what was most on my mind—respecting the one awful to me because so awfully dear to you—(for there is a *religion in all deep love*, but the love of a Mother is, at your age, the veil of softer light between the Heart and the Heavenly Father!) Mrs. Gillman likewise has been thinking of you both asleep and awake: and so, though I know not how to direct my letter, yet a letter I am resolved to write.

I am sure, my dear Friend! that if aught can be a comfort to you in affliction or an addition to your joy in the hour of Thanksgiving, it will be to know, and to be reminded of your knowledge, that I feel as your own heart in all that concerns you. Next to this I have to tell you, that the Sea Air and the Sea Plunges, and the leisure of mind, with regular devotion of the Daylight to exercise (for I write only after tea), have been auspicious, beyond my best hopes, to my health and spirits. The change in my looks is beyond the present reality, but may be veracious as *prophecy*, though somewhat exaggerating as *history*. The same in all essentials holds good of Mrs. Gillman; and I am most pleased that the improvement in her looks and strength has been gradual though rapid. First she got rid, in the course of four or five days, of the *Positives* of the wrong sort—*e. g.* the blackness under the eyes and the thinness of the cheeks—and now she is acquiring the Positives of the right kind, her eyes brightening, her face becoming plump, and a delicate, yet cool and steady colour, stealing upon her cheeks. Mr. Gillman too is uncommonly well since his second arrival here. The first week his arm, the absorbents of which had been perilously poisoned by opening a body, was a sad drawback, and prevented his bathing. In short, we are all better than we could have anticipated; and the better we are, the more I long, and we all wish you to be with us. If you *can* come, though but for a few days, I pray you come to us. In grief or gladness, we shall grieve less, and (I need not say) be more glad, by seeing you, by having you with *us*. I will not say *write*, for I would a thousand times rather have you plump in on me, unannounced; but yet write, unless this be possible. We have an excellent house, with beds enough for half a dozen Allsops, if so many there were or could be. The situation the very best in all Ramsgate (Wellington Crescent, East Cliff, Ramsgate); and we, or rather Mrs. Gillman's voice and manner, procured it *shameful cheap* for the size and accommodations.

I am called to dinner; so God bless you, and receive all our loves, my very dear friend.

T. Allsop, Esq. S. T. Coleridge.

My birth-day, 51; or, as all my collegiates and Mrs. Coleridge swear, 50.

In reading these letters—so full of love and kindness—my first wish had been to keep them sacred to my own perusal, and to my own bitter and most painful regrets; but they contain so lively a portraiture of the writer's mind, express so clearly what he so entirely felt, that I have judged it meet and fitting, as well as an act of justice to the memory of the dead, to give them place. I am reminded whilst I write this of an opinion—I fear not altogether a heresy—of Lamb's, that all strong affection, whether it be love of man, to woman, or pure and abiding friendship between men, is not merely of no interest, but that it is, to a certain degree, positively distasteful to all others. As I write for men as they are, not as they *may* be, or as I think they should, *and yet will be*, I should not have published these personal and individual communications during the life of their author under any conceivable circumstances, even if such publications were usual or conceivable. Adhering, therefore, to the rule I have laid down for myself—to publish exactly that which I myself should like most to know of any man, in whom I felt sufficient interest to wish to know anything—I have given every letter, not in itself a repetition in words or tone of feeling of some preceding communication; being determined not to incur justly the regret expressed in the Biographia Literaria, at Spratt's refusing to allow Cowley to appear in "his dressing gown and slippers."

Of the Conversations about this period I possess the following:—

"We are none of us tolerant in what concerns us deeply and entirely."

"A man who admits himself to be deceived, must be conscious that there is something upon, or respecting which, he cannot be deceived."

"A man who wishes for an *end*, the *means* of which are criminal, is chargeable with all the guilt."

"I was told by one who was with Shelley shortly before his death, that he had in those moments, when his spirit was left to prey inwards, expressed a wish, amounting to anxiety, to commune with me, as the one only being who could resolve or allay the doubts and anxieties that pressed upon his mind."

"Leigh Hunt (I think he said) having stated that it was my opinion that Byron only *made believe* when he painted himself in his poems, Shelley expressed his fears, his belief that there was no counterfeiting, that it was too real; that he was a being incapable of true sympathy, that he was selfish and sensual beyond his own portraiture."

The enclosed extract of a letter written about this time, I give for the sake of the conclusion.

"I am glad to learn that the dwellers at Rydal perceived an amendment in me. In self-management, in the power of keeping my eyes more, and my heart less open, in aversion to baseness, intrigue, in detestation of apostacy, to *

* * * * * *

and *silent* or suggestive detraction it would be well for me if I were as I was at twenty-five. Amendment! improvement in outward appearance, in health and in manners, I owe to my friends here; who as they would not admit any improvement in innocence or blamelessness of life, so they would indignantly reject and repel any alteration for the worse."

"I am much delighted with Lamb's letter to Southey, I have read it many times; Lamb feels firm and has taken sure ground."

"I used to be much amused with Tobin and Godwin. Tobin would pester me with stories of Godwin's dullness; and upon his departure Godwin would drop in just to say that Tobin was more dull than ever."

"Mentioned many things of, and concerning, Godwin; which, to me, at that time not yet familiar with the ignorance of the learned, with the contradictions, which I have since seen, between the knowledge so called and the practices of men, surprised me much."

---

* I have now no means of supplying this hiatus.

"Spoke in the highest terms of affection and consideration of Lamb. Related the circumstance which gave occasion to the 'Old Familiar Faces.' Charles Lloyd, in one of his fits, had shown to Lamb a letter, in which Coleridge had illustrated the cases of vast genius in proportion to talent and predominance of talent in conjunction with genius, in the persons of Lamb and himself. Hence a temporary coolness, at the termination of which, or during its continuance, these beautiful verses were written."

"Jeffery, speaking of Campbell, said 'He is one of the best fellows in the world. If, however, he has a fault, it is that he is envious, and to that degree that he wishes the walls may fall and crush any one who may excel him. He is one of my most intimate friends, and with that *little* drawback, one of the best fellows in the world.'"

"Spoke of the cold and calculating character of the Scotch; agreed that they were in this the same drunk or sober: their heads seemed always so full that they could not hold more, adding, 'We value the Scotch without however liking them; and we like the Irish without however *over*-valuing them. Instanced Dr. Stoddart as having most of the unamiable traits of the Scotch character without the personally useful ones—doing dirty work for little pay.'"

"Came to me very much heated and fatigued, stayed to refresh before proceeding to Sir George Beaumont's. Had received a letter from Colin Mackenzie, stating that he was occupied in attending the Privy Council, and that he feared he should not be able to dine with him at Sir George Beaumont's. Coleridge not being able to decipher the letter, said, 'It is an excellently contrived kind of hand for the purpose of disguising false orthography. I had before this conceived strong suspicions, that my good friend Colin Mackenzie could not spell, and they are now confirmed.'"

"Met Wilkie at this dinner, who expressed his opinion that patronage did no good but much injury. Said also, that he should never think painting properly estimated until a painter should make his fifteen, twenty, or thirty thousand a year like a man at the bar;—an opinion which did him no service with Sir George Beaumont.—Speaking of the Queen's trial, I said, 'It was a most atrocious affair.'

'I am delighted to hear *you* sanction my use of that opinion,' said Lady Sarah Bathurst, 'indeed it was a most 'atrocious" business; and if any iniquity could withdraw the sun's light, *that* would surely have occasioned a physical, as well as moral, eclipse.' A general outcry; an earnest entreaty on the part of Lady Sarah, put an end to this extraordinary scene."

"Quoted with great glee, as one of the best practical jokes extant, if indeed a thing so good must not be true, a story from an old Spanish humourist which had, by some strange oversight or lapsus, escaped the shears of the Inquisition.

"At the sacrament, a Priest gave, without perceiving it, a counter instead of a wafer. The communicant thinking it would melt, very patiently waited, but without effect. The Priest seeing him hesitate, inquired what was the matter? 'Matter,' said he, 'I hope you have not made a mistake and given me God the Father, he is so hard and tough there is no swallowing him.' These stories abound in all Catholic countries, especially in Italy. Indeed the religious of all countries are, in the eye of Reason, the greatest blasphemers, seeing that though all affirm God made man in his own *image*, they make God after their own *imaginations*."

LETTER XXIII

MY DEAR FRIEND, *Ramsgate, Nov. 2nd*, 1821.

First, let me utter the fervent, God be praised! for the glad tidings respecting your dear Mother, which would have given an abounding interest to a far less interesting letter. May she be long preserved both to enjoy and reward your love and piety! And now I will try to answer the other contents of your letter, as satisfactorily I *hope*, as I am sure it will be sincerely and affectionately. Conscious how heedfully, how watchfully I cross-examined myself whether or no my anxiety for your earthly happiness and free exercise of head and heart had not *warped* the attention which it was my purpose to give whole and undivided to the one Question—What is the Right, I can repeat (with as much confidence as the slippery and Protean nature of all self-inquisition and the great *à priori* likelihood of my reason being tampered with by my affections, will sanction me in expressing) what I have already more than once said, viz., that I hold it incredible, at least improbable to the utmost extent, that you and I should decide differently in any one definite instance. Let a case be stated with all its *particulàrs*, personal and circumstantial, with its antecedents and *involved* (*n. b.*—not its contingent or apprehended) consequents—and my faith in the voice within, whenever the heart desiringly listens thereto, will not allow me to fear that our verdict should be diverse. If this be true, as true it is, it follows—that we have attached a different import to the same terms in some general proposition;—and that, in attempting to generalise my convictions briefly, and yet comprehensively, I have worded it either incorrectly or obscurely. On the other hand, your communications likewise, my dear friend! were indefinite—" taught light to counterfeit a gloom;" and love left in the dusk of twilight is apt to fear the worst, or rather, to think of worse than it fears, and the momentary transformations of posts and bushes into apparitions and foot-pads must not be interpreted as symptoms of brain fever or depraved vision.

And now, my dearest Allsop! why should it be "a *melancholy* reflection, that the three most affectionate, gentle, and estimable women in your world are the three from whom you have learnt almost to undervalue their sex?" In other words those who in their reasonings have supposed as possible, not even improbable, that women can be unworthy and insincere in their expressions of attachment to men, the frequency of which it is as impossible, living open-eyed, not to have ascertained, as it is with a heart awake to what a woman ought to be, and those of whom you speak substantially* are. Why should this be a melancholy reflection? (Thursday, Nov. 1st. A fatality seems to hang over this letter; I will not, however, defer the continuation for the purpose of explaining its suspension.) Why, dearest friend, a melancholy reflection? Must not those women who have the highest sense of womanhood, who know what their sex may be, and who feel the rightfulness of their own claim to be loved with honour, and honoured with love, have likewise the keenest sense of the contrary? Understand a few foibles as incident to humanity; take as matters of course that need not be mentioned, because we know that in the least imperfect a glance of the womanish will shoot across the womanly, and there are Mirandas and Imogens, a Una, a Desdemona, out of fairy land; rare, no doubt, yet less rare than their counterparts among men in real life. Now can such a woman not be conscious, must she not feel how great the happiness is that a woman is capable of communicating, say rather *of being* to a man of sense and sensibility, pure of heart, and capable of appreciating, cherishing, and repaying her virtues? Can she feel this, and not shrink from the contemplation of a contrary lot? Can she know this, and not know what a sore evil, fearful in its heart-withering affliction in

* Thus in original letter.

proportion to the capacity of being blessed, a weak, artful, or worthless woman is—perhaps in her *own* experience has been? And if she happen to know a young Man, know him as the good, and only the good, know each other—if he were precious to her, as a younger brother to a matron sister—and so that she could not dwell on his principles, dispositions, manners, without the thought—"If I had an only daughter, and she all a mother ever prayed for, one other prayer should I offer—that, freely chosen and choosing, she should enable me to call this man my son!" would you not more than pardon even an excess of anxiety, even an error of judgment, proceeding from a disinterested dread of his taking a step irrevocable, and, if unhappy, miserable beyond all other misery, that of guilt alone excepted? Especially if there were no known particulars to guide her judgment—if that judgment were given avowedly, on the mere unbelieved possibility, on an unsupposed supposition of the worst.

In Mrs. Gillman I have always admired, what indeed I have found more or less an accompaniment of womanly excellence wherever found, a high opinion of her own sex comparatively, and a partiality for female society. I know that her strongest prejudices against individual men have originated in their professed disbelief of such a thing as female friendship, or in some similar brutish forgetfulness that woman is an immortal soul; and as to all parts of the female character, so chiefly and especially to the best, noblest, and highest—to the germs and yearnings of immortality in the man. I have much to say on this, and shall now say it with comfort, because I can think of it as a pure Question of Thought. But I will not now keep this letter any longer.

God bless you, and your friend,

T. Allsop, Esq. S. T. COLERIDGE.

P.S. The morning after our arrival, a card with our address and *all our several* names was delivered in at the post office and to the Postmaster; and this morning, Monday, Oct. 29, I received your letter dated 16th, which ought to have been delivered on Wednesday last—lying at the Post-office while I was hour by hour fretting or dreaming about you. And you, too, must have been puzzled with mine, written on my birthday. A neglect of this kind may be forgivable, but it is utterly inexcusable; a Blind-worm sting that has sensibly quickened my circulation, and I have half a mind to write to Mr. Freeling, if my wrath does not subside with my pulse, and I should have nothing better to do.

Earnest, affectionate, and impressive as this letter was to me, and must be to others, I find in it a proof, if such were not upheaped and overflowing in the preceding letters, of the love and abounding sympathy of this wonderful being; the more admirable as his own experience and trials had been of a nature rather to sear and to embitter, than to cherish and extend hope and the sympathetic affections. I may yet undertake a full exposition of this particular question, which, though unsuited to this work, would be of the highest possible value, not merely or chiefly for those to whom it would be addressed, but by reflex to parents and young children. The vice of the present day, a *spurious* delicacy, which exceeding all propriety is essentially indelicate, prevents the communication of many of the most valuable truths to the gentler sex, and thus tends to perpetuate those evils which are admitted to exist, and of which the removal is felt—known—to be co-existent with the public or open denunciation. Do I regret this delicacy? No; or if so, only as a pseudo-economist, from its rendering necessary a fresh *translation* of all the treasures of our ancient literature, not one volume of which is in accord with the finical expressions, with the sickly sentimentality of our modern reading public. To what end is this? Are our morals more pure, our conduct more manly, than that of our ancestors?

I fear much, that judged by any *fixed standard*, it will be found to be the reverse, and that the greater the fastidiousness the greater the *real* immorality. But this subject I will not farther pursue; it will be more fully discussed in the exposition I contemplate, should it be necessary to prepare it.

The subjoined fragment of an essay printed more than twenty years ago, and given to me with several others about this time, I subjoin, as being, in my opinion, and, what is of more worth, in the opinion of its author, of much value.

"The least reflection convinces us that our sensations, whether of pleasure or of pain, are the incommunicable parts of our nature, such as can be reduced to no universal rule, and in which, therefore, we have no right to expect that others should agree with us, or to blame them for disagreement. That the Greenlander prefers train oil to olive oil, and even to wine, we explain at once by our knowledge of the climate and productions to which he has been habituated. Were the man as enlightened as Plato, his palate would still find that most agreeable to which he had been most accustomed. But when the Iroquois Sachem, after having been led to the most perfect specimens of architecture in Paris, said that he saw nothing so beautiful as the cooks' shops, we attribute this without hesitation to the savagery of intellect, and infer with certainty that the sense of the beautiful was either altogether dormant in his mind, or at best very imperfect. The beautiful, therefore, not originating in the sensations, must belong to the intellect, and therefore we declare an object beautiful and feel an inward right to expect that others should coincide with us. But we feel no right to demand it; and this leads us to that which hitherto we have barely touched upon, and which we shall now attempt to illustrate more fully, namely, to the distinction of the beautiful from the good.

"Let us suppose Milton in company with some stern and prejudiced puritan, contemplating the front of York Cathedral, and at length expressing his admiration of its beauty. We will suppose it too, at that time of his life when his religious opinions, feelings and prejudices more nearly coincided with those of the rigid anti-prelatists.

"PURITAN. Beauty! I am sure it is not the beauty of holiness.

"MILTON. True: but yet it *is* beautiful.

"PURITAN. It delights not me. What is it good for? Is it of any use but to be stared at?

"MILTON. Perhaps not: but still *it is* beautiful.

"PURITAN. But call to mind the pride and wanton vanity of those cruel shavelings that wasted the labour and substance of so many thousand poor creatures in the erection of this haughty pile.

"MILTON. I do. But *still* it is *very* beautiful.

"PURITAN. Think how many score of places of worship incomparably better suited both for prayer and preaching, and how many faithful ministers might have been maintained, to the blessing of tens of thousands, to them and their children's children, with the treasures lavished on this worthless mass of stone and cement.

"MILTON. Too true! but nevertheless it is *very beautiful.*

"PURITAN. And it is not merely useless, but it feeds the pride of the prelates, and keeps alive the popish and carnal spirit amongst the people.

"MILTON. Even so: and I presume not to question the wisdom nor detract from the pious zeal of the first Reformers of Scotland, who for these reasons destroyed so many fabrics, scarce inferior in beauty to this now before our eyes. But I did not call it GOOD, nor have I told thee, brother, that if this were levelled with the ground, and existed only in the works of the modeller or engraver, that I should desire to reconstruct it. The Good consists in the congruity of a thing with the laws of the reason and the nature of the will, and in its fitness to determine the latter to actualise the former, and it is always discursive. The BEAUTIFUL arises from the preconceived harmony of an object, whether sight or sound, with the inborn and constitutional rules of the judgment and imagination; and it is always intuitive. As light to the eye, even such is beauty to the mind, which cannot but have complacency in whatever is perceived, as pre-configured to its living faculties.

"Hence the Greeks called a beautiful object *καλον*, *quasi καλουν*, *i.e.*, calling on the soul, which receives instantly and welcomes it as something con-natural."

LETTER XXIV.

Saturday Afternoon, Nov. 17th.

At length, my dear friend! we are safe and (I hope) sound at Highgate. We would fain have returned, as we went, by the Steam-vessel, but for two reasons; one that there was none to go by, the other, that Mr. Gillman thought it hazardous from the chance of November fogs on the river. *Likewise*, my dear Allsop, I have *two* especial reasons for wishing that it may be in your power to dine with us to morrow; first, it will give you so much real pleasure to see my improved looks, and how *very well* Mrs. Gillman has come back. I need not tell you, that your sister cannot be dearer to *you*—and you are no ordinary brother—than Mrs. Gillman is to me; and you will therefore readily understand me when I say, that I look at the manifest and (as it was gradual), I hope permanent change in her countenance, expression, and motion, with a sort of *pride* of comfort; second (and in one respect more urgent), my anxiety to consult you on the subject of a proposal made to me by Anster, before I return an answer, which I must do speedily. I cannot conclude without assuring you how important a part your love and esteem constitute of the happiness, and through that (I will yet venture to hope) of the utility, of your affectionate friend,

T. Allsop, Esq. S. T. Coleridge.

"I have somewhere read a story of a Turk, who, when in Paris, was prevailed upon to turn Christian, having been promised plenty of wine in this life, and a Paradise of *eternal delights* in the next. He was regularly instructed in the doctrine of the Church of Rome, and after a time had the sacrament administered to him. The next day, when his instructor was interrogating him, he asked how many gods there were?

"'None at all,' said Mustapha.

"'How! none at all?' said the priest.

"'No,' replied the sincere believer; 'you have always taught that there was only one God, and yesterday I eat him.'

"Verily there is no absurdity, how glaring soever in theology, that has not had at one time or other believers and supporters amongst men of the greatest powers and most cultivated minds."

"In one respect, and in one only, are books better than conversation. In a book, the mind of the writer is before you, and you can read and re-peruse it in case of doubt, whilst in conversation a link once lost is irrecoverable. Thus in all reported conversations, unless we are intimate with the mind of the person speaking, we often draw a wrong conclusion, and attribute *that* to discontent, to envy, or some other unworthy feeling, which, if we were in possession of the author's reasons and feelings, we should sympathise with, if indeed we did not in every case acquiesce in, his conclusions."

"In order to escape the government regulations, and with a view to contribute as little as possible to a war against freedom, it was decided that I should publish the 'Watchman' every eighth day, by which the stamp duty became unnecessary—was, in fact, evaded."

When my friend was with me, I one day, about this time, placed in his hands a volume of Letters from Swift, Bolingbroke, Pope; and it was indeed delightful to hear him read and comment upon these very interesting records of the thoughts, feelings, and principles which actuated and impelled the distinguished men of a hundred years ago.

Bolingbroke, always my favourite, was, in his letters at least, the first in my friend's estimation. He dwelt with affectionate and almost reverential interest upon the few manly, philosophical, yet easy and graceful, letters and half letters in this collection. Entirely agreeing as I do with Lamb in the opinion, that Coleridge gave value to what he read, and that, if not for the writer's, yet for *his* sake, you admired it,—I will gratify myself by giving a few of the passages upon which my friend dwelt with most *onction*.

POPE TO SWIFT.

"*Dawley*.

"I now hold the pen for my Lord Bolingbroke, who is reading your letter between two hay-cocks; but his attention is somewhat diverted by casting his eyes to the clouds, not in admiration of what you say, but for fear of a shower. He is pleased with your placing him in the triumvirate between yourself and me, though he says that he doubts he shall fare like Lepidus, while one of us runs away with all the power like Augustus, and another with all the pleasures like Antony. His great temperance and economy are so signal, that the first is fit for my constitution, and the latter would enable you to lay up so much money as to buy a bishopric in England. As to the return of his health and vigour, you might inquire of his hay-makers; but as to his temperance, I can answer that, for one whole day, we have had nothing for dinner but mutton broth, beans and bacon, and a barn-door fowl.

"Now his lordship is run after his cart, &c."

SWIFT TO POPE.

"*Dublin*.

"You give a most melancholy account of yourself, and which I do not approve. I reckon that a man, subject like us to bodily infirmities, should only occasionally converse with great people, notwithstanding all their good qualities, easinesses, and kindnesses. There is another race which I prefer before them, as beef and mutton for constant diet before partridges; I mean a middle kind both for understanding and fortune, who are perfectly easy, never impertinent, complying in every thing, ready to do a hundred little offices that you and I may often want; *who dine and sit with me five times for once that I go to them, and whom I can tell, without offence, that I am otherwise engaged at present.*"

POPE TO SWIFT.

"*London.*

"At all events, your name and mine shall stand linked as friends to posterity, both in prose and verse; and (as Tully calls it) *in consuetudine studiorum.* Would to God our persons could but as well, and as surely, be inseparable! I find my other ties dropping from me; some worn off, some torn off, and others relaxing daily: my greatest, both by duty, gratitude, and humanity, Time is shaking every moment, and it now hangs but by a thread! *I am many years the older for living with one so old;* much the more helpless for having been so long helped and tended by her; and much the more considerate and tender, for a daily commerce with one who required me justly to be both to her; and consequently the more melancholy and thoughtful, and the less fit for others, who want only in a friend or companion to be amused or entertained.

* * * *

"As the obtaining the love of valuable men is the happiest end I know of in this life, so the next felicity is to get rid of fools and scoundrels."

BOLINGBROKE TO SWIFT.

"DEAR SWIFT,

"Take care of your health: I'll give you a receipt for it, *à la Montaigne;* or, which is better, *à la Bruyère.*

"'Nourisser bien votre corps; ne le fatiguer jamais: laisser rouiller l'ésprit, meuble inutil, votre outil dangereux: laisser souper nos cloches le matin pour éveiller les chanoines, et pour faire dormir le doyen d'un sommeil doux et profond, qui lui procure de beaux songes; levez vous tard,' &c. &c. I am in my farm, and here I shoot strong and tenacious roots; I have caught hold of the earth (to use a gardener's phrase), and neither my friends nor my enemies will find it an easy matter to transplant me again.

SWIFT TO POPE.

"I have conversed with some freedom with more ministers of state of all parties than usually happens to men of my level; and I confess, in their capacity of ministers, *I look upon them as a race of people whose acquaintance no man would court, otherwise than upon the score of vanity or ambition.*

"As to what is called a revolution of principle, my opinion was this,

—that whenever those evils which usually attend and follow a violent change of government, were not in probability so pernicious as the grievance we suffer under a present power, then the public good will justify such a revolution.

"I had likewise in those days a mortal antipathy against standing armies in times of peace; because I always took standing armies to be only servants hired by the master of the family for keeping his own children in slavery, and because I conceived that a prince, who could not think himself secure without mercenary troops, must needs have a separate interest from that of his subjects; although I am not ignorant of those artificial necessities which a corrupted ministry can create, for keeping up forces to support a faction against the public interest.

"As to Parliament, I adored the wisdom of that Gothic institution which made them ANNUAL;* and I was confident our liberty could never be placed upon a firm foundation until that ancient law were restored among us: *for who sees not that, while such assemblies are permitted to have a longer duration, there grows up a commerce of corruption between the ministers and the deputies, wherein they both find their accounts, to the manifest danger of liberty?—which traffic would neither answer the design nor expense if Parliament met once a year.*

"I ever abominated that scheme of politics (now about thirty years old) of setting up a monied interest in opposition to the landed: for I conceived there could not be a truer maxim in our government than this,—that the possessors of the soil are the best judges of what is for the advantage of the kingdom.

* * * * * *

"I have ever hated all nations, professions, and communities, and all my love is towards individuals: for instance, I hate the tribe of lawyers, but I love Counsellor Such-a-one and Judge Such-a-one. But principally I hate and detest that animal *man*, although I love Peter, John, Thomas, and so forth. I have got materials towards a treatise, proving the falsity of that definition, 'animal rationale,' and to show it should be only 'rationis capax.' Upon this great foundation of misanthropy (though not in Timon's manner) the whole building of my travels is erected. The matter is so clear that it will admit of no dispute.

* * * * * *

"Dr. Arbuthnot likes the Projectors (in Gulliver's Travels) least; others you tell me the Flying Island; some think it wrong to be so

* This from Swift—the Arch Tory!

hard upon whole bodies or corporations; yet the general opinion is, that reflections on particular persons are most to be blamed: in these cases, I think the best method is to let censure and opinion take their course. *A Bishop here said that book was full of improbable lies; and for his part, he hardly believed a word of it.* So much for Gulliver.

"I hope my Whitehall landlord is nearer to a place than when I left him: as the preacher said "*the day of judgment was nearer than ever it had been before.*"

POPE TO SWIFT.

"I often imagine, if we all meet again after so many varieties and changes, after so much of the old world and the old man in each of us has been altered, that scarce a single thought of the one any more than a single atom of the other remains the same. I have fancied, I say, that we shall meet like the righteous in the Millenium, quite in peace, divested of all our former passions, smiling at our past follies, and content to enjoy the kingdom of the just in tranquillity; but I find you would rather be employed as an avenging angel of wrath, to break your vial of indignation over the heads of the wretched creatures of this world.

* * * * * *

"I enter as fully as you can desire into the principle of your love of individuals; and I think the way to have a public spirit is first to have a private one; for who can believe that any man can care for a hundred thousand men who never cared for one? No ill-humoured man can ever be a patriot any more than a friend.

* * * * * *

"I take all opportunities of justifying you against these friends, especially those who know all you think or write, and repeat your slighter verses. It is generally on such little scraps that witlings feed; and it is hard that the world should judge of our housekeeping *from what we fling to the dogs.*"

* * * * * *

"My lord, in the first part of the letter, has spoken justly of his lady; why not I of my mother? Yesterday was her birthday, now entering on the ninety-first year of her age, her memory much diminished, but her senses very little hurt, her sight and hearing good; she sleeps not ill, eats moderately, drinks water, says her prayers; *this is all* she does. I have reason to thank God for continuing so long to me a very good and tender parent, and for allowing me to exercise for some years those cares which are now as necessary to her as hers have been to me.

"An object of this sort daily before one's eyes very much softens the mind, but, perhaps, may hinder it from the willingness of contracting other ties of the like domestic nature, when one finds how painful it is even to enjoy the tender pleasures. I have formerly made some strong efforts to get and deserve a friend; perhaps it were wiser never to attempt it, but live *extempore, and look upon the world only as a place to pass through, just pay your hosts their due, disperse a little charity, and hurry on.*

* * * * *

"While we do live we must make the best of life.

"'Cantantes licet usque (minus via lædet) eamus,' as the shepherd said in Virgil when the road was long and heavy.

* * * * *

"Can you possibly think he can neglect you? If you catch yourself thinking such nonsense, your parts are decayed; for, believe me, great geniuses must and do esteem one another, *and I question if any others can esteem or comprehend uncommon merit. Others only guess at that merit, or see glimmerings of their minds; a genius has the intuitive faculty;* therefore, imagine what you will, you cannot be so sure of any man's esteem as of his. If I can think that neither he nor you despise me, it is a greater honour to me by far, and will be thought so by posterity, than if all the House of Lords writ commendatory verses upon me, the Commons ordered me to print my works, the Universities gave me public thanks, and the King, Queen, and Prince crowned me with laurel. You are a very ignorant man; you do not know the figure his name and yours will make hereafter. I do, and will preserve all the materials I can that I was of your intimacy. *Longo, sed proximus, intervallo.*

* * * *

"The world will certainly be the better for his (Lord Bolingbroke's) change of life. He seems, in the whole turn of his letters, to be a settled and principled philosopher, thanking Fortune for the tranquillity he has been forced into by her aversion, like a man driven by a violent wind, into a calm harbour. The most melancholy effect of years is that you mention, the catalogue of those we loved, and have lost, perpetually increasing. You ask me if I have got a supply of new friends to make up for those who are gone? I think that impossible; for not our friends only, but so much of ourselves is gone by the mere flux and course of years, *that, were the same friends restored to us, we could not be restored to ourselves to enjoy them.* But as, when the continual washing of a river takes away our flowers and plants, it throws weeds and sedges in their room, so the course of time brings us something as it deprives us of a great deal, and instead of leaving us what we cultivated, and expected to flourish and adorn us, gives us only what is of some little use by accident. Thus, I have acquired a few chance acquaintance of young men who look rather to the past age than the present, and *therefore* the future may have some hopes of them. *I find my heart hardened and blunted to new impressions; it will scarce receive or retain affections of yesterday, and those friends who have been dead these twenty years are more present to me now than those I see daily.*

* * * *

"I am rich *enough*, and can afford to give away £100 a year. I would not *crawl* upon the earth without doing a little good. I will enjoy the pleasure of what I give, *by giving it alive, and seeing another enjoy it.* When I die, I should be ashamed to leave enough for a monument, *if there were a wanting friend above ground.*"

SWIFT TO BOLINGBROKE.

"My Lord,—I have no other notion of economy than that it *is the parent of liberty and ease*, and I am not the only friend you have who have chid you in his heart for the neglect of it, though not with his mouth as I have done. And, my lord, I have made a maxim that should be writ in letters of diamonds,—*That a wise man ought to have money in his head, but not in his heart.* I am sorry for Lady Bolingbroke's ill-health; but I protest I never knew a *very* deserving person of that sex who had not too much reason to complain of ill health.* I never wake without finding life a more insignificant thing than it was the day before; but my greatest misery is recollecting *the scene of twenty years past, and then all of a sudden dropping into the present. I remember, when I was a little boy, I felt a great fish at the end of my line, which I drew up almost on the ground, but it dropt in, and the disappointment vexes me to this very day*, and I believe it was the type of all my future disappointments.

* * * * *

---

* Is not this an additional ground, if any more were needed, in support of the conclusion that all men, and indeed all women, who have been very remarkable or very loveable, owe the original tendency of their characters to *physical* structure.

"I tell you it is almost incredible how opinions change by the decline or decay of spirits.

* * * * *

"I was forty-seven years old when I began to think of death, and the reflections upon it now begin when I wake in the morning, and end when I am going to sleep.

"My Lord, what I would have said of fame is meant of fame which a man enjoys in this life, because I cannot be a great lord I would require a kind of *subsidium*. I would endeavour that my betters should seek me, by being in something distinguishable, instead of my seeking them. The desire of enjoying it in aftertime is owing to the spirit and folly of youth; but with age we learn to know that the house is so full that there is no room for above one or two at most in an age through the whole world.

BOLINGBROKE TO SWIFT.

"I am under no apprehension that a glut of study and retirement should cast me back into the hurry of the world; on the contrary, the single regret which I ever feel, is, that I fell so late into this course of life; my philosophy grows confirmed by habit, and if you and I meet again, I will extort this approbation from you; 'Jam non consilio bonus, sed more eo perductus, ut non tantum recte facere possim, sed nisi recte facere non possim.' The incivilities I meet with from opposite parties have been so far from rendering me violent or sour to any, that I think myself obliged to them all; some have cured me of my fears by showing me how impotent the world is; others have cured me of my hopes by showing how precarious popular friendships are; all have cured me of surprise. *In driving me out of party they have driven me out of cursed company; and in stripping me of titles, and rank, and estate, and such trinkets, which every man that will, may spare, they have given me that which no man can be happy without.*

"Perfect tranquillity is the general tenor of my life; good digestion, serene weather, wind me above it now and then, but I never fall below it; *I am sometimes gay, but I am never sad.* As soon as I leave this town I shall fall back into that course of life which keeps knaves and fools at a great distance from me: I have an aversion to them both, but in the ordinary course of life I think I can bear the sensible knave better than the fool. One must, indeed, with the former, be in some or other of the attitudes of those wooden men whom I have seen before a sword-cutler's shop in Germany: but even in those constrained postures the witty rascal will divert me, and he that diverts me does me good, and lays me under an obligation to him, which I am not obliged to pay in any other coin: the fool obliges me to be almost as much upon my guard as the knave, and he makes me no amends; he numbs me like the torpor or teases me like a fly.

* * * * * *

"I used to think sometimes formerly of old age and of death enough to prepare my mind, not enough to anticipate sorrow, to dash the joys of youth, and be all my life a dying. I find the benefit of this practice now, and find it more as I proceed on my journey; little regret when I look backwards, little apprehension when I look forward.

* * * * * *

"You know that I am too expensive, and all mankind knows that I have been cruelly plundered; and yet I feel in my mind the power of descending without anxiety two or three stages more. In short, Mr. Dean, if you will come to a certain farm in Middlesex, you shall find that I can live frugally without growling at the world or being peevish *with these whom fortune has appointed to eat my bread, instead of appointing me to eat theirs;* and yet I have naturally as little disposition to frugality as any man alive.—I am sure you like to follow reason, not custom; through this medium you will see few things to be vexed at, few persons to be angry at; and yet there will frequently be things which we ought to wish altered, and persons whom we ought to wish hanged.

"In your letter to Pope, you agree that a regard for fame becomes a man more towards his exit than at his entrance into life, and yet you confess that the longer you live the more you are indifferent about it. Your sentiment is true and natural; your reasoning, I am afraid, is not so on this occasion. Prudence will make us desire fame, because it gives us many real and great advantages in all the affairs of life. *Fame is the wise man's means; his ends are his own good, and the good of Society. Your poets and orators have inverted this order; you propose fame as the end, and good, or at least great actions as the means.* You go farther; you teach our self-love to anticipate the applause which we suppose will be paid by posterity to our names, *and with idle notions of immortality you turn other heads besides your own.*

Fame is an object which men pursue successfully by various and even contrary courses. Your doctrine leads them to look on this end as essential, and on the means as indifferent; so that Fabricius and Crassus, Cato and Cæsar, pressed forward to the same goal. After all, perhaps it may appear from the depravity of mankind, that you could do no better, nor keep up virtue in the world, without calling up this passion or this direction of self-love to your aid. Tacitus has crowned this excuse for you, according to his manner, into a maxim, *contemptu famæ, contemni virtutes.*

* * * * * *

"I know not whether the love of fame increases as we advance in age; sure I am that the force of friendship does. I loved you almost twenty years ago; I thought of you as well as I do now, better was beyond the power of conception, or, to avoid an equivoque, beyond the extent of my ideas. *Whether you are more obliged to me for loving you as well when I knew you less, or for loving you as well after loving you so many years, I shall not determine.* What I would say is this: whilst my mind grows daily more independent of the world, and feels less need of leaning on external objects, the ideas of friendship return oftener; they busy me, they warm me more. *Is it that we grow more tender as the moment of our great separation approaches?* or is it that they who are to live together in another state (for *vera amicitia non nisi inter bonos*) begin to feel more strongly that divine sympathy which is to be the great band of their future society? There is no one thought which soothes my mind like this; I encourage my imagination to pursue it, and am heartily afflicted when another faculty* of the intellect comes boisterously in, and wakes me from so pleasing a dream, if it be a dream.

"I will dwell no more on economics than I have done in my former letter; thus much only will I say, that *otium cum dignitate* is to be had with £500 as well as with £5,000 a year; *the difference will be found in the value of the man, not of the estate.*

* * * * *

"I have sometimes thought that if preachers, hangmen, and moral writers, keep vice at a stand, or so much as retard its progress, they do as much as human nature admits. A real reformation is not to be brought about by ordinary means; it requires those extraordinary means which become punishments as well as lessons. National corruption must be purged by national calamities.

* * * * *

"I was ill in the beginning of the winter for near a week, but in no danger either from the distemper *or from the attendance of three physicians.* Since that I have had better health than the regard I have paid to health deserves. We are both in the decline of life, my dear Dean, and have been some years going down the hill; let us make

---

* Reason.

the passage as smooth as we can; let us fence against physical evil by care, and the use of those means which experience must have pointed out to us; let us fence against moral evil by philosophy. The decay of passion strengthens philosophy; for passion may decay and stupidity not succeed. What hurt does age do us in subduing what we toil to subdue all our lives? It is now six o'clock in the morning; I recall the time (I am glad it is over) when about this hour I used to be going to bed, *surfeited with pleasure or jaded with business; my head often full of schemes, and my heart as often full of anxieties.*

"Is it a misfortune, think you, that I rise at this hour refreshed, serene, calm? that the past and even the present affairs of life stand like objects at a distance from me, where I can keep off the disagreeable so as not to be strongly affected by them, and from whence I can draw the others nearer to me? Passions in their force would bring all these, nay even future contingencies, about my ears at once, and reason would but ill defend me in the scuffle.

* * * * *

"My wife says she would find strength to nurse you if you was here; and yet, God knows she is extremely weak. The slow fever works under, and mines the constitution. We keep it off sometimes, but still it returns and makes new breaches before nature can repair the old ones. I am not ashamed to say to you, that I admire her more every hour of my life. Death is not to her the King of Terrors; she beholds him without the least fear. When she suffers much, she wishes for him as a deliverer from pain; when life is tolerable, she looks on him with dislike, because he is to separate her from those friends to whom she is more attached than to life itself.—You shall not stay for my next as long as you have done for this letter; and in every one Pope shall write something better than the scraps of old philosophers, which were the presents, *munuscula*, that stoical fop, Seneca, used to send in every epistle to his friend Lucilius.

* * * * *

"As to retirement and exercise, your notions are true; *the first should not be indulged in so much as to render us savages, nor the last neglected so much as to impair health;* but I know men who, for fear of being savage, live with all who will live with them; and who, to preserve their health, saunter away half their time."

LETTER XXV.

MY DEAR FRIEND, *Monday Morning.*

Ab Hydromania, Hydrophobia: from Water-lust comes Water-dread. But this is a violent metaphor, and disagreeable to boot. Suppose then, by some caprice or colic of nature, an Aqueduct split on this side of the slider or Sluice-gate, the two parts removed some thirty feet from each other, and the communication kept up only by a hollow reed split lengthways, of just enough width and depth to lay one's finger in; the likeness would be fantastic to be sure, but still it would be no inapt likeness or emblem of the state of mind in which I feel myself as often as I have just received a letter from you!—and when, after the first flush of interest and rush of thoughts stirred up by it, I sit down, or am about to sit down, to write in answer, a poor fraction, or finger-breadth of the intended reply fills up three-fourths of my paper; so, sinking under the impracticability of saying what seemed of use to say, I substitute what there is no need to say at all—the expression of my wishes, and the Love, Regard, and Affection, in which they originate.

For the future, therefore, I am determined, whenever I have any time, however short, to write whatever is first in mind, and to send it off in the self-same hour.

I do not know whether I was most affected or delighted with your last letter. It will endear Flower de Luce Court to me above all other remembrances of past efforts; and the pain, the restless aching, that comes instantly with the thought of giving out my soul and spirit where you cannot be present, where I could not see your beloved countenance glistening with the genial *spray* of the outpouring; this, in conjunction with your anxiety and that of Mr. and Mrs. Gillman concerning my health, is the most efficient, I may say, imperious of the *retracting* influences as to the Dublin scheme.

Basil Montagu called on me yesterday. I could not but be

11

amused to hear from him, as well as from Mrs. Chisholm and two other visitors, the instantaneous expression of surprise at the apparent change in my health, and the certain improvement of my looks. One lady said, "Well! Mr. Coleridge really *is* very handsome."

Highgate is in high feud with the factious stir against the governors of the chapel, one of whom I was advising against a reply addressed to the inhabitants as an *inconsistency*. "But, sir, we would not carry any thing to an extreme!" THIS IS THE DARLING WATCH-WORD OF WEAK MEN, *when they sit down on the edges of two stools. Press them to act on fixed principles, and they talk of extremes;* as if there were or could be any way of avoiding them but by keeping close to a fixed principle, *which is a principle only because it is the one medium between two extremes.*

God bless you, my ever dear friend, and

Your affectionately attached

T. Allsop, Esq. S. T. COLERIDGE.

P.S. Our friend Gillman sees the factious nature and origin of the proceedings in so strong a light, and feels so indignantly, that I am constantly afraid of his honesty spirting out to his injury. If I had the craft of a Draughtsman, I would paint Gillman in the character of Honesty, levelling a pistol (with "Truth" on the barrel) at Sutton, in the character of Modern Reform, and myself as a *Dutch* Mercury,* with rod in hand, hovering aloft, and —— pouring water into the touchhole. The superscription might be "Pacification," a little finely pronounced on the first syllable.

The passage in italics, at the close of the last letter, may *now* fitly be applied to the present unsorted or *mis*-sorted

* Mercury, the god of lucre and selfish ends, patron god of thieves, tradesmen, stock-jobbers, diplomatists, pimps, harlots and go-betweens: the soothing, pacifying god.

ministry; though the possibility of such men being, by any conjunction of circumstances, placed in a situation to influence the destinies of a mighty nation in its struggles for self-government, never, in the most extravagant mood of the Poet's mind, occurred to *him*. If the old Chancellor Oxenstiern chided his son's under-estimation of himself and over-estimate of others, by telling him "to go and see with how little wisdom the world is governed," what words would he have used had he wished to express a correct notion of *our rulers?* Either we have no choice, or not the wisdom to choose aright. At the moment that a modification or the abolition of the Peerage is sought, we have a Government consisting of Peers, or sons of Peers; a Government, the necessity of whose existence precludes their carrying reform beyond the point to which they are pledged, *if indeed they have any intention to go even that length.* This is the parent defect in our present social condition; and until we shall have virtue and self-reliance enough to place power in the middle classes at first, and in all classes almost *immediately* after, the onward progress will be slow, and exposed to the greatest danger, by the occurrence of any adverse circumstances.

I am well aware that the "greatest and wisest minds are those of whom the world hears least;" still, when it is our interest to be well governed, we shall *seek* and *choose* for ourselves, and distrust those who *seek* us. *I speak advisedly:* in the district in which I reside, self-government has been obtained; and I speak from observation, and a *thorough* knowledge of its results, when I say, that imperfect as it is at present (and chiefly so from the inferior circumstances by which it is environed), yet that its superiority in practice is in the highest degree satisfactory to those who have watched its progress and seen its results. When the basis upon which representation is founded is extended to *all*, then *all* will have an interest in good Government; and this so far from being to be feared, is of all things the most to be desired. In proportion as power is diffused, the *rewards* of public service *lessened* and its *labours increased*, will the public be served well; and the public functionary will become the mere organ for the *expression of the universal public will.*

If this were an untried scheme, it would be well to urge caution; but when we know that it is in existence, and that practically it acts well, it is discreditable to our public spirit, and to the character of our age, that self-government has not been adopted, or that approximation to this desirable state has not taken place to a much greater extent.

"On one occasion Godwin took me to Purley, where we met Sir Francis Burdett. Altogether, during the whole day,

'The feast of reason and the flow of soul'

was without drawback. It was indeed an Attic Feast.

"I was pressed to go again. I went: but how changed! No longer did I see gentlemen or scholars, I only saw drunkards, who to obscenity, scurrility, and malignity, added every species of grossness and impurity. I had been in the company of sceptics, of Pyrrhonists, but never before had I seen wickedness exhibited so completely without disguise, and in all its naked deformity.

"The only emulation was, which could utter the most senseless, the most horrid impurities, uttered in all the uproarious mirth and recklessness of lost souls. I became sick; I left the room and got into a hackney coach, which happened to be at the door. I was followed by Sir Francis Burdett, who earnestly entreated me to visit him at Wimbledon. I made no promise, nor did I ever go, and I now blame myself that political predilections should have hindered me from visiting him, as it is possible I might have assisted, if not to reclaim, to recall at least the truant energies of one who, in spite of my disgust at the orgies in which he participated, so respectfully entreated me."

I find the following lines amongst my papers, in my own writing, but whether an unfinished fragment, or a contribution to some friend's production, I know not.

"What boots to tell how o'er his grave
She wept, that would have died to save;
Little they know the heart, who deem
Her sorrow but an infant's dream
  Of transient love begotten;
A passing gale, that as it blows
Just shakes the ripe drop from the rose—
  That dies, and is forgotten.

Oh woman! nurse of hopes and fears,
All lovely in thy spring of years,
  Thy soul in blameless mirth possessing;
Most lovely in affliction's tears,
  More lovely still those tears suppressing."

LETTER XXVI.

DEAREST FRIEND, *January 25th*, 1822.

My main reason for wishing that Mrs. Gillman should have made her call on Mrs. Allsop, or that Mrs. Allsop would waive the ceremony, and taking the willingness for the act, and the præsens *in rus* (if Highgate deserves that name) for the future *in urbe*, would accompany you hither, on the earliest day convenient to you both, is, that I cannot help feeling the old inkling to press you to spend the Sunday with me, and yet feel a something like impropriety in so doing. Speaking confidentially, *et inter nosmet*, if it were prognosticable that dear Charles would be half as delightful as when we were last with him, and as pleasant relatively to the probable impressions on a stranger to him as Mary always is, I should still ask you to fulfil our first expectation. As it is, I must be content to wish it; and leave the rest to your knowledge of the circumstantial pro's and con's. Only remember, that what is dear to you becomes dear to me, and that whatever can in the least add to happiness in which you are interested, is a duty which I cannot neglect without injury to my own. *I am convinced that your happiness is in your own possession.*

One part of your letter gave me exceeding comfort—that in which you spoke of the peculiar sentiment awakened or inspired *at first sight. This is an article of my philosophic creed.*

And now for my pupil schemes. Need I say that the verdict of your judgment, after a sufficient hearing, would determine me to abandon a plan of the expediency and probable result of which I was less sceptical than I am of the present? But first let me learn from you whether you had before your mind, at the moment that you formed your opinion, the circumstance of my being already in some sort engaged to *one* pupil already: that with Mr. Stutfield and Mr. Watson I have already proceeded on two successive Thursdays, and completed the introduction and the first chapter, amounting to somewhat more than a closely-printed octavo sheet, requiring no such revision as would render transcription necessary; and that three or four more young men at the table will make no addition, or rather no change. Mr. Gillman thought my agreeing to receive Stutfield advisable. Mrs. G. did not indeed influence me by any express wish, but thought that this was the most likely way in which my work would proceed with regularity and constancy; in short, it was, or seemed to be, a *bird in the hand*, that, in conjunction with other reliable resources, would remove my anxiety with regard to the *increasing* any positive pressure on their finances of former years; so that if I could not lessen, I should prevent the deficit from growing. On all these grounds I did—I need not say down right—*engage* myself, but I certainly permitted Mr. Stutfield to make the trial in such a form that I scarcely know whether I can, in the spirit of the expectation I excited, be the first to cry *off*, he appearing fully satisfied and in good earnest. Now, supposing this to be the state of the case, how would my work fare the better by dictating it to two amanuenses instead of five or six, if I get so many? For the occasional explanations, and the necessity of removing difficulties and misapprehensions, are a real advantage in a work which I am peculiarly solicitous to have "level with the plainest capacities." To be sure, on the other hand, I *might* go on three days in the week instead of one, and let the work outrun the lectures, but just so I *might* on the plan of an increased number of auditors; and secondly, so many little obstacles start up when it is not *fore*-known that on such a day I *must* do so and so. I need not explain myself further. You can understand the "I would not ask you, but it is only—" "and but that—" "I pray do not take any *time* about it," &c., &c., added to my *startings* off.

If I do not see you on Sunday, do not fail to write to me, for of course I shall take no step till I am quite certain that your judgment is *satisfied* one way or other, for I am with unwrinkled confidence and inmost reclination,

Your affectionate friend,

S. T. COLERIDGE.

T. Allsop, Esq.

I have preserved the prospectus of a course of Lectures which were delivered in Flower de Luce Court in 1818, and were constantly thronged by the most attentive and intelligent auditory I have ever seen. This prospectus I insert. I wish the same care had been taken of the notes made at the time. I still cling to the hope that I shall recover them, or that the notes said to have been taken by a reporter will be made available in the forthcoming biography.

"*Prospectus of a Course of Lectures by S. T. Coleridge.*

"There are few families at present in the higher and middle classes of English society, in which literary topics and the productions of the Fine Arts, in some one or other of their various forms, do not occasionally take their turn in contributing to the entertainment of the social board, and the amusement of the circle at the fire-side. The acquisitions and attainments of the intellect ought, indeed, to hold a very inferior rank in our estimation, opposed to moral worth, or even to professional and specific skill, prudence, and industry. But why should they be *opposed*, when they may be made subservient merely by being *subordinated?* It can rarely happen that a man of social disposition, altogether a stranger to subjects of taste (almost the only ones on which persons of both sexes can converse with a common interest), should pass through the world without at times feeling dissatisfied with himself. The best proof of this is to be found in the marked anxiety which men who have succeeded in life without the aid of these accomplishments show in securing them to their children. A young man of ingenuous mind will not wilfully deprive himself of any species of respect. He will wish to feel himself on a level with the average of the society in which he lives, though he may be ambitious of *distinguishing* himself only in his own immediate pursuit or occupation.

"Under this conviction, the following Course of Lectures was planned. The several titles will best explain the particular subjects and purposes of each; but the main objects proposed, as the result of all, are the two following:—

"I. To convey, in a form best fitted to render them impressive at the time, and remembered afterwards, rules and principles of sound judgment, with a kind and degree of connected information, such as the hearers, generally speaking, cannot be supposed likely to form, collect, and arrange for themselves, by their own unassisted studies. It might be presumption to say that any important part of these Lectures could not be derived from books; but none, I trust, in supposing, that the same information could not be so surely or conveniently acquired from such books as are of commonest occurrence, or with that quantity of time and attention which can be reasonably expected, or even wisely desired, of men engaged in business and the active duties of the world.

"II. Under a strong persuasion that little of real value is derived by persons in general from a wide and various reading; but still more deeply convinced as to the actual *mischief* of unconnected and promiscuous reading, and that it is sure, in a greater or less degree, to enervate even where it does not likewise inflate, I hope to satisfy many an ingenuous mind, seriously interested in its own development and cultivation, how moderate a number of volumes, if only they be judiciously chosen, will suffice for the attainment of every wise and desirable purpose; that is, *in addition* to those which he studies for specific and professional purposes. It is saying less than the truth to affirm, that an excellent book (and the remark holds almost equally good of a Raphael as of a Milton) is like a well-chosen and well-tended fruit tree. Its fruits are not of one season only. With the due and natural intervals, we may recur to it year after year, and it will supply the same nourishment and the same gratification, if only we ourselves return with the same healthful appetite.

"The subjects of the lectures are indeed very *different*, but not, in the strict sense of the term, *diverse:* they are *various* rather than *miscellaneous*. There is this bond of connection common to them all, that the mental pleasure which they are calculated to excite is not dependent on accidents of fashion, place, or age, or the events or the customs of the day, but commensurate with the good sense, taste, and feeling, to the cultivation of which they themselves so largely contribute, as being all in *kind*, though not all in the same *degree*, productions of GENIUS.

"What it would be arrogant to promise, I may yet be permitted to hope,—that the execution will prove correspondent and adequate to the plan. Assuredly, my best efforts have not been wanting so to select and prepare the materials, that, at the conclusion of the lectures, an attentive auditor, who should consent to aid his future recollection by a few notes, taken either during each lecture or soon after, would rarely feel himself, for the time to come, excluded from taking an intelligent interest in any general conversation likely to occur in mixed society.

"S. T. COLERIDGE."

LETTER XXVII.

MY DEAREST FRIEND, *March 4th*, 1822.

I have been much more than ordinarily unwell for more than a week past—my sleeps worse than my vigils, my nights than my days;

———"The night's dismay
Sadden'd and stunned the intervening day;"

but last night I had not only a calmer night, without roaming in my dreams through any of Swedenborg's Hells *modéré;* but arose this morning lighter and with a sense of *relief*.

I scarce know whether the enclosed Detenu is worth enclosing or reading. I fancy that I send it because I cannot write at any length that which is even tolerably adequate to what I wish to say. Mrs. Gillman returned from town—very much pleased with her reception by Mrs. Allsop, and with the impression that it would be her husband's fault if she did not make him a happy home.

I shall make you smile, as I did dear Mary Lamb, when I say that you sometimes mistake my position. As individual to individual, from my childhood, I do not remember feeling myself either superior or inferior to any human being; except by an act of my own will in cases of real or imagined moral or intellectual superiority. In regard to worldly rank, from eight years old to nineteen, I was habituated, nay, naturalised, to look up to men circumstanced as you are, as my superiors—a large number of our governors, and almost *all* of those whom we regarded as greater men still, and whom we saw most of, *viz.* our committee governors, were such—and as neither awake nor asleep have I any other feelings than what I had at Christ's Hospital, I distinctly remember that I felt a little flush of pride and consequence—just like what we used to feel at school when the boys came running to us—"Coleridge! here's your friends want you—they are quite *grand*," or "It is quite a *lady*"—when I first heard who you were, and laughed at myself for it with that pleasurable sensation that, spite of my sufferings at that school, still accompanies any sudden re-awakening of our school-boy feelings and notions. And oh, from sixteen to nineteen what hours of Paradise had Allen and I in escorting the Miss Evanses home on a Saturday, who were then at a milliner's whom we used to think, and who I believe really was, such a nice lady;—and we used to carry thither, of a summer morning, the pillage of the flower gardens within six miles of town, with Sonnet or Love Rhyme wrapped round the nose-gay. To be feminine, kind, and genteelly (what I should now call neatly) dressed, these were the only things to which my head, heart, or imagination had any polarity, and what I was then, I still am.

God bless you and yours,

T. Allsop, Esq. S. T. Coleridge.

Letter to a Young Lady.

If there be any one subject which it especially concerns a young woman to understand, both in itself generally, and in its application to her own particular habits and circumstances, IT IS THAT OF MARRIAGE; and if there be any one subject of more perplexing delicacy than any other to advise a young woman about, above all for one of a different sex, and of no marked inequality in respect of age, however the attempt may seem authorised by intimacy and nearness of kindred; if there be one that at once attracts by its importance and repels by its difficulty, IT IS THAT OF MARRIAGE. To both sexes, indeed, it is a state of deep and awful interest, and to enter into it without proportionate Forethought is in both alike an act of Folly and Self-degradation. But in a Woman, if she have sense and sensibility enough to deserve the name, it is an act tantamount to Suicide—for it is a state which, once entered into, fills the *whole* sphere of a Woman's moral and personal Being, her Enjoyments and her Duties, dismissing none, adding many, and modifying all. Even those Duties (if such there be) which it may seem to* leave behind, it does but *transfer;* say rather, it re-imposes and re-consecrates them under yet dearer names (though names more dear than those of Daughter and Sister it is not easy to imagine); at all events, with obligations, additionally binding on her conscience, because undertaken by an act of her own free will. A woman—mark me! in using that term I still have before my

* Too often, I fear, on the supposed sanction of the *mistranslated,* and still worse *interpreted,* text, Genesis ii. 29.

mind the *idea* of Womanhood, and suppose the individual to possess its characteristic constituents—a woman in a single state may be happy and may be miserable; but *most* happy, *most* miserable—these are epithets which, with rare exceptions, belong exclusively to a Wife. The tree of *full* life, and that "whose mortal taste brings death" into the heart, these, my dear——, grow in the probationary Eden of courtship alone. To the Many of both sexes I am well aware this Eden of matrimony is but a Kitchen-garden, a thing of Profit and convenience, in an even temperature between *indifference* and *liking;* where the beds, bordered with *Thrift*, reject all higher attractions than the homely charms of *Mary-gold* and *Penny-royal*, or whatever else is good to boil in the Pot, or to make the Pot boil; or if there be aught of richer fragrance and more delicate hues, it is put or suffered there not for the *Blossom* but for the Pod. But this, my dear ——, is neither the soil, climate, nor aspect, in which *your* "Heart's-ease" or your "Herbs of grace" would bloom or burgeon. To be happy in Marriage Life, nay (unless you marry with the prospect of sinking into a lower state of moral feeling, and of gradually quenching in yourself all hope and all aspiration that looks beyond animal comforts and the outside shows of worldly respectability), in order not to be miserable, *you* must have a *Soul*-mate as well as a *House* or a *Yoke*-mate; *you* must have a Husband whom before the Altar, making yourself at that moment distinctly conscious of the presence of the Almighty God to whom you appeal, you can safely, that is, according to your confident belief, grounded on sufficient opportunities of observation, *conscientiously* vow to love, *honour*, and *respect*. With what disgust would you not turn from a sordid, with what horror would you not recoil from a contagious or infectious garment offered to you? you would not suffer it to come near your *skin*. And would you surrender your *person*, would you blend your whole personality, as far as God has put it in your power to do so, all that you call "I"—soul, body, and estate—

with one, the contagion of whose Principles, the infection or sordidness of whose habits and conversation you would have to guard against in behalf of your own soul; and the insidious influence of which on the tone and spirit of your thoughts, feelings, objects, and unconscious tendencies and manners, would be as the atmosphere in which you lived! Or were the Man's character merely negative in these respects, were he only incapable of understanding the development of your moral Being, including all those minor duties and objects of quiet pursuit and enjoyment which constitute the moral *Taste;* were he only indifferent to the interest you felt for his and your own salvation, and for the conditions of your re-union in the world to come—still it would be a *benumbing* influence, and the heart may be *starved* where it is neither stabbed nor poisoned. God said that it was not well for the human Being to be alone; to be what *we* ought to be, we need support, help, communion in good. What, then, if instead of a Helpmate we take an Obstacle, a daily counteraction? But the mere want of what God has rendered necessary or most desirable for us is itself an obstacle. Virtue sickens in the air of the Marshes, loaded with poisonous Effluvia; but even where the air is merely deficient in the due quantity of its vital Element, and where there is too little, though what there is may be faultless, human virtue lives but a *panting* and anxious life. For as to a young woman's marrying in the hope of reforming the man's principles, you will join with me in smiling at the presumption, or more probably the *pretext;* as if the Man was likely to appreciate as of very serious importance a danger which the Wife had not feared to risk on so slender a chance, or be persuaded by her to feel as hateful the very qualities which she had taken to her Bosom, as a few weeds in a Nosegay that she might pick out at leisure.

Well (you will perhaps reply), you would have convinced me, if I had not been convinced before, of the misery attendant on an unfit choice, and the criminal folly of a rash and careless one. But by what marks am I to distinguish the suitable from the unsuitable? What are the criteria, or at least the most promising signs of a man likely to prove a good husband to a good wife? And as far as you can judge from your knowledge of my character, principles, and temper, likely to find his happiness in me, and to make me happy and deserving to be so? For perfection can be expected on neither side.

Most true; and whilst the Defects are both in their *kind* and their degree within the bounds of that Imperfection which is common to all in our present state, the best and wisest way that a Wife can adopt, is to regard even faulty trifles as serious faults in herself, and yet to bear with the same or equivalent faults as trifles in her Husband. If the Fault is removable, well and good; if not, it is a speck in a Diamond—set the jewel in the Marriage Ring with the speck downmost. But it is one thing to choose for the companion of our life a man troubled with occasional Headaches or Indigestions, and another to run into the arms of *inveterate Gout*, or consumption (even though the consequent Hectic should render the countenance still more winning and beautiful), or of Hemiplegia, that is, of Palsy on one side. For, as you will see that I am speaking figuratively, and under the names of bodily complaints am really thinking, and meaning you to think, of moral and intellectual Defects and Diseases, I have hazarded the hard word "*Hemiplegia*;" as I can conceive no more striking and appropriate Image or Symbol of an Individual with one-half of his Being, that is, his person, manners, and circumstances, well and as it should be, while the other and inestimably more precious Half is but half alive, blighted and insensate. Now for the prevention of the perilous mistake, into which a personal prepossession is too apt to seduce the young and marriageable, and females more often, perhaps, than males, from the very gentleness of their sex, the mistake of looking through the diminishing end of the Glass and confounding vices with foibles,—I know no better way than by attempting to answer the questions, which I have supposed you to put, overleaf; viz.—What are the marks, &c., first, generally, and, secondly, in particular application to yourself? In the latter I can of course only speak conjecturally, except as your outward circumstances and relative Duties are concerning; in all else you must be both Querist and Respondent. But the former, the knowledge of which will be no mean assistance to you in solving the latter for your own satisfaction, I think I can answer distinctly and clearly; and with this, therefore, we will begin.

You would have reason to regard your sex affronted, if I supposed it necessary to warn any good Woman against open viciousness in a Lover, or avowed indifference to the great principles of moral obligation, religious, social, or domestic.

By "religious" I do not *here* mean matters of opinion or differences of belief in points where good and wise men have agreed to differ. Religious (in my present use of the word), is but morality in reference to all that is *permanent* and *imperishable*, God and our souls, for instance; and Morality is Religion in its application to individuals, circumstances, the various relations and spheres in which we *happen* to be placed; in short, to all that is contingent and transitory, and passes away, leaving no abiding trace but the conscience of having or not having done our duty in each.

I would fain, if the experience of Life would permit me, think it no less superfluous to dissuade a Woman of common foresight and information, from encouraging the addresses of one, however unobjectionable or even desirable in all other respects, who, she knew, or had good reason to believe, was by acquired or hereditary constitution affected by those mournful complaints, which, it is well known, are ordinarily transmitted to the offspring, to one or more, or all. But, alas! it often happens, that afflictions of this nature are united with the highest worth and the most winning attractions of Head, Heart, and Person; nay, that they often add to the native good Qualities of the Individual a tenderness, a sensibility, a quickness of perception, and a vivacity of Principle, that cannot but conciliate an interest in behalf of the Possessor in the affections of a Woman, strong in proportion to the degree in which she is herself characterised by the same excellences. Manly virtues and manly sense with feminine manners without effeminacy, form such an assemblage, a *tout ensemble* so delightful to the Womanly Heart, that it demands a hard, a cruel struggle to find in any ground of objection an effective counterpoise, a *decisive* negative. Yet the struggle must be made, and must end in the decisive and, if possible, the preventive "NO;" or all claims to Reason and Conscience, and to that distinctive seal and impress of divinity on Womanhood, the *Maternal* Soul, must be abandoned. The probable misfortunes attendant on the early death of the Head of the Family are the least fearful of the consequences that may rationally, and therefore *ought*, morally, to be expected from such a choice. The *Mother's* anguish, the *Father's* heart-wasting self-reproach, the recollection of that Innocent lost, the sight of this Darling suffering, the Dread of the future,—in fine, the conversion of Heaven's choicest Blessings into sources of anguish and subjects of Remorse. I have seen all this in more than one miserable, and *most* miserable because amiable and affectionate couple, and have seen that the sound constitution of one parent has not availed against the Taint on the other. Would to God the picture I have here exhibited were as imaginary in itself as its exhibition is unnecessary and the reality of improbable occurrence for *you*.

Dismissing, therefore, as taken for granted or altogether inapplicable, all objections grounded on gross and palpable unfitness for a state of moral and personal union and life-long interdependence,—and less than this is not Marriage, whether the unfitness result from constitutional or from moral defect or derangement; and with these, and only not *quite* so bad, dismissing too the objections from want of competence, on both sides, in worldly means, proportional to their former rank and habits; and yet what worse or more degradingly selfish (yea, the very Dregs and Sediment of Selfishness, after the more refined and *human* Portion of it, the sense of self-*interest*, has been drawn off), what worse, I repeat, can be said of the Beasts of the Field, without reflection, without forethought, of whom and for whose Offspring, Nature has taken the responsibility upon herself?—Putting all these aside, as too obvious to require argument or exposition, I will now pass to those marks which too frequently *are* overlooked, however obvious in themselves they may be; but which *ought* to be *looked for*, and *looked after*, by every woman who has ever reflected on the words, "my future Husband" with more than *girlish* Feelings and Fancies. And if the *Absence* of these *Marks* in an Individual *furnishes* a decisive reason for the rejection of his addresses, there are others the *presence* of which forms a sufficient ground for hesitation, and I will begin with an instance.

When you hear a Man making exceptions to any fundamental Law of Duty in favour of some particular pursuit or passion, and considering the dictates of *Honour* as neither more nor less than motives of selfish Prudence in respect of character; in other words, as conventional and ever-changing regulations, the breach of which will, if detected, *blackball* the offender, and send him to Coventry in that particular Rank and Class of Society of which he was born or has become a member; when, instead of giving instantaneous and unconditional obedience to the original Voice from within, a man substitutes for this, and listens after, the mere echo of the Voice from without; his knowledge, I mean, of what is commanded by *Fashion* and enforced by the foreseen consequences of non-compliance on his Worldly reputation (thus I myself heard a buckish Clergyman, a clerical Nimrod, at Salisbury avow, that he would *cheat his own Father in a* HORSE), then I say, that to smile, or show yourselves *smiling angry*, as if a

Tap with your Fan was a sufficient punishment, and a "for shame! you don't think so, I am sure," or "you should not *say* so," a sufficient reproof, would be an ominous symptom either of your own laxity of moral Principle and deadness to true honour, and the unspeakable *Contemptibleness* of this gentlemanly Counterfeit of it, or of your abandonment to a blind passion, kindled by superficial Advantages and outside Agreeables, and blown and fuelled by that most base and yet frequent thought, "one must not be over nice, or a woman may say No till no one asks her to say Yes." And what does this amount to (with all the other pretty common places, as, "What right have *I* to expect an angel in the shape of a man?" &c., &c.) but the plain confession, "I *want* to be married, the better the man the luckier for me; I have made up my mind to be the Mistress of a Family; in short, I *want* to be married!"

Under this head you may safely place all the knowing Principles of action, so often and so boastingly confessed by your clever fellows—"I take care of *Number* One; hey, Neighbour: what say you?"—"Each for himself, and God for us all: that's my maxim." And likewise, as the very same essentially, though in a more dignified and seemly Form, the principle of determining whether a thing is right or wrong, by its supposed Consequences.

There are men who let their life pass away without a single effort to do good, either to Friend or Neighbour, to their country or their religion, on the strength of the question—"What *good* will it do?" But woe to the man who is incapable of feeling, that the greatest possible good he can do for himself or for others, is to *do his duty* and to leave the consequences to God. But it will be answered, "How can we ascertain that it is our duty but by weighing the probable *consequences?* Besides, no one can act without *Motives;* and all motives must at last have respect to the agent's own self-interest; *and that is the reason why Religion is so useful, because it carries on our Self-interest beyond the grave!*"

O my dear . . . . ! so many worthy persons, who really, though unconsciously, both act from, and are actuated by, far nobler impulses, are educated to talk in this language, that I dare not expose the folly, turpitude, immorality, and *irreligion* of this system, without premising the necessity of trying to discover, previous to your forming a fixed opinion respecting the true character of the Individuals from whom *you* may have heard declarations of this kind, whether the sentiments proceed from the Tongue only, or at worst, from a misinstructed Understanding, or are the native growth of his Heart."

* * * * *

S. T. C.

The following verses were pointed out to me by my friend about this time. They are worthy of the age to which they belong.

I.

And what is love, I praie thee tell?
It is that fountain and that well
Where pleasure and repentance dwell;
It is, perhaps, that passing bell
Which tolls all into heaven or hell:
And this is love, as I heare tell.

II.

Yet what is love, I praie thee say?
It is a work—a holiday,
It is December matched with May;
When lusty Blood's in fresh arraie
Heare ten months after of the plaie,
And this is love, as I heare saie.

III.

* * *
* * * *
* * *

It is a game where none doth gaine;
The lasse saithe no, and would full faine;
And this is love, as I heare saine.

IV.

Yet what is love, I pray thee say?
It is a yea, it is a nay,
A pretie kind of sporting fray;
It is a thing will soon away,
Then take advantage while you may;
And this is love, as I heare say.

V.

Yet what is love, I pray thee shoe?
A thing that creeps, it cannot goe,
A prize, that passeth to and fro;
A thing for one, a thing for two,
And they that prove must find it so;
And this is love (sweet friend) I tro.

LETTER XXVIII.

MY DEAR FRIEND, *March 22nd,* 1822.

Mr. Watson is but now returned. I was about to set off to your house and take turns with Mrs. Allsop in watching you. It is a comfort to hear from Watson that he thinks you look not only better than when he saw you before, but more promisingly.

Si tibi deficiant medici, medici tibi fiant
Hæc tria: mens hilaris, requies, moderata dieta.

is the adage of the old Schola Salernitana, and his belief and judgment. Would to God that there were any druggist or apothecary within the king's dominions where I could procure for you the first ingredient of the recipe, fresh and genuine. I would soon make up the prescription, have the credit of curing you, and then make my fortune by advertising the nostrum under the name of Dr. Samsartorius, *Carbonifugius's Panacea Salernitana——iensis.*

You will have thought, I fear, that I had forgotten my promise of sending you Charles Lamb's *epistola porcinæ.* But it was not so. I now enclose it, and when you return it

I will make a copy for you if you wish it, for I think that writing in your present state will be most injurious to you.

I am interrupted—"a poor lad, very ragged, he says Mr. Dowling has sent him to you to show you his poetry."—"Well! desire him to step up, Maria!"

As soon as Mr. Green left me, Mrs. Gillman delivered your letter. I am not sorry, therefore, that the "Wild Irish Boy" made it too late to finish the above for that day's post. His name, poor lad! is Esmond Wilton; his mother, I guess, was poetical. But I will reserve him for a dish on our table of chat when we meet.—In reply to your affectionate letter what can I say, but that from all that you say, write or do, I receive but two impressions; first, a full, cordial, and unqualified assurance of your love towards me, a genial, unclouded faith in the entireness and steadfastness of your more than friendship, sustained and renewed by the consciousness of a responsive attachment in myself, that blends the affections of parent, brother and friend,—

"A love of thee that seems, yet cannot greater be;"

and secondly, impressions of grief or joy, according, and in proportion to, the information I receive, or the inferences that I draw, respecting your health, ease of heart and mind, and all the events, incidents, and circumstances, that affect, or are calculated to affect, both or either. Only this in addition—whatever *else* may pass through your mind, never, from any motive, or with any view, withhold from me your thoughts, your feelings, and your sorrows. What if they be momentary, winged thoughts, not native, that blowing weather has driven out of their course, and to which your mind has allowed thorough flight, but neither nest, perch, nor halting room? Send them onward to pass through mine; and between us both, we shall be better able to give a good account of them! What if they are the offspring of low or perturbed spirits—the changelings of ill health or disquietude? So much the rather communicate them. When on the white paper, they are already out of *us;* and when the letter is gone, they will not stay long behind; the very anticipation of the answer will have answered them, and superseded the need, though not the wish, of its arrival. And shall I not, think you, take them for what they are? With what comfort, with what security, could I receive or read your letters, or you mine, if we either of us had reason to believe, that whatever affliction had befallen, or discomfort was harassing, or anxiety was weighing on the heart, the other would say no word of or about it, under the plea of not transplanting thorns, or whatever other excuse a depressed fancy might invent, in order to transmute *unfriendly withholding* into a self-sacrifice of tenderness. If you had come to stay with me while I lay on a bed of pain, it would grieve you indeed, if, from an imagined duty of not grieving you, I should suppress every expression of suffering, and not tell you where my pain was, or whether it was greater or less. *Grant* that I was rendered anxious or heavy at heart, or keenly sorrowful, by any tidings you had communicated respecting yourself! *Should* it not be so? Ought it not to be so? Will not the Joy be greater when the Cloud is passed off—greater in *kind*, nobler, better—because I should feel it was my *right?* And is there not a dignity and a hidden Healing in the suffering itself—which is soothed in the wish and tempered in the endeavour of removing, or lessening, or supporting it, in the Soul of a dear Friend? However trifling my vexations are, yet if they vex me, and I am writing to you, to you I will unbosom them, my dear . . . . . and my serious sorrows and hindrances I will still less keep back from you. General Truths, Discussions, Poems, Queries—all these are parts of my nature, *often* uppermost; and when they are so, you have them—and I like well to write to, and to hear from you on them—but these I might write to the Public: and, with all Christian respect for that gentleman, I love your little finger better than his whole multitudinous Body.

Give my love to Mrs. Allsop, and tell her I will try to deserve hers.

Ever and ever God bless you, my dearest friend.

T. Allsop, Esq. S. T. Coleridge.

The letter here alluded to is a most delightful communication from Charles Lamb; which, with the hints thrown out by Manning, as to the probable origin of roast meat, were afterwards interwoven into that paper on Roast Pig, one of the most, if not the most, *delightful* Essay in our Language.

A collection of Lamb's very curious letters—more especially those written during the last twenty years—would be invaluable. Indeed, if I judge aright from the numberless Letter*lets* in my possession, and from those longer letters now I fear lost, a selection, if made from *various* sources, would be one of the most interesting in our Literature.

"Dear C.,

"It gives me great satisfaction to hear that the Pig turned out so well—they are interesting creatures at a certain age. What a pity such buds should blow out into the maturity of rank bacon! You had all some of the crackling—and brain sauce—did you remember to rub it with butter, and gently dredge it a little, just before the crisis? Did the eyes come away kindly with no Œdipean avulsion?—was the crackling the colour of the ripe pomegranate?—had you no damned complement of boiled neck of mutton before it to blunt the edge of delicate desire?—did you flesh maiden teeth in it?

"Not that I sent the Pig, or can form the remotest guess what part Owen (our landlord) could play in the business. I never knew him give any thing away in his life—he would not begin with strangers. I suspect the Pig after all was meant for me—but at the unlucky juncture of time being absent, the present, somehow, went round to Highgate.

"To confess an honest truth, a Pig is one of those things I could never think of sending away. Teals, widgeons, snipes, barn-door fowls, ducks, geese, your tame villatic things—Welsh mutton—collars of brawn—sturgeon, fresh and pickled—your potted char—Swiss cheeses—French pies—early grapes—muscadines,—I impart as freely to my friends as to myself,—they are but *self*-extended; but pardon me if I stop somewhere—*where the fine feeling of benevolence giveth a higher smack than the sensual rarity; there my friends* (or any good man) *may command me;* but pigs are pigs; and I myself am therein nearest to myself; nay, I should think it an affront, an undervaluing done to Nature, who bestowed such a boon upon me, if, in a churlish mood, I parted with the precious gift. One of the bitterest pangs I ever felt of remorse was when a child—my kind old aunt had strained her pocket-strings to bestow a sixpenny whole plum-cake upon me. In my way home through the Borough, I met a venerable old man—not a mendicant—but thereabouts; a *look-beggar*—not a verbal petitionist—and, in the coxcombry of taught charity, I gave away the cake to him. I walked on a little *in all the pride of an evangelical peacock*, when of a sudden my old aunt's kindness crossed me—*the sum it was to her—the pleasure that she had a right to expect that I, not the old impostor, should take in eating her cake*— the damned ingratitude by which, under the colour of a Christian virtue, I had frustrated her cherished purpose. I sobbed, wept, and took it to heart so grievously, that I think I never suffered the like. And I was right; it was a piece of unfeeling hypocrisy, and proved a lesson to me ever after. The cake has long been masticated, consigned to the dunghill, with the ashes of that unseasonable pauper.

"But when Providence, who is better to us all than our aunts, gives me a Pig, remembering my temptation and my fall, I shall endeavour to act towards it more in the spirit of the donor's purpose.

"Yours (short of Pig) to command in everything,

"C. L."

"When I first heard from Stewart of the Courier that Buonaparte had declared that the interests of small states must always succumb to great ones, I said, 'Thank God! he has sealed his fate: from this moment his fall is certain.'"

"Clarkson (the moral steam engine, or Giant with one idea) had recently published his book, and being in a very irritable state of mind, his wife expressed great fears of the effect of any severe review in the then state of his feelings. I wrote to Jeffrey, and expressed to him my opinion of the cruelty of any censure being passed upon the work *as a composition.* In return I had a very polite letter, expressing a wish that I should review it. I did so: but when the Review was published, in the place of some just eulogiums due to Mr. Pitt, and which I stated were upon the best authority (in fact, they were from Tom Clarkson himself), was substituted some abuse and detraction.* Yet Clarkson expressed himself gratified and satisfied with the effect of the review, and would not allow me to expose the transaction. Again, Jeffrey had said to me that it was hopeless to persuade men to prefer Hooker and Jeremy Taylor to Johnson and Gibbon. I wrote him two letters, or two sheets, detailing, at great length, my opinions. *This* he never acknowledged; but in an early number of the Review he inserted the whole of my communication in an article of the Review, and added at the conclusion words to this effect: 'We have been anxious to be clear on this subject, as much has been said on this matter by men who evidently do not understand it. Such are Wordsworth, Southey, Coleridge, and Miss Baillie.'"

"One day, when I had not a shilling which I could spare, I was passing by a cottage not far from Keswick, where a carter was demanding a shilling for a letter, which the woman of the house appeared unwilling to pay, and at last declined to take. I paid the postage; and when the man was out of sight, she told me that the letter was from her son, who took that means of letting her know that he was well: the letter was *not to be paid for*. It was then opened, and found to be blank!"

"On my return I found a double letter, for which two shillings had been paid. I tore it open, and found it to contain a long communication from Haydon the Artist, which, in allusion to my Poem on Mont Blanc, ended thus: 'From this moment you are immortal.' I was ungrateful enough to consider Mr. Haydon's immortality dear at two shillings! And though

* Was not this a fraud, a moral forgery? And this man, who attained notoriety and influence by conduct and practices like these, is he not a Judge, whose office it is to punish such acts in another?

I can now smile at the infliction, my judgment remains the same; and to this day my thanks have not been given to Mr. Haydon for his apotheosis."

"Darwin was so egregiously vain, that, after having given to his son a thesis upon Ocular Spectra, in itself an entire plagiarism from a German book published at Leipsig, he became jealous of the praise it received, and caused it to be given out that he was the real author. Nay, he even wrote letters and verses to himself, which he affixed to his own Poems as being addressed to him, by (I think) Billsborough, a young admirer of his. He asked his friends whether they had not frequently heard him express opinions like these twenty years ago?"

LETTER XXIX.

MY DEAREST FRIEND, *April 18th 1822.*

There was neither self nor unself in the flash or jet of pleasurable sensation with which I saw the old

T P
PALL MALL
3

tea canister top surmounting my own name, but a mere unreflecting gladness, a sally of inward welcoming, on finding you near to me again. I am indebted to it, however, for this, and the dear and affectionate letter that sustained and substantiated it, like a gleam of sunshine ushering in a genial south-west, and setting all the birds a singing; while the joy at the recall of the old, dry, *scathy*, viceroy of the discouraged spring, the Tartar laird from the north-east, augments yet loses itself in the delight at the arrival of the long wished-for successor to his native realm, gave a sudden spur and kindly sting to my spirits, the restorative effects of which I felt on rising this morning, as soon after, at least, as the pain which always greets me on awaking, and never fails to be my Valentine for every day in the year, had taken its leave.

Charles and Mary Lamb are to dine with us on Sunday next, and I hope it will be both pleasant and possible for you and Mrs. Allsop to complete the party; and if so, I will take care to be quite *free* to enjoy your society from the moment of your arrival, and I hope that Mrs. Allsop will not be too much tired for me to show her some of our best views and walks; and perhaps the nightingales may commence their ditties on or by that day, for I have daily expected them.

Need I say what thoughts rush into my mind when I read a letter from you, or think of your love towards me.

God bless you, my dear, dear friend,

T. Allsop, Esq. S. T. Coleridge.

The following observations preface a chronological and historic assistant to a course of lectures, delivered in 1818.

"The history of philosophy commences with the birth of Thales. Of the three different dates given by three several chronologists—namely, 640, 629, and 594th, year before Christ—I have chosen the second, not only as a mean, but as best agreeing with his manhood being contemporary with Solon's, and with the recorded fact of his having foretold an eclipse of the sun in the fourth year of the 45th Olympiad, or 597 B.C.: thus making an interval of 322 years between the birth of Thales and the era in which Hesiod and Homer are generally supposed to have flourished; that is, about the year B.C. 907. In the great poems of this era we find a language already formed, beyond all example adapted to social intercourse, to description, narration, and the expression of the passions. It possesses pre-eminently the perfections which our Milton demands of the language of poetry. It is simple, sensuous and impassioned. And, if in the word 'sensuous' we include, as Milton doubtless intended that we should, the gratification of the sense of hearing as well as that of sight, sweetness as well as beauty, these few pregnant words will be found a full and discriminative character of the Greek language, as it appears in the Iliad and Odyssey; and expressing with no less felicity the desideratum or ideal of poetic diction in all languages. But our admiration must not seduce us to extend its perfections beyond the objective into the subjective ends of language. It is the language of poetry, not of speculation; an exponent of the senses and sensations, not of reflection, abstraction, generalisation, or the mind's own notice of its own acts. It was, in short, what the state of society was—the best and loveliest *of its kind*, but of an imperfect kind; an heroic youth, but still a youth, and with the deficiencies and immaturity of youth.

"In all countries, the language of intellect has been posterior to, and the consequence of, settled LAW and an ESTABLISHED RELIGION. But in the Homeric times laws appear to have been extemporaneous, made for the occasion by tumultuary assemblage, with or without the consent of their king, whose sovereignty (or effective power) depended chiefly on his superior wealth,* though the royal title resulted from birth and ancestry, as is always the case in countries the aborigines of which have been conquered by new settlers who regarding themselves, of course, as a superior race, constitute and leave an order of nobility.

"Concerning the state of religion, it would be as difficult, as for the purpose in hand it is unnecessary, to speak otherwise than *negatively*. It is sufficient to see, that it neither had nor could have any bearing on philosophy; inasmuch as all the problems, which it is the peculiar

---

* Thus Ulysses (OD. l. xi.) tells Alcinous that kings must be rich, if they would be respected by their people, and the larger the estate the more the obedience. And of himself we are told (l. xiv.)—

> Ulysses his estate and wealth were such,
> No prince in Greece, nor Argos, nor Epire,
> In Ithica no twenty, had so much:
> And, if to have it reckoned you desire,
> Upon the continent twelve herds of kine,
> Twelve herds of goats, as many flocks of sheep,
> As many swine-houses replete with swine;
> And here, upon the island's farthest end,
> There be eleven herds of goats.

Hobbes' Odyssey;

which, homely as it is throughout and too often vulgar, scarcely falls below the point more than the other translators strain above it. In easy flow of narration Hobbes has few rivals; and his metre in alternate rhyme is so smooth (*negatively* smooth, I mean), so lithe, without bone or muscle, that you soon forget that it is metre, and read on with the same kind and degree of interest as if it were a volume of the "Arabian Nights."

object of philosophy to solve, the Hesiodic theology, or rather theogony, precludes, by resolving the absolute origin and ground of all things into night and chaos. The gods differed from animals only by a right of primogeniture. Will, Intelligence, and Love, are an equivocal generation of Death, Darkness, and Passive Necessity. The scheme, therefore, as delivered by Hesiod, is an anti-philosophic Atheism, of which a sensual Polytheism was but the painted veil.

"During the long interval from Homer to Solon all the necessary conditions and antecedents of Philosophy had been gradually evolved; the governments had ripened into constitutions; legislation had become a science, in which the disposition of the parts was predetermined by some one predominant object, to which they were to be all alike subservient and instrumental. Thus, in Sparta, the country as the efficient object SELF of each citizen; self-sufficing fortitude in the individuals, and self-sufficing strength in the state; and, as the means to those ends, war and the exclusion of trade: in Athens, political equilibrium by the balance of artificial and physical force, so as to prevent revolution and faction, without checking progressiveness and public spirit. In this manner, the minds of men were accustomed to principles, and ideal ends: and the faculties, more especially intellectual —Abstraction, Comparison, and Generalisation, the contemplation of unity in the balance of differences and the resolution of differences into unity by the establishment of a common object; all the powers. in short, by which the mind is raised from the things to the *relations* of things,— were called forth and exercised. In the meantime, the Phœnicians and Egyptians were successively the masters of the Mediterranean: and to the former, and their close connection with Palestine, it is more than merely probable, we must ascribe the institution of the Cabiric Mysteries* in Samothrace, for the influence of which, as the foster-mother of Philosophy, we refer to our first lecture. We have only to add the appearance of individuality in conception and style, as manifested in the rise of the Lyric Poets, Thales, the immediate predecessors or contemporaries, the connection of which with the awakening of the speculative impulse, will be likewise shown, in the first lecture, to explain and justify our choice in the point from which we have made the Chronology of Philosophy commence, and conducted it to the final extinction of Philosophy (or, at least, its long trance of

* "That Orpheus and Jason were initiated, or that Ulysses was the founder, must be regarded as mere poetic fictions, contradictory in themselves and inconsistent with the earliest genuine poems of Greece."

LETTER XXX.

MY VERY DEAR FRIEND, *May* 30*th*, 1822.

On my arrival at Highgate after our last parting, I ought to have written, if it were only that I had fully resolved to do so, and when I feel that I have not done what I ought, and what you would done in my place, I will, as indeed too safely to make a merit of it I may do, leave the palliative and extenuating circumstance to your kindness to think of. This only let me say, that mournful as my experience of Messrs.——— and———* in my own immediate concerns had been, of the latter especially, I was not prepared for their late behaviour, or, to use Anster's words on the occasion, for "so piteous a lowering of human nature," as the contents of Mr. W.'s letters were calculated to produce.

I have *at length*—for I really tore it out of my brain, as it were piecemeal, a bit one day and a bit the day after—finished and sent off a letter of two folio *large* and close-written sheets —nine sides equal to twelve of this size paper—to Mr. Dawes, of Ambleside, the rough copy of which I will show you when we meet.

The exceeding kindness and uncalculating instantaneous and decisive generous Friendship of the Gillmans, and the presence of *you* to my Thoughts, prevent all approach to misanthropy in my Feelings, but *for that reason* render those feelings more *acutely* painful. If I did not know that Genius, like Reason, though not perhaps so entirely, is rather a presence vouchsafed, like a guardian spirit, to an Individual, which departs whenever the Evil Self becomes decisively predominant, and not like Talents or the Powers of the Understanding, a personal property—the contemplation of . . . . . 's late and present state of Head and Heart would overwhelm me. But

---

* Great as was the shock my friend sustained from the unkind conduct of the gentlemen here alluded to, it is to me a great solace to be assured that he forgave them fully and entirely.

I must not represent my neglect as worse than I myself hold it to be; for I feel that I could not have omitted it had I not known that you were so busily engaged.

Charles and Mary Lamb and Mr. Green dine with us on Sunday next, when we are to see Mathews' Picture Gallery. Can you and Mrs. Allsop join the party? or, if Mrs. Allsop's health should make this hazardous or too great an exertion, can you come yourself? I am sure she will forgive me for putting the question.

God bless you and your affectionate

S. T. COLERIDGE.

"The most extraordinary and the best attested instance of enthusiasm existing in conjunction with perseverance is related of the *founder* of the Foley family. This man, who was a fiddler living near Stourbridge, was often witness of the immense labour and loss of time, caused by dividing the rods of iron, necessary in the process of making nails. The discovery of the process called splitting, in works called splitting mills, was first made in Sweden, and the consequences of this advance in art were most disastrous to the manufacturers of iron about Stourbridge. Foley the fiddler was shortly missed from his accustomed rounds, and was not again seen for many years. He had mentally resolved to ascertain by what means the process of splitting of bars of iron was accomplished; and, without communicating his intention to a single human being, he proceeded to Hull, and thence, without funds, worked his passage to the Swedish iron port. Arrived in Sweden, he begged and fiddled his way to the iron foundries, where, after a time, he became a universal favourite with the workmen; and, from the apparent entire absence of intelligence or anything like ultimate object, he was received into the works, to every part of which he had access. He took the advantage thus offered, and having stored his memory with observations and all the combinations, he disappeared from amongst his kind friends as he had appeared, no one knew whence or whither.

On his return to England he communicated his voyage and its results to Mr. Knight and another person in the neighbourhood, with whom he was associated, and by whom the necessary buildings were erected and machinery provided. — When at length every thing was prepared, it was found that the machinery would not act, at all events it did not answer the sole end of its erection—it would not split the bar of iron.

Foley disappeared again, and it was concluded that shame and mortification at his failure had driven him away for ever. Not so: again, though somewhat more speedily, he found his way to the Swedish iron works, where he was received most joyfully, and to make sure of their fiddler, he was lodged in the splitting mill itself. Here was the very aim and end of his life attained beyond his utmost hope. He examined the works and very soon discovered the cause of his failure. He now made drawings or rude tracings, and, having abided an ample time to verify his observations and to impress them clearly and vividly on his mind, he made his way to the port, and once more returned to England. This time he was completely successful, and by the results of his experience enriched himself and greatly benefited his countrymen. This I hold to be the most extraordinary instance of *credible* devotion in modern times."

"Phillips left Nottingham, where he had first established himself, at an early age. He afterwards kept a hosiery shop in St. Paul's, and sold the Magazine at the back. He used to boast that he could do more by puffing than all the other booksellers. It is certain that he was a great annoyance to them at one time. He had a host of writers in his pay, whom however, he never retained. A gross flatterer. I recollect hearing him address some fulsome compliments to Dr. Beddoes, to which the Doctor appeared to listen with patience. He was, after a peroration of ten minutes' duration, told by the Doctor that he was wrong in his chronology.

"'Not right in my chronology!" said the surprised bookseller; "what has chronology to do with the matter?"

"'Only this: that so far back as the year 1540, this kind of complimentary insult had become obsolete.'

"The Knight said no more, but decamped at once.

"Once, when in an abstruse argument with Mrs. Barbauld on the Berkleian controversy, she exclaimed,—'Mr. Coleridge! Mr. Coleridge!'

"The Knight was present. No sooner did he hear my name mentioned than he came up to my chair, and after making several obsequious obeisances, expressed his regret that he should have been half-an-hour in the company of so great a man without being aware of his good fortune, adding shortly afterwards, 'I would have given nine guineas a sheet for his conversation during the last hour and half?' This too at a time when I had not been at all publicly known more than a month.

"He avowed, indeed, afterwards, that he never feared offending by flattery, being convinced that for one man who was offended ninety-nine were pleased with that, which, if presented to others, they would have deemed nauseating and disgusting."

LETTER XXXI.

MY DEAR FRIEND, *June 29th*, 1822.

As fervent a prayer, as glow-trembling a joy, thanksgiving that seeks to steady itself by prayer, and prayer that dissolves itself into thanks and gladness, as ever eddied in or streamed onward from of love and friendship for pain and dread, for travail of body and spirit passed over, and a mother smiling over the first-born at her bosom, have sped toward you from the moment I opened your Letter. For as if there had been a light suffused along the paper at that part, "birth of a Daughter after a very short illness," were the first words I saw. "Well pleased!" To be sure you are. It was scarcely a week ago that—during the only hour free from visits, visitors, and visitations that we have had to ourselves for I do not know how long—Mrs. Gillman and I had settled the point; and, after a strict, patient, and impartial poll of the *pro's* and *con's* on both sides, a Girl it was to be, and a Girl was returned by a very large majority of wishes. But as wishes, like strawberries, do not bear carriage well, or at least require to be poised on the *head*, I will send a scanty specimen of the Reasons by way of *Hansel. Imprimis*, A Girl takes five times as much spoiling to spoil her. *Item.*—It is a great advantage both in respect of Temper, Manners, and the Quickening of the Faculties, for a Boy to have a Sister or Sisters a year or two older than himself.—But I devote this brief scroll to Feeling: so no more of disquisition, except it be to declare the entire coincidence of my experience with yours as to the very rare occurrence of strong and deep Feeling in conjunction with free power and vivacity in the expression of it. The most eminent Tragedians, Garrick for instance, are known to have had their emotions as much at command, and almost as much on the surface, as the muscles of their countenances; and the French, who are all Actors, are proverbially heartless. Is it that it is a false and feverous state for the Centre to live in the Circumference? The vital warmth seldom rises to the surface in the form of sensible Heat, without becoming hectic and inimical to the Life within, the only source of real sensibility. Eloquence itself—I speak of it as habitual and at call—too often is, and is always like to engender, a species of histrionism.

In one of my juvenile poems (on a Friend who died in a Frenzy Fever), you will find* that I was jealous of this in

* To me hath Heaven with bounteous hand assigned
Energic Reason and a shaping mind,

myself; and that it is (as I trust it is), otherwise, I attribute mainly to the following causes:—A naturally, at once searching and communicative disposition, the necessity of reconciling the restlessness of an ever-working Fancy with an intense craving after a resting-place for my Thoughts in some *principle* that was derived from experience, but of which all other knowledge should be but so many repetitions under various limitations, even as circles, squares, triangles, &c., &c., are but so many positions of space. And, lastly, that my eloquence was most commonly excited by the desire of running away and hiding myself from my personal and inward feelings, *and not for the expression of them*, while doubtless this very effort of feeling gave a passion and glow to my thoughts and language on subjects of a general nature, that they otherwise would not have had. I fled in a Circle, still overtaken by the Feelings, from which I was ever more fleeing, with my back turned towards them; but above all, my growing deepening conviction of the *transcendency of the moral to the intellectual*, and the inexpressible comfort and inward strength which I experience myself to derive as often as I contemplate truth realised into Being by a human Will; so that, *as I cannot love without esteem, neither can I esteem without loving.* Hence I *love* but few, but those I love as my own Soul; for I feel that without them I should—not indeed cease to be kind and effluent, but by little and little become a soul-less fixed Star, receiving no rays nor influences

---

The daring ken of Truth, the Patriot's part,
And Pity's sigh, that breathes the gentle heart.

Sloth jaundiced all! and from my graspless hand
Drop Friendship's precious pearls, like hour-glass sand.
I weep, yet stoop not! the faint anguish flows,
A dreamy pang in Morning's feverish dose.

Is this piled earth our Being's passless mound?
Tell me, cold grave! is Death with poppies crowned?
Tired sentinel! 'mid fitful starts I nod,
And fain would sleep, though pillowed on a clod.

into my Being, *a Solitude which I so tremble at, that I cannot attribute it even to the Divine Nature.*

*God*father or not (have not Girls Godfathers?), the little lady shall be to me a dear Daughter, and I will make her love me by loving her own Papa and Mamma. God bless you.

T. Allsop, Esq. S. T. Coleridge.

"Once, when in the Roman States, I entered a house of entertainment on a Friday, accompanied by a German artist, and, being hungry, asked for some ham or meat. The woman to whom I addressed myself said I could not have it; it was fast day. I replied we were heretics. She still hesitated, when her husband growled out,—'Let them have it, let them have it; they are *damned already.*' Thus satisfying himself that, as we were heretics, or what, singular enough, is here considered synonymous, philosophers, and therefore already damned, he could not injure us farther, but might benefit himself by ministering to our guilty appetites."

"I have been reading Antony and Cleopatra. It is with me a prime favourite. It is one of the most gorgeous and sustained of all Shakspeare's dramas. In particular do I dote upon the last half of the fifth act."

"An American, by his boasting of the superiority of the Americans generally, but more especially in their language, once provoked me to tell him that 'on that head the least said the better, as the Americans presented the extraordinary anomaly of a *people without a language.* That they had mistaken the English language for baggage (which is called plunder in America), and had stolen it.' Speaking of America, it is I believe a fact verified beyond doubt, that, some years ago it was impossible to obtain a copy of the Newgate Calendar, as they had all been bought up by the Americans, whether to suppress this blazon of their forefathers, or to assist in their genealogical researches, I could never learn satisfactorily."

LETTER XXXII.

MY DEAREST FRIEND, *Ramsgate, Oct. 8th,* 1822.

In the course of my past life I count four griping and grasping sorrows, each of which seemed to have my very heart in its hands, compressing or wringing. The first, when the Vision of a Happy Home sunk for ever, and it became impossible for me any longer even to hope for domestic happiness under the name of Husband, when I was doomed to know

> That names but seldom meet with Love,
> And Love wants courage without a name!

The second commenced on the night of my arrival (from Grasmere) in town with Mr. and Mrs. Montagu, when all the superstructure raised by my idolatrous Fancy during an enthusiastic and self-sacrificing Friendship of fifteen years—the fifteen bright and ripe years, the strong summer of my Life—burst like a Bubble! But the Grief did not vanish with it, nor the love which was the stuff and vitality of the grief, though they pined away up to the moment of . . . . . 's last total Transfiguration into Baseness; when, with £1,200 a year, and just at the moment that the *extraordinary* Bankruptcy of Fenner and Curtis had robbed me of every penny I had been so many years working for, every penny I possessed in the world, and involved me in a debt of £150 to boot, he *first* regretted that he was not able to pay a certain bill of mine to his . . . . . . 's wife's brother, himself, 'never wanted money so much in his life,' &c. &c.; and an hour after attempted to extort from me a transfer to himself of all that I could call my own in the world—my books—as the condition of his paying a debt which in *equity* was as much, but in honour and gratitude was far more, *his* debt than mine!

My third sorrow was in some sort included in the second; what the former was to Friendship the latter was to a yet more inward bond. The former spread a wider gloom over the world around me, the latter left a darkness deeper within myself; the former is more akin to indignation, and moody scorn at my own folly in my weaker moments, and to contemplative melancholy and alienation from the Past in my ordinary state; the latter had more of self in its character, but of a Self, emptied—a gourd of Jonas: and is *this* it under which I hoped to have prophesied?

My fourth commenced with the tidings of the charge against J . . . —remitted with the belief and confidence of the Falsehood of the charge—relapsed again—and again—and again—blended with the sad convictions, that neither E. nor I. thought of or felt towards me as they ought, or attributed any thing done for them to me; and lastly, reached its height on the nineteenth day of E.'s fever by J.'s desertion of him, when it trembled in the scales whether he should live or die, and the cause of this desertion first awakening the suspicion that I had been deliberately deceived and made an accomplice in deceiving others.

And yet, in all these four griefs, my recollection, as often as they were recalled to my mind, turned not to *what* I suffered, but on what *account*—at worst, I never thought of the sufferings apart from the causes and occasions of them; but the latter were ever uppermost. It was reserved for the interval between six o'clock and twelve on *that Saturday* evening to bring a suffering which, do what I will, I cannot help thinking of and being *affrighted* by, as a terror of itself—a self-subsisting, separate something, detached from the cause. I cannot help hearing the sound of my voice at the moment when I . . . took me by surprise, and asked me for the money to pay a debt to, and take leave of, Mr. Williams, promising to overtake me if possible before I had reached his aunt Martha's, but at latest before five. "Nay, say *six*. Be, if you can, by five, but *say* six." Then, when he had passed a few steps—"J... six; O my God! think of the *agony*, the *sore agony*, of every moment after six!" And though he was not three yards from me, I only saw the colour of his Face through my Tears!—No more of this! I will finish this scrawl after my return from the Beach.

When I had left behind me what I had no power to make better or worse, and arrived at the sea side, I had soon reason to remember that I was not at *home*, or at Muddiford, *or* at Little Hampton, or at Ramsgate, but under the conjunct signs of Virgo and the Crab; the one in the wane, the other in advance, yet in excellent agreement with the former, by virtue of its rare privilege of advancing backward. In sober prose, I verily believe we should have found as genial a birth in a nest hillock of Termites or Bugaboos as with this single Ant-consanguineous. As soon therefore as dear Mr. Gillman returned to us, you will not hold it either strange or unwise that, in agreeing to accompany him to Dover, the kingdom of France west of Paris, Ramsgate, Sandwich, and foreign parts in general, I determined to give myself up to each moment as it came, with no anticipations and with no recollections, save as far as is involved in the wish every now and then, that you had been with me; and in this resolve it was that I destroyed the kit-cat or bust at least of the letter I had meant to have sent you. But oh! how often have I wished, and do I wish, that you and Mrs. Allsop could form a household in common at Ramsgate with us next year.

And now for your second Letter. What shall I say? When our Griefs and Fears and agitations are strongly roused towards one object, we almost want some fresh memento to remind us that we have other Loves, other Interests. Forgive me if I tell you that your last letter did, in something of this way, make me feel afresh, that there was that in my very heart that called you Son as well as Friend, and reminded me that a Father's affection could not exist exempt from a Father's anxiety. I am fully aware that every syllable in the latter half of your letter proceeded from the strong two-fold desire at once to comfort and to conciliate, and that I ought to regard your remarks as the mere straining of the Soul towards an End felt and known to be pure and lovely; and even so I do regard them, yet I cannot read them without anxiety: not indeed anxious Thoughts, but anxious Feeling. Sane or insane, fearful thing it is, when I can be comforted by an assurance of the latter; but I neither know nor *dare* hear of any mid state, of no vague necessities dare I hear. Our own wandering thoughts may be suffered to become Tyrants over the mind, of which they are the Offspring and the most effective Viceroys, or substitutes of that dark and dim spiritual Personëity, whose whispers and fiery darts holy men have supposed them to be, and that these may end in the loss, or rather Forfeiture of Free agency, I doubt not. But, my dearest friend, I have both the *Faith of Reason* and the Voice of Conscience and the assurance of Scripture, that, "resist the evil one, and he will flee from you." But for self-condemnation, J. . . . would never have tampered with Fatalism; and but for Fatalism, he would never have had such cause to condemn himself. With truest love,

Yours,

T. Allsop, Esq. S. T. Coleridge.

P.S. Affectionate remembrances to Mrs. Allsop, in short, to you and *yours*. While I write the two last words, my lips felt an appetite to kiss the baby.

This and the preceding letters are painful, very painful, to me. I know not whether they have not given birth to sensations more afflicting in the re-perusal, than they caused me to feel even at the time. Then, I could hope that the clouds which darkened the life of hope would pass away, and that the genial sunshine of my friend's mind would again shine, inward at least, with unobscured brilliancy. *Now*, I can but garner in my heart the experience of the past, to be conveyed, as all personal experience must be, to unwilling or inattentive ears: to be part of that experience which he himself so beautifully and so truly describes, as like the stern-lights of a vessel, illuminating only the past. In the instance alluded to, the extreme sensitiveness of my *young* friend caused him, to avoid a little present pain, so to act, as to give a far greater amount of pain to Mr. Coleridge than he could ever compensate, and to store up for himself the most acute and protracted regrets. Moral courage, my dear children, the daring to suffer the present evil, be it an expiation for the past, or as an offering or a testimony to convictions, not *lightly* attained, *is always its own great reward.*

To say nothing, or to say all you think, and at all times, provided no personal offence is intended or sought to be given, is the course for an honest man, for a lover of truth, invariably to pursue. It may be said that the course of affairs is so complicated and so tortuous, that conduct to harmonise with it must be tortuous also, and that in the necessity that exists for numerous and skilful combinations, simplicity must altogether be cast aside as unsuited to the present state and necessities of the social condition. I have come to a wholly different conclusion. I deem it most important, even on these very grounds, and for these (to me, at least) always secondary objects, to preserve sincerity in the means, and simplicity in the end, however extensive may be the combinations by which that end is sought to be obtained. For if, in addition to the complications of society, and to the combinations necessary to our individual success, we superadd suppressions and those moral falsehoods which are worse and every way more injurious than direct lies, we render success *far less probable*, and even in its attainment, less valuable, from the recollection of the very unworthy means by which it has been achieved.

I well know the process by which men are led on to this fearful state of constant insincerity in matters of worldly interest, whether of fame, riches, or power, all of which might and *yet will*, I hope, be estimated at their proper value (whilst they are permitted to have any value at all), as means and not as ends.

LETTER XXXIII.

MY VERY DEAR FRIEND, *Dec.* 26*th*, 1822.

I might with strict truth assign the not only day after day, but hour after hour employment, if not through the whole period of my waking time, yet through the whole of my writing power, as the cause of my not having written to you with my own hand; but then I ought to add that it was enforced and kept up by the expectation of seeing you. There are two ways of giving you pleasure and comfort; would to God I could have made the one *compossible* with the other and done both! The first, the having finished the Logic in its three main divisions,—as the Canon, or that which prescribes the rule and form of all *conclusion* or conclusive reasoning; second, as the Criterion, or that which teaches to distinguish truth from falsehood, containing all the sorts, forms, and sources of error, and means of deceiving or being deceived; third, as the Organ, or positive instrument for discovering truth, together with the general introduction to the whole.

The second was to come to town, and pass a week with you and Mrs. Allsop. The latter I could not have done, and yet have been able to send you the present good tidings that with regard to the former we are in sight of land; that Mr. Stutfield will give three days in the week for the next fortnight; and that I have no doubt, notwithstanding Mrs. Coleridge and my little Sarah's expected arrival on Friday next, that by the end of January the whole book will not only have been finished, for *that* I expect will be the case next Sunday fortnight, but ready for the press. In reality, I have *now* little else but to transcribe, and even this would in part only be necessary, but that I must of course dictate the sentences to Mr. Stutfield and Mr. Watson, and shall therefore avail myself of the opportunity for occasional correction and improvement. When this is done, and can be offered as *a whole* to Murray or other Publisher, I shall have the Logical Exercises, or the Logic exemplified and applied in a critique on—1. Condillac; 2. Paley; 3. The French Chemistry and Philosophy, with other miscellaneous matters from the present Fashions of the age, moral and political, ready to go to the Press with by the time the other is printed off; and this without interrupting the greater work on Religion, of which the first Half, containing the Philosophy or ideal Truth, possibility, and *a priori* probability of the articles of Christian Faith, was completed on Sunday last.

Let but these works be once done, and the responsibility off my conscience, and I have no doubt or dread of afterwards obtaining an honourable sufficiency, were it only by school books, and compilations from my own memorandum volumes. The publication of my Shakspeare and other similar lectures, sheet per sheet, in Blackwood, with the aid of Mr. Frere's short-hand copies, and those on the History of Philosophy in one volume, would nearly suffice.

I was unspeakably delighted to see Mrs. Allsop look so *charmingly* well. My affectionate regards to her, and a heart-uttered Happy, Happy, Happy Christmas to you both, one for each, and the third for the little girl, who (Mr. Watson assures me) has now the ground work and necessary pre-condition of thriving, though it may be some time before a notable change in the appearances may take place for the general eye.

God bless you, and your friend,

T. Allsop, Esq. S. T. Coleridge

"It is good to get and good to spend; but it is not well or seemly to carry the *spirit* of thrift into kind acts, nor a profuse spirit into thrift."

"Men are not more generous than women. Men desire the happiness of women apart from themselves, chiefly, if not only, *when and where* it would be an imputation upon a woman's affections for her to be happy; and women, on their part, seldom cordially carry their wish for their husband's happiness and enjoyment beyond the threshold. Whether it is that women have a passion for nursing, or from whatever cause, they invariably discourage all attempts to seek for health itself, beyond their own abode. When balloons, or these new roads upon which they say it will be possible to travel fifteen miles an hour, for a day together, shall become the common mode of travelling, women will become more locomotive;—the health of all classes will be materially benefited. Women will then spend less time in attiring themselves—will invent some more simple head gear, or dispense with it altogether.

"Thousands of women, attached to their husbands by the most endearing ties, and who would deplore their death for months, would oppose a separation for a few weeks in search of health, or assent so reluctantly, and with so much dissatisfaction as to deprive the remedy of all value—rather make it an evil. I speak of affectionate natures and of the various, but always selfish, guises of self-will.

"Caresses and endearment on this side of sickening *fondness*, and affectionate interest in all that concerns himself, from a wife freely chosen, are what every man loves, whether he be communicative or reserved, staid or sanguine. But affection, where it exists, will always prompt or discover its own most appropriate manifestation. All men, even the most surly, are influenced by affection, even when little fitted to excite it. I could have been happy with a servant girl had she only in sincerity of heart responded to my affection."

On this matter I could enlarge, but shall defer it for the present, seeing that all the materials are not yet collected upon which to form a correct judgment.

LETTER XXXIV

MY DEAR ALLSOP, *Grove, Highgate, Dec. 10th,* 1823.

I shall be alone on Sunday, and shall be happy to spend it with you. Ever since the disappearance of a most unsightly eruption on my Face I have been, with but short intermission, annoyed with the noise as of a distant Forge hammer incessantly sounding, so that for some time I actually supposed it to be an outward sound. To me, who never before *knew* by any sensation that I had a head upon my shoulders, this you may suppose is extremely harrassing to the spirits and distractive of my attention. Mrs. Gillman, on stepping from my attic, slipt on the first step of a steep flight of nine high stairs, precipitated herself and fell head foremost on the fifth stair; and when at the piercing scream I rushed out, I found her lying on the landing place, her head at the wall. Even now the Image, and the Terror of the Image, blends with the recollection of the Past a strange expectancy, a fearful sense of a something still to come; and breaks in, and makes stoppages, as it were, in my Thanks to God for her providential escape. For an escape we all must think it, though the small bone of her left arm was broken, and her wrist sprained. She went without a light, though (Oh! the vanity of Prophecies, the truth of which can be established only by the proof of their uselessness) two nights before I had expostulated with her on this account with some warmth, having previously more than once remonstrated against it, on stairs not familiar and without carpeting.

As I shall *rely* on your spending Sunday here, and with me

alone, I shall defer to that time all but my tenderest regards to Mrs. Allsop, and the superfluous assurance that I am evermore, my dearest Allsop,

Your most cordial, attached, and
Affectionate friend,

T. Allsop, Esq. S. T. Coleridge.

P.S.—You will be delighted with my new room.

"The notion, that affections are of less importance than advantages, or that the latter dare even be weighed in the same scales, is less truly described as opposite to my opinion than as alien from my very nature. As to accomplishments, I do not know whether it is right to cherish a positive opinion of an indifferent thing, that is neither good nor evil. If we leave all moral relations out of view, such as vanity, or the disposition to underrate the solidities of the soul, male or female, &c., &c., the question of *accomplishments* (as they are absurdly called) seems to me to depend on the individual woman, in the same way that dress does. Of two equally amiable and equally beloved women, one looks better in an evening, the other in a morning dress. It is just as it *suits*, and so with accomplishments. There are two women, to whom, though in different ways, I have been *deeply* attached in the course of my life. The one had no so-called *accomplishments*, and not only at the time when I had faith in the return, did I say, "And I love her all the better," but I am still convinced that such would be my opinion of any such woman. Accomplishments (in which nothing good, useful, or estimable, is or can be accomplished) would not suit her. Just as I should say to a daughter, or should have said to the lassy in question, had she been my wife, "My dear! I like to see you with bracelets; but your hand and fingers are prettiest without any ornament, they don't suit *rings*." The other lady, on the contrary, became them; they were indeed so natural *for* her that they never strike me *as* accomplishments. And, to do her justice, I must say that I am persuaded that the consciousness of them occupies as little room in her own thoughts.

"Accomplishments, what are they? why truly the very want of the French, Italian, smattering of terms without relation to things or properties of any kind, and piano-fortery, which meets one now with Jack-o'-lantern ubiquity, in every first and second story, in every street, is become a presumptive accomplishment *as the being free from debt is a negative stock.* Mrs. C . . . had no meretricious *accomplishments.* Did you ever suspect, from anything I ever said, that this lay in the way of my domestic happiness? And she, too, had no accomplishments, to whom *the man* in the poet sighed forth the

'Dear maid! no prattler at a mother's knee
Was e'er so deeply prized as I prize *thee*,
Why was I made for love, and love denied to me?'"

The following letter addressed to me, arrived on Christmas-Eve, and was opened by Mrs. . . . . ; who replied that I was spending my Christmas with my parents, but that, had I been at home this was a season of *family* re-unions.

This will serve to explain the letter which follows; which I give to show the pain caused by a slight misapprehension, and the great anxiety of the writer to remove an erroneous impression.

LETTER XXXV.

MY DEAREST ALLSOP, *Dec. 24th*, 1823.

I forgot to ask you, and so did Mr. and Mrs. G. . . , whether you could dine with us on Christmas-day—or on New Year's-day—or on both! If you can, need I say that I shall be glad.

My noisy forge-hammer is still busy; quick, thick, and fervent.

With kindest regards to Mrs. Allsop,
Your ever faithful and affectionate,

T. Allsop, Esq. S. T. Coleridge.

LETTER XXXVI.

My dear Mrs. Allsop,

Indeed, indeed you have sadly misunderstood my last-hurried note. So over and over again has Mr. Allsop been assured that every invitation to him included you, so often has he been asked to consider one meant for both, that in a few lines scrawled in the dark, with a distracting, quick, thick, and noisy beating as of a distant forge-hammer in my head, and, lastly, written, not so much under any expectation of seeing him (in fact for *Christmas*-day I had none), as from a nervous jealousy of any customary mark of respect and affection being omitted, the ceremony of EXPRESSING your name did not occur to me. But the blame, whatever it be, lies with me, wholly, exclusively on me; for on asking *Mr.* Gillman whether an invitation had been sent to you, he replied by asking me if I had not spoken, and on my saying it was now too late, he still desired me to write, his words being,—"For though Allsop must know how glad we always are to see him, yet still, as far as it is a mark of respect, it is his due." Accordingly I wrote. But after the letter had been sent to the post, on going to Mrs. Gillman to learn how she was, and saying that I had just scrawled a note in the dark in order not to miss the post, *she* expressed her disapprobation as nearly as I can remember in these words:—"I do not think a mere ceremony any mark of respect to intimate friends. How, in such weather as this, and short days, can it be supposed that Mrs. Allsop could either leave the children or take them?

But to expect Mr. Allsop to dine away from his family at this time is what I would not even appear to do, for I should think it very wrong if he did." I was vexed, and could only reply, —"This comes of doing things of a hurry. However, Allsop knows me too well to attribute to me any other feeling or purpose than the real ones." I give you my word and honour, my dear madame, that these were, to the best of my recollection, the very words; but I am quite CERTAIN that they contain the same substance. And for this reason, knowing how it would vex and fret on her spirits that you had been offended, and (if the letter of itself without any interpretation derived from the character or known sentiments of the writer were to decide it), justly offended, I have not shown her your note, nor mentioned the circumstance to her; for this sad accident has pulled her down sadly, coming too in conjunction with the distressful state of my health and spirits; for such is my state at present, that though I would myself have run any hazard to have spent to-morrow with Miss Southey, my own Sarah's friend and twin-sister, and with Miss Wordsworth at Monkhouse's, in Gloster-place; yet Mr. Gillman has both dissuaded and forbidden me as my medical adviser. I trust, therefore, that, finding Mrs. Gillman *more* than *blameless*, and that in me the blame was in the judgment and not in the *intention*, you will think no more of it, but do me the *justice* to believe that any intentions or feelings of which I have been conscious have ever been of a kind most contrary to any form of disrespect, omisive or commissive; to which, let me add, that *I should* be doing what Mr. Allsop (I am sure) would *not* do, *if having* shown you *consciously* any *dis*respect I continued to subscribe myself *his* friend, not to speak of any profession of being what in very truth I am, my dear Mrs. Allsop,

Sincerely and affectionately *yours*,

S. T. COLERIDGE.

This letter is written in a very hurried and irregular

manner, showing the exceeding pain the writer suffered from the thought of having hurt or offended another. Truly did he exemplify his own position, that great minds are ever gentle and affectionate.

LETTER XXXVII.

DEAR MRS. ALLSOP, *Grove, Highgate, April 8th*, 1824.

There are three rolls of paper, Mr. Wordsworth's translation of the first, second, and third books, two in letter-paper, one in a little writing-book, in the drawer under the side-board in your dining-room. Be so good as to put them up and give them to the bearer should Mr. Allsop not be at home.

MY DEAR ALLSOP,

You I know will have approved of my instant compliance with Mr. Gillman's request of returning with him; and I know, too, that both Mrs. Allsop and yourself will think it superfluous in me to tell you what you must be sure I cannot but feel. I trust that when I next return from you, I shall have—not to thank you less—but with less painful recollections of the trouble and anxiety I have occasioned you.

In the agitation of leaving Mrs. Allsop, I forgot to take with me the translation of Virgil. Could I, that is, dared I, wait till Sunday, I might make it one way of inducing you to spend the day with me. Upon the whole, however, I had better send than increase my anxieties, so I will send Riley with this note.

My Grandfatherly love and kisses to the Fairy Prattler and the meek boy. I did heave a long-drawn wish this morning, as the sun and the air too were so genial, that the latter had been in the good woman's house at Highgate well wrapped up. A fortnight would do wonders for the dear little fellow.

You and Mrs. Allsop may rely on it that I would see him every day during his stay here, if there were only one hour in which it did not rain vehemently.

God bless you,
And your obliged and most
affectionately attached friend,

T. Allsop, Esq. S. T. COLERIDGE.

Thus early, my dear children, did you become the objects of his affection and affectionate solicitude. It is pleasant to me, almost as pleasant as it is painful, to recall those days, days when from many causes my anxieties were great and my position altogether most ungenial, and which, but for your dear sakes, and for one, then as now, dearer to me than all beside, would have been one of unmixed evil. From this position I have now happily escaped into a state of greater freedom, which, if it shall permit me to realise the objects of my earliest and steadfast aspirations, objects in which you, as Friends rather than as children, will have active and *pleasant* duties allotted, will leave me little more to wish, hardly anything to hope.

This letter was written after a sojourn of about ten days in London, respecting which I have preserved the correspondence, but which, as it is of interest chiefly to myself, would be out of place here. It is a painful fact, if any general condition or facts can with propriety be said to be painful, that those alone who have been steeped in anxieties and in suffering can appreciate the anxieties or sufferings of others. Prosperous men avoid and eschew all approximation to distress or uneasiness in *real* life, however they may indulge in *mental* sympathy with suffering, or occasionally afford pecuniary assistance through the hands of third parties. Hence those who have themselves passed through mental and pecuniary distress are alone found to make sacrifices as a tribute to, or from sympathy with, their own past trials; though it may fairly be doubted whether suffering ever yet produced *patient* consideration for the anxieties of another, or increased the *real charities*, though it may greatly enlarge the sympathies and the sensibility which pass current as charity, that greatest of all the virtues.

LETTER XXXVIII.

MY DEAREST FRIEND, *April* 14*th*, 1824.

I am myself at my ordinary average of Health, and beat off the blue Devils with the Ghosts of defunct hopes, chasing the Jack-o'-lanterns of foolish expectation as well as I can, in the which, believe me, I derive no small help from the Faith that in *your* affection and sincerity I have at least one entire counterpart of the Thoughts and Feelings with which I am evermore and most sincerely

Your affectionate friend,

T. Allsop, Esq. S. T. COLERIDGE.

My kindest love and remembrance to Mrs. Allsop, and assure her that I called this morning at Mrs. Constable's, induced by the very fine though unwarm day, to hope I might find the little boy there, and was rather disappointed to see her return without him. But, doubtless, we are entitled every day to expect a change of the present to a more genial wind. If the meek little one does not crow and clap his wings in a week or so from Thursday, it shall not be for want of being looked after.

LETTER XXXIX.

MY DEAREST FRIEND, *April* 27*th*, 1824.

I direct this to your *house*, or *firm* should I say? because I should not think myself justified in exciting in Mrs. Allsop an alarm, for which I have no more grounds than my own apprehensions and unlearned conjectures. And yet having these bodings, I cannot feel quite easy in withholding them from you. On Saturday, the morning Mrs. Allsop was here, I was in high hope, the little boy looking so much clearer and livelier than on the Thursday; but the weather since then being on the whole genial, and the baby showing no mark of progress, but rather the reverse, and it seeming to me each returning day to require a stronger effort to rouse its attention, and the relapse to a dulness, which it is evident the upright posture alone prevented from being a doze, becoming more immediate, I cannot repel the boding that there is either some mesenteric affection, which sometimes exists in infants without betraying itself by any notable change in the ingestion or the egestæ, yet producing on the brain an effect similar to that which flatulence, or confined gas pressing on the nerves of the stomach, will do; or else that it is a case of chronic (slow) hydrocephalus. Against this fear I have to say, first, that I have not been able to detect any insensibility to light in the pupil of its eyes, and that the little innocent has no convulsive twitches, and neither starts nor screams in its sleep. For the first I have no opportunity (the sun being clouded) of making a decisive experiment, and requested Mrs. Constable to try it with a candle, as soon as it was taken up after dark; and though the presence of this symptom is an infallible evidence of the presence of effusion, or some equivalent cause of pressure, its absence is no sure proof of the absence of the disease, though it is a presumption in favour of the *degree*. The freedom from perturbation in sleep, however, is altogether a favourable circumstance, and allows a hope that the continued heaviness and immediate relapse into slumber on being placed horizontally may be the effect of weakness. But then the poor little fellow habitually keeps its hand to its head, and there is a sensible heat and throbbing at the temples. On the whole, you should be prepared for the possible event, and Mrs. Constable is naturally very anxious on this point, not merely lest any neglect should be suspected on her part, but likewise from an anticipation of the mother's agitation, should she at any time come up just to witness the baby's last struggles, or to find no more what she was expecting to see in incipient recovery.

Do not misunderstand me, my dearest friend, nor let this letter alarm you beyond what the facts require. I have seen no decisive marks, no positive change for the worse, no measurable *retro*-gression. I have of course repeatedly spoken to Mr. Gillman, but he says it is impossible to form any conclusive opinion. There is no proof that it may not be weakness at present and hitherto, but neither dare he determine what the continuanee of the weakness may not produce. Nothing can warrantably be attempted in this uncertainty but mild alteratives, watchful attention to the infant's regularity, with as cordial nourishment as can be given withont endangering heat or inflammatory action.

I do not think that I have been able to remain undisturbed an hour together for the last three days, such a tumble in of persons with requests or claims on me has there been. House-hunting, &c., &c.

* * * * *

* * * *

The genial glow of Friendship once deadened can never be rekindled.

> "Idly we supplicate the Powers above—
> There is no Resurrection for a Love
> That uneclipsed, unthwarted, wanes away
> In the chilled heart by inward self-decay.
> Poor mimic of the Past! the love is o'er,
> That must *resolve* to do what did itself of yore."

God bless you, and your ever affectionate

T. Allsop, Esq. S. T. COLERIDGE.

P.S. To my great surprise and delight, Mr. Anster came in on us this afternoon, and in perfect health and spirits.

To you, my dear Rob, this letter will be a reminiscence of interest in after life, should life and health be preserved to you; and I cannot choose but think that it must also find a response in the heart of every parent, still more of every mother. Of all the men, ordinary or extraordinary, I have ever known, Coleridge was the one in whom the *child-like*, the almost infantile, love and joyance, giving birth to or rather intermingled with perfect sympathy and identity of feeling, most predominated. His mind was at once the most masculine, feminine, and yet *child-like* (and, in that sense, the most innocent) which it is possible to image. The expressions which conclude this letter I know were only forced from him in a moment of imperfect sympathy, a short interval of ebb in the genial current of affection and love, and a proof how entirely his being yearned for sympathy; not similarity in taste, in feeling, or in judgment, but a love for the good, the beautiful, and the loveable, which become *more good*, *more beautiful*, and *more loveable*, when contemplated by minds essentially individual and independent under the *same* aspect.

LETTER XL.

MY DEAREST FRIEND, *March* 20*th*, 1825.

I should have answered your last but for three causes: first, that I had proofs to correct and a passage of great nicety to add, neither of which could be deferred without injustice to the Publishers, and the breach of a definite promise on my part; second, that I was almost incapacitated from thinking of and doing anything as it ought to be done by poor Mrs. G.'s restless and interrogating anxieties, which in the first instance put the whole working Hive of my Thoughts in a whirl and a Bur; and then, when I see her care-worn countenance, and reflect on the state of her health (and it is difficult to say which of the two, ill-health or habitual anxiety, is more cause and more effect), a sharp fit of the Heart-ache follows.

But enough of this Subject. I ought to be ashamed of myself for troubling you with it; you have enough frets and frictions of your own. And so I proceed to the third cause, which is that (how far imputable to the mood of mind I was in, I cannot say) I did not understand your letter.

Is there any definite service, or any chance of any definite service, great or small, that I can do or promote, or expedite, by coming to town? If there be, let me have a line or a monosyllable *Yes*, and mention the time. I would have set off and taken the chance without asking the question, but that I have so many irons in the fire at this present moment,—1, my Preface; 2, my Essay; 3, a Work prepared for the Press by my Hebrew Friend, in which I am greatly interested, morally and *crumenically*, though not like the Modern Descendants of Heber, one of a *crumenimulga Natio*, *i. e.* a purse-milking set; and 4, Revisal, &c., for a friend only less near than yourself.

Mr. Chance, I take it for granted, has written to you. My opinion is, that he will be a valuable man, not only generally, but *especially* to that which alone concerns *me*—*your* comfort and happiness. He is a self-satisfied man, but of the very kindest and best sort. Prosperous in all his concerns, and with peace in his own conscience and family, I regard such vainness but as the overflow of humanity. I do not like him the better *for* it; but I should not like him the better *without* it. Meantime he is active, shrewd, a thorough man of business; *sanguine* I should think, both by constitution and habitual success: and, under any sudden emergency, I think that Mr. Chance, not so deeply interested, and yet (such is his nature) with equal liveliness in feeling, would be a comfort to you.

I shall miss the post if I do more than add, that whatever really serves *you*, will (and on his death-pillow quite as much as in his present garret) delight

Your sincere and affectionate friend,

T. Allsop, Esq. S. T. COLERIDGE.

It will be necessary to the better understanding of some passages of this letter, to refer very briefly to matters affecting myself, and my position at that time.

At the date of this letter I had been for nearly six years actively engaged in an extensive business, which, owing partly to want of unity of opinion and action amongst those most interested, and partly to changes which were beyond control, had resulted in serious loss, and still more serious deterioration in the value of the property embarked; a loss and a deterioration which I even then saw could never be retrieved, and could only be parried by a system of contrivances, with anxiety and discredit attendant upon the means, and loss and ruin as the assured end.

Under these circumstances, and not with any view to get rich in haste, did I adventure in one of the undertakings with which the time abounded. I owe it to truth to state, that it was a sound, useful, practicable project,* and that it only failed from the unfitness of the men who were associated in its management, and from the general discredit into which *all* similar undertakings fell at this era.

I here state as a beacon to others, that, great as my losses had been, first, in the business in which I had, for six years, incurred yearly pecuniary damage; second, by the very serious losses attendant upon the relinquishment of the undertaking, these would have been parried, and, such is the force of custom, I should probably still have clung to the business in which I had been so great a loser, had I not, in the plenitude of my confidence, accepted a draft for a very great amount, for the use and accommodation of parties, upon whose means I had the most entire confidence, and in their honour, if possible, a still more implicit reliance. Will it be credited that, before

* This very project has been revived, and is now carried on with advantage by a private company. It was, as *I always* foresaw it would be, adopted by those on the spot out of the necessities of their condition.

this draft reached maturity (a dissolution of partnership having taken place between the drawers), that the senior and more affluent partner placed this very bill in the hands of the worthy Member for Leominster, and himself, being an attorney, commenced proceedings for its recovery, although the circumstances were detailed, and the undertaking of the parties, this very attorney being one, were known to that representative of the People: and that this very person so placing the draft in the Honourable Member's hands, knew it was accepted on the faith of *his* means, and that I held his and his partner's joint undertaking? Above all, will it be believed that this very man, whom I had thus assisted with my acceptance, was the attorney in the action? I mention these circumstances neither in anger nor in pity. Me they have not injured, unless the anxiety of those days, and the anxiety they caused to one most dear to me, may in some degree have impaired those buoyant and joyous hopes (common to ardent temperaments) before their appointed time. On the contrary, by severing a connexion I was not in a condition to abandon of myself, I have been saved years of continued and hopeless anxiety, and have thus arrived at a position from whence I can look forward to the realisation of the hope, which has been to me an abiding source of comfort in all my strivings, the prospect of which has ever soothed and supported me—a country life; to end my life in the pursuits and amid the occupations of my childhood. That you, my dearest children, may be free from the soiling influences of buying and selling, from the frightful insincerity and heartlessness which they engender, that you may find a happy home away from scenes of self-seeking competition and the debasing motives which may yet be said to be natural in large communities, is now almost the only wish I have ungratified. I have ever made, as much as possible, "the chosen *employments* of the years in *hope*, the relaxations of the time present; of the years devoted to present duties, and among them to the means of realising that hope; thus have I kept my inward trains of thought, my faculties, and my feelings, in a state of fitness, and as it were contempered to a Life of ease, and capable of enjoying Leisure, because both able and disposed to employ it." Not having been able to lift my means to the extent of the wants sanctioned, almost necessitated, by conventional habits, I have succeeded in reducing my needs to the measure of my condition. I have attained, though somewhat seared in the conflict, content and mental repose, without having passed through or sought refuge in that most *cheerless* condition, *Resignation*. I can yet say,

"Homo sum; a me alienum nihil humani puto."

"So was it when my life began,
So is it now I am a man,
So let it be when I grow old,
Or let me die."

I recollect well—as it were only yesterday—a little excursion I made into the wilder parts of the Peak with my worthy friend and schoolfellow, Mr. John Bromley of Derby. It was a very sultry day, when having with some difficulty led our horses down the precipitous declivity, which from the summit of the shivering Mountain leads into the beautiful Dale of E., or E-dale, we proceeded through that most interesting and most secluded spot on our return to Bakewell, and arrived, weary and heated, at the village (how beautifully named) of Hope. There, having refreshed and rested ourselves, we were preparing to continue our ride, when the appearance of a man, who, by an expression of meekness and benevolence, at once created an interest in my heart, detained me for some time.

From this man of many sorrows, with whom I had long and fervid colloquy, I first learned that Resignation was only acquiescence in that which was felt to be wrong or unjust, or undeserved; and was a very different condition from content. Whilst the impressions were yet vivid, or rather whilst they were yet fresh in my recollection, I wrote to my revered friend, expressing more clearly than I can hope to convey to you now, my repugnance and utter dislike of Resignation. Resignation to, or acquiescence in, that which is felt to be an evil, a sorrow, or a grievous injury, loss or infliction, is of very doubtful value, is at best but suffering superseded, not Enjoyment superinduced; whilst Content, whatever may be the condition of mind, body, or estate with which it co-exists, leaves a man to hope, that highest of human delights, whilst at the same time it secures him from its opposite, fear. It seems that condition in which the energies, mental and physical, find their equipoise and equilibrium; where they all exist and act in harmony; where the discords are neutralised, if not entirely withdrawn; where the atmosphere is such, that they can no longer make themselves heard.

"For this the best preparative is a belief in philosophical necessity." Read again and again this passage, which I would more frequently impress upon your attention did I not fear that the iteration might defeat the effect I seek to produce.

LETTER XLI.

My dearest Friend, *April 30th*, 1825.

Having disburthened myself of the main loads of outward obligation at least that pressed upon me, my Essay for the R. S. L., and my Aids to Reflection, with other matters not so expressly my own, but having the same, if not greater, demands on such quantity of time, as bodily pain and disqualification, with unprecludible interruption, have enabled me to make use of, I take the *very* first moment of the Furlough to tell you that I have been perplexed both by your silence and your absence. In fact, I had taken for granted you were in Derbyshire, till this afternoon, when I saw one who had met you yesterday.

Now I cannot recollect anything that can—I am sure, ought

to have given you offence, unless it were my non-performance of the request communicated to me by Mr. Jameson.

I was ever in the *stifle* of my *reflected* anxieties, *i. e.* anxieties felt by reflection from those of others, and my *Tangle* of *Things-to-be-done*, solicitous to see and talk with you. You must not feel wounded if, loving you so truly as I do, and feeling more and more every week that nothing is worth living for but the consciousness of living aright, I was *nervous* if you will, with regard to the effect of this undertaking on the frame of your moral and intellectual Being. In the meantime, you never came near me, so that I might have been able to rectify my opinions, or rather to form them; and I felt, and still feel, that I would gladly go into a garret and work from morning to late night, at any work I could get money by, and more than share my pittance with you and yours, than see you unhappy with twenty thousand at your command.

Do not, my dearest Friend, therefore let my perplexities, derived in great measure from my unacquaintance with the facts, and to which my ever-wakeful affection gave the origin, prevent you from treating, as you were wont to do,

Your truly sincere

T. Allsop, Esq. S. T. Coleridge.

Whilst I write, my attention is called to a work where this Great and Gentle Being is called bigoted, uncharitable, and I know not what harsh terms are huddled and upheaped upon his Honoured name. If I had no other object but to disabuse the minds of those who are likely to be influenced by this work, I should persevere; regarding, though I may, an injustice done to another as the greatest misfortune that can befall the perpetrator. Well indeed has the Departed said, that the world is a great Labyrinth in which all men take different ways, and abuse all who do not take the same way. Hence I hold it safe at all times to say *I* instead of *it*. What do we really express? *our* opinions. Why not then couple the opinion with the Being who holds or propounds it? To what then does the opinion thus impersonally expressed amount? That *he*, the writer of this Review, thinks wisely, or it may be otherwise. Is he not, however, dishonest in bringing to bear upon the character, the reputation, or the conduct of another man, not facts, not merely the weight of his own arguments or opinions, whatever may be their worth, but the ponderous WE, or the more insidious and dishonest IT. Let us have the opinion of Henry Brougham, of Sydney Smith, of *Francis Jeffery*, of any one man, young or old, and he will be careful in his affirmations. I am inclined to honour and hope well of the attempts of Mr. Roebuck, Mr. Fox, and *my high purposed* and *honest* Friend, John Bell, who have nobly set the example of writing on subjects so important to all without the Stamp, and have given their opinions, under their own names, in their own Journals, and for every word of which they are thus *morally* and legally responsible.

"I think the praise of Folly is the most pleasant Book of Erasmus."

"The distich which he returned to Sir Thomas More in the place of the Horse he had borrowed, is as good as was any Steed in the Stable of that most excellent Utopian. I cannot see how a good Catholic could refuse to receive it. *He* ought to be prepared to renounce *his* religion who shrinks from the necessary, inevitable, and legitimate consequences to which it must lead. Here it is:

"Quod mihi dixisti
De corpore Christi
Crede quod edas et edis,
Sic tibi rescribo
De tuo Palfrido
Crede quod habeas et habes."

Garrick.

"The warmest admirers of histrionic merit would not willingly be supposed to overlook the difference, both in kind and degree, between an excellence that in its very nature is transient, or continuing, only as an echo, in the memory of a single generation, while the name alone remains for posterity, and a power, enduring as the Soul of Man and commensurate with the human language.

But, without dreading the imputation of a wish to balance weights so unequal, we may assert that if ever two great men might seem to have been made for each other, we have this correspondency presented to us in the instance of Garrick and Shakspeare. It will be sufficient for me to direct attention to one peculiarity, the common and exclusive characteristic of both,—the union of the highest Tragic and Comic Excellence in the same Individnal. This indeed supersedes the necessity of mentioning the particular merits which it implies and comprehends, while it is eminently and in the exactest sense of the word *characteristic*, inasmuch as this transcendent power sprung from the same source in both,—from an insight into human nature at its fountain head, which exists in those creations of Genius alone, in which the substance and essential forms are the Gifts of Meditation and self-research, and the individualising accidents, and the requisite drapery, are supplied by observation and acquaintance with the world. We may then hope for a second Garrick or of an approach to a Shakspeare where we find a knowledge of Man united to an equal knowledge of Men, and both co-existing with the power of giving Life and Individuality to the products of both. For such a being possesses the rudiments of every character in himself, and acquires the faculty of *becoming*, for the moment, whatever character he may choose to represent. He combines in his own person at once the materials and the workman. The precious proofs of this rare excellence in our Greatest Dramatic Poet are in the hands of all men. To exhibit the same excellence

15

in our greatest actor, we can conceive no more lively or impressive way than by presenting him in the two extreme Poles of his Creative and almost Protean Genius—in his Richard the Third and his Abel Drugger."

"In the language of prophecy, the first and prominent symptom of a good or evil will, or influencing tendency, is brought forward as the condition or occasion of all that follows. The first link in the chain of effects is made the representative of the common cause of them all, or the good or evil state of the moral Being of the agents. So, for instance, a turbulent malcontent disposition in large classes of a country, with the assertion of *Rights*, unqualified by, and without any reference to, duties, a vague Lust for Power, mistaken for, and counterfeiting the love of, Liberty—

'Licence they mean when they cry Liberty,
For who loves *that*, must first be wise and good—'

show themselves first in clubs, societies, political unions, &c., &c. And this, as the first prominent symptom, foretels and becomes itself a powerful efficient cause of the disruption, disorganisation, and anarchy that follow. Most truly, therefore—indeed what great truth and principle of State Wisdom can be mentioned which is not to be found in the oracle of the Hebrew Prophets—most truly doth Isaiah proclaim—ch. viii. v. 9, "Associate yourselves, O ye people! and ye shall be broken in pieces. Give ear, all ye of far countries! Gird yourselves (*i.e.* form yourselves into Clubs as with Girdles), and ye shall be broken in pieces."

"It at once soothes and amuses me to think—nay, to know, that the time will come when this little volume of my dear, and well nigh oldest friend, dear Mary Lamb, will be not only enjoyed but acknowledged as a rich jewel in the treasury of our permanent English Literature; and I cannot help running over in my mind the long list of celebrated writers, astonishing Geniuses! Novels, Romances, Poems, Histories, and dense Political Economy quartos, which, compared with Mrs. Leicester's School, will be remembered as often and prized as highly as Wilkie's and Glover's Epics and Lord Bolingbroke's Philosophics compared with Robinson Crusoe!"

All my recollections of Sir James Mackintosh were mislaid, or, I fear, lost, together with many letters of Charles Lamb and of Coleridge, on the occasion of a removal about six years ago. The only thing that I distinctly retain is a *bon mot* which Coleridge considered very felicitous.

Speaking of Mr. Hume, who had recently distinguished himself by something connected with finance—a loan for Greece, I think—as an extraordinary man,—"Yes," said Mackintosh, "he is: he is an extraordinary man—an extraordinary ordinary man."

LETTER XLII.

MY DEAR FRIEND, *Saturday, May 2nd,* 1825.

I am sure you did not mean that the interest I feel in this undertaking was one which I was likely to *throw* off, or one which there was any chance of my not retaining; but I would fain have you not even speak or write below that line of friendship and mutual implicit reliance, on which you and I stand. We are in the world, and obliged to chafe and chaffer with it; *but we are not of the world, nor will we use its idioms or adopt its brogue.*

God bless you, and your affectionate Friend,

T. Allsop, Esq. S. T. COLERIDGE.

Goldsmith makes one of his Characters say of the Magazines or Reviews of his day, "They hate each other, but I like them all." I have known, with less or greater intimacy, many men of note and great attainments, who have hated or mistaken (if indeed these are not convertible terms) each other, and yet I have found something not only to admire, but something to *love*, in them all. You have seen the expression applied to Cobbett, and you will see what is said of Hazlitt, O'Connell, and Owen, in the subsequent portion of these reminiscences. Now first of the First.

With William Cobbett, I once passed three days; three days of the most delightful interest throughout. He was, perhaps, at the zenith of his influence (it was before he *sunk* into Parliament), and in the meridian of his powers. It was in the Five *hard* Parishes, as he always called them, in Hampshire, in the stronghold of the Parsons—the large sheep and arable Farms.

He then and there held a Court of Enquiry touching the misdeeds of the millionaires, the Barings: and truly, if what was there stated and confirmed and corroborated to iteration by all who were likely to be cognisant of the facts, is worthy of any credit, MOST FOUL WRONG was done to those, who had been previously *only* oppressed. Fear is always cruel; and I cannot doubt that the Barings considered themselves justified in their *shameful* conduct to Mrs. Deacle, not to mention the case of Farmer Boyes, or Boyce, and the atrocious execution, or, to speak honestly, the legal murder, or murder under legal forms, of Henry Cook, for striking Bingham Baring. I mention this now, at a period of political calm, not to point indignation at misdeeds long since perpetrated, but to awake compunction in the breasts of rich men, who, themselves never exposed to want, cannot conceive or image to themselves the sufferings of the very poor. To them, the reply of the young lady, when told that the poor could not get bread, "then why not eat pie-crust?" is natural; how can it be otherwise? And yet from this class, who are necessarily ignorant of all that it really imports man, in his social condition, to know, are nearly all our Legislators; and not merely those who misrepresent Counties, but the misrepresentatives of Towns. Colonel Sibthorp may sneer at Bulwer as an author, and in his return be contemned as an unreasoning soldier; but they are both of the useless class. Manchester could not find amongst its active and intelligent population a second member, but must have a *rich* man from London: whilst Liverpool—aristocratic and refined Liverpool—must have *a Lord*. The chosen haunts of idleness and profligacy have rejected the idle and the worthless, who are received and cherished in the hives of industry. Brighton, Bath, and Mary-le-bone, are well and truly served by men who belong to the people; whilst Manchester, Liverpool, and Derby, have chosen Lords or Lord-lings to attend to the interests of cotton, calico, and hosiery!

The first day the fine and sturdy Yeoman, with his bold, and, it may be, somewhat burly, bearing, feasted under an immense Tent, more than a thousand Visitors, to whom he gave Food and Drink in ample quantities, a speech after dinner, and a dance in the evening. The gathering came far and near; the best proof, if *any* were needed of the favourable impression he had made in his own neighbourhood.

The following morning I was up about half-past three, and was shortly after joined by this very noticeable Man, with whom I walked across the Fields in the direction of Micheldever. It was delightful at that hour of a fine summer's morning to see him quiet, calm, like the time. Nothing escaped him. Not a flower—especially a honeysuckle—which he did not figuratively sniff up if he could approach it; not a feature of rural beauty which he did not notice, and explain in what lay its distinguishing excellence. Although living at that time constantly in the country, he seemed, in the freshness of his joy and enjoyment, like one who had "been long in dismal cities pent." My pencil recollections of that day are few and scant.

On the morning following, I was one of a party which proceeded to the Church-yard of Micheldever, and strewed the grave of Henry Cook with flowers. Ill-fated youth! hadst *thou* been struck even to the earth, a small gratuity would have been offered to thee, and thou wouldst have been envied by thy poor comrades for thy luck. In what, then, consists thy crime? Truly *thou wert poor*. Had a Prince struck Bingham Baring, he might have been made a Baronet, as his father has since been made a Baron, and the blow would have been esteemed fortunate, and have been added to the Escutcheon of a Loan Jobber; but to be struck by a Ploughman or a Carpenter, *that* is the difference. What matter whether it was in self-defence or in the resistance of wrong done? Fear is ever cruel, is only appeased with Blood!

It was touching and painful, an hour after, to find the mother of this ill-fated victim of the panic of property, so utterly prostrated by the fear of offending the owner of Stratton, employed in removing the flowers from her son's grave, fearful lest the wrath of these Parvenu's should follow her and her husband even unto the Parish Workhouse, in which they had taken refuge, and that this touching tribute to the dead, should be remembered in vengeance against the unoffending bereaved Parents, driven by the death of their son, in old age, to the wretched workhouse of Micheldever. Again, on the arrival of Mr. Cobbett, were flowers strewed on the Grave; again and more quickly were they removed by the *in soul affrighted* Parent. I do not know when I have been more affected.

To you, my dear children, I wish to point out what may else escape your attention whilst young—that these oppressors, these *soul enslavers* of the Poor, are either conscious of the enormity of their conduct or they are not. If not conscious, if totally alienated from *all* sympathies with their kind unless it be in their own especial class, what sympathies, what sources of pleasure and pure delight, are for ever closed to them!

These are fit and appropriate punishments for them. Pleasures withheld for punishments vouchsafed.

If they are awakened to the consciousness of the Blood they have shed, the Widows and the Fatherless that owe their bereaved condition to them, think you that vengeance—ample though unseen vengeance—has not been taken? *Oh! never doubt but that, in some form or other, retribution for misdeeds, for taking, or mistaking, the power for the right, will assuredly arrive to every man during his life.*

Pleasant was it to see the stout Yeoman, the *Country* Gentleman (for such he was in his bearing and general demeanour), go over the ground which he had visited under other and quieter aspects. "Here lived Mr. . . . and there Tom . . .; they were very kind to my sons whilst at school with the Parson at Micheldever." And the recollection of kindness from those who had passed away "from this visible diurnal sphere," caused his eyes to glisten and his voice to soften. The Widow of the Clergyman with whom his sons had been placed, hearing that he was in Micheldever, sent most earnest entreaties that he would not leave the Village without visiting her. He refused, saying "it may injure her: she receives assistance, countenance, or support, from Baring." Again the good lady sent; he went, abusing her *in words*, springing, however, from, and associated with, the finest and purest feelings of our nature; and after a colloquy of some half hour, I rejoined him as he descended the steps of the Widow's house, his face streaming with tears—weeping like a child.

Kind and cordial, frank, hearty, and generous, with energies and powers of mind unequalled in his day, it will indeed be a deep disgrace to the national character, if those who have been benefited, delighted, and instructed by his multifarious writings, shall not evince their sense of his transcendent powers, in the only mode now possible, by prompt contributions to the Statue about to be erected to his Memory.

I am grateful for the delightful days I have passed in communion with a mind, whose matchless energy was softened and attempered by a kindness, which can only have its highest value when allied to, or springing out of, great powers. It was of this man, thus gifted, that Hunt, after he had become a personal enemy, said, when asked what was his opinion of Cobbett's powers, "I have seen him engage the attention of a company for hours by his energy, variety, and the extent of his resources; I have seen him the life and soul of every domestic or social circle, attracting and engaging the attention alike of all—from the child of three years to the old woman of eighty." I gratify myself by inserting the two following letters; the first addressed to the Daughter of an old Friend, on his return from a visit of recreation, the second addressed to the Father upon the death of his excellent Wife. I yet hope that we shall be able to profit by a collection of Mr. Cobbett's letters to private friends, though I much fear that the value he attached to time, deterred him from writing many familiar and friendly letters.* In this view, therefore, these letters, as well as from their kindness and delicate attention, to those who had been heretofore his assistants, are of great interest.

DEAR MISS . . . . *Normandy Farm, Aug. 26th*, 1834.

Your father and mother return in pretty good health; and they have the great consolation to reflect that they owe their recovery to the air which their just confidence in your prudence and diligence have enabled them to avail themselves of.

I have to thank you also, which I do most sincerely, for that very great service which has been rendered me by the great care of your father, at a time when I knew not which way to turn. This he could not have rendered me if he had not had you to confide his business to.

I hope that your mother will come here as often as she may find it necessary for her health, and I hope your health will not suffer on account of your confinement. Your conduct has

---

* This economy of time he also carried into conversation. I recollect his observing, to the clever and pretty girl who ministered to him at Sutton Scotney, "Time is valuable; never throw away your words. I never do."

been so excellent, that I should have deemed it a neglect of my duty had I failed thus to express my sentiments regarding it.

I am your faithful friend,
And most obedient servant,
WM. COBBETT.

Mr. . . . . . *Normandy, April 9th*, 1835.

DEAR SIR,

I am sure I need not tell you what grief your melancholy loss has occasioned me. I do not believe that a better human being ever existed in the world. Nor is it much consolation to know that you must have parted first or last. It is a great calamity, and all I can say is that I most deeply lament it.

Pray remember me to poor little Emma. I wish you could so manage as to come here for a while to withdraw your mind from the scene.

I beg you to be assured that I feel for this event *more* than I have felt for any misfortune of my own in my whole life, for I never yet had a death in my family. I am,

Most sincerely your friend,
WM. COBBETT.

It is well to bear in mind that the last words of William Cobbett were for and concerning the country, and those who make the food to be.

That even when his senses became dim, he still muttered,—"I have ever been their* friend. *They make all things to come: it is right they should have their full share first.*"

That he never swerved; that, contemning imposture whilst living, he was consistent in his Death as in his Life.

Peace to the memory of a Great, and, if words have any meaning, a GOOD man.

---

* The friend of the agricultural classes.

LETTER XLIII.

MY DEAREST FRIEND, *May* 10*th*, 1825.

I have been reflecting earnestly and actively on the subject of a Metropolitan University, now in agitation, and could conveniently comprise the results in three Lectures.

On the Histories of Universities generally, the most interesting Features in the History of the most celebrated Universities in Great Britain, Germany, France, &c. Reduction of all Universities of any name, with respect to their construction and constitution, to three Classes. 2. The Meaning of the Term, University, and the one true and only adequate Scheme of a University stated and unfolded from the Seed (*i. e.* the idea) to the full Tree with all its Branches. 3. The advantages, moral, intellectual, national, developed from reason and established by proofs of History; and, lastly, a plan (and sketch of the *means*) of approximating to the Ideal, adapted and applied to this Metropolis. (N.B. The Plan *in detail*, salaries only not mentioned—the particular sums, I mean). The obstacles, the favourable circumstances, the *pro* and *con* regarding the question of Collegiate Universities, &c. &c. That I could make these subjects not only highly interesting but even entertaining, I have not the least doubt. But would the subject excite an interest of *curiosity?* Would the anticipation of what I might say attract an audience of respectable smallclothes and petticoats sufficiently large to produce something more than, with the same exertions of Head and Hand, I might earn in my Garret (to give the precise Top-ography of my abode) here at Nemorosi, *alias* Houses in the Grove. For the expense of coach-hire, the bodily fatigue, and (to borrow a phrase from poor Charles Lloyd) "*the hot huddle of indefinite sensations*" that hustle my inward man in the *monster* city and a Crown and Anchor Room demand a +, and would an =, after all expenses paid, but ragged economy, unless I were certain of effecting more good in this than in a quieter way of industry.

I wrote to Mr. B. Montagu for his advice; but he felt no interest himself in the subject, and naturally therefore was doubtful of any number of others feeling any. But he promised to talk with his friend Mr. Irving about it! On the other hand, I heard from Mr. Hughes and a Mr. Wilkes (a clever Solicitor-sort of a man who lives in Finsbury-square, has a great sway with the Slangi yclept the Religious Public, and, *this I add as a whitewasher*, was a regular attendant on *my* lectures), that the subject itself is stirring up the Mud-Pool of the Public Mind in London with the vivacity of a Bottom wind. If you can find time, I wish you would talk with Jameson about it, and obtain the opinion of as many as are likely to think aright; and let me know your own opinion and anticipation above all, and at all events, and as soon as possible. We dine on Friday with Mr. Chance. I wish you were with us, for I am sure he would be glad to see you. Need I say that my thoughts, wishes, and prayers follow you in all your doings and strivings, for I am evermore, my dearest friend,

Yours, with a friend and a father's
affection and solicitude,

T. Allsop, Esq. S. T. Coleridge.

My kindest remembrances to Mrs. Allsop, with kisses for little Titania Puckinella.

Years have passed since I heard the Nightingales sing as they did this evening in Mr. Robart's Garden Grounds; *so many, and in such full song, particularly that giddy voluminous whirl of notes which you never hear but when the Birds feel the temperature of the air voluptuous.*

P.S. If I undertook these Lectures, I should compose the three, and write them out with as much care and polish as if for the Press, though I should probably make no use of the MS. in speaking, or at all attempt to recollect it. It would, relatively to my *vivâ voce* addresses, be only a way of premeditating the subject.

It has been charged against the writer of this letter, that he had latterly secluded himself from the world, and had confined his communications chiefly to inferior and subordinate minds. I wish to believe that I have mistaken this writer; I would fain persuade myself that he must be a *very young man;* one, who having no settled or satisfactory opinions, *neither knowledge, experience, or judgment,* seeks in an eternal *gabble* of words, disconnected from thoughts, to impose upon his readers. If, however, he should prove to be a man to whom Age has brought Evil alone, one, who to restlessness, which is *more* than disease, adds treachery of the blackest nature and in all its forms, I would remind him of the communications which he made to the man he now slanders, at the time when the necessities of our *gracious* and *religious* King rendered necessary the resumption of the hundred guineas granted from what is called the Privy Purse to the Fellows of the Society of Literature.

To you, my dear Children, it will be important to know that my dear Friend, with impaired health and in old age, found it a more fit vocation to instruct others in that Knowledge he had with so great labour and research amassed, than any longer to waste time (to him most precious) in vain dispute and idle colloquies. He comprehended not only the view or the objection taken by the clever and restless minds with which he occasionally came in contact, but the opposite and contrary views or objections, and had established for himself a harmony and co-unity, which it was latterly the whole business of his life to convey to others—to those who sought his instructions and the results of his long experience, great knowledge, and *most wonderful* genius.

I will frankly own that I dissuaded my Friend from wasting his powers upon ungenial subjects and ungenial minds, and am therefore open to the charge of having in some measure withdrawn him from an arena to which his health, genius, and modes of thinking, were alike unsuited. To convey to you an adequate *individual* notion or image of the Friend you have lost is with me quite hopeless; the next thing to this is to present to you as many individual pictures or views of his mind as are within my power. To begin with the first— here is the Estimate formed by one of my earliest Friends; hear what was said of him by T. N. T., now Sergeant Talfourd, who, more than any man I know, himself a Poet of the highest order, is best fitted to appreciate the Poets of our time.

" Not less marvellously gifted, though in a far different manner, is Coleridge, who by a strange error has usually been regarded of the same school. Instead, like Wordsworth, of seeking the sources of sublimity and beauty in the simplest elements of humanity, he ranges through all history and science, investigating all that has really existed, and all that has had foundation only in the strangest and wildest minds, combining, condensing, developing, and multiplying the rich products of his research with marvellous facility and skill; now pondering fondly over some piece of exquisite loveliness brought from an unknown recess, now tracing out the hidden germ of the eldest and most barbaric theories, and now calling fantastic spirits from the vasty deep, where they have slept since the dawn of reason. The term 'myriad-minded,' which he has happily applied to Shakspeare, is truly descriptive of himself. He is not one, but Legion, 'rich with the spoils of time,' richer in his own glorious imagination and sportive fantasy. There is nothing more wonderful than the facile majesty of his images, or rather of his worlds of imagery, which, whether in his poetry or his prose, start up before us self-raised and all perfect, like the palace of Aladdin. He ascends to the sublimest truths by a winding track of sparkling glory, which can only be described in his own language:—

" 'The Spirit's Ladder,
That from this gross and visible world of dust,
Even to the starry world, with thousand rounds
Builds itself up; on which the unseen powers
Move up and down on heavenly ministries—
The circles in the circles, that approach
The central sun with ever narrowing orbit.'

"In various beauty of versification he has never been exceeded. Shakspeare, doubtless, in linked sweetness and exquisite continuity, and Milton in pure majesty and classic grace—but this in one species of verse only; and taking all his trials of various metres, the swelling harmony of his blank verse, the sweet breathing of his gentle odes and the sybil-like flutter with the murmuring charm of his wizard spells, we doubt if even these great masters have so fully developed the music of the English Tongue. He has yet completed no adequate memorials of his genius, yet it is most unjust to assert that he has done little or nothing.

"To refute this assertion, there are his *Wallenstein;* his love poem s of intensest beauty; his *Ancient Mariner*, with its touches of profoundest tenderness amidst the wildest and most bewildering terrors; his holy and sweet tale of *Christabel*, with its rich enchantments and richer humanities; the depths, the sublimities, and the pensive sweetness of his *Tragedy;* the heart-dilating sentiments scattered through his '*Friend;*' and the stately imagery which breaks upon us at every turn of the golden paths of his metaphysical labyrinths. And if he has a power within him mightier than that which even these glorious creations indicate, shall he be censured because he has deviated from the ordinary course of the age in its development, and instead of committing his imaginative wisdom to the press has delivered it from his living lips? He has gone about in the true spirit of an old Greek bard, with a noble carelessness of self, giving fit utterance to the divine spirit within him. Who that has ever heard can forget him? his mild benignity, the unbounded variety of his knowledge, the fast succeeding products of his imagination, the child-like simplicity with which he rises from the driest and commonest theme into the wildest magnificence of thought, pouring on the soul a stream of beauty and of wisdom to mellow and enrich it for ever? The seeds of poetry, the materials for thinking, which he has thus scattered will not perish. The records of his fame are not in books only, but on the fleshly tablets of young hearts, who will not suffer it to die even in the general ear, however base and unfeeling criticism may deride their gratitude."

Quoted the passage from Southey, in which he declares the Church to be in danger from the united attacks of Infidels, Papists, and Dissenters. Expressed his surprise at Southey's extreme want of Judgment. "*Any Establishment which could fuse into a common opposition, into an opposition on Common Grounds, such heterogeneous and conflicting materials, would deserve, ought, to be destroyed.* I *almost* wish that Southey had been one of the audience, *fit though few,* who attended my Lectures on Philosophy; though I fear that in his present state of mind, he would have perverted, rather than have profited, by them."

The prospectus of these Lectures is so full of Interest, and so well worthy of attention, that I subjoin it; trusting that the Lectures themselves will soon be furnished by or under the auspices of Mr. Green, the most constant, and the most assiduous of his Disciples.

That gentleman will, I earnestly hope—*and doubt not*—see, *feel,* the necessity of giving the whole of his Great Master's views, opinions, and anticipations; not those alone in which he more entirely sympathises, or those which may have more ready acceptance in the present time. He will not shrink from the Great, the *Sacred duty* he has voluntarily undertaken, from any regards of prudence, still less, from that most hopeless form of fastidiousness, the wish to conciliate those who are never to be conciliated, *inferior minds* smarting under a sense of inferiority, and the imputation *which they are conscious is just,* that but for Him *they* never could have been; that distorted, dwarfed, changed, as are all his views and opinions, by passing *athwart* minds with which they could not assimilate, they are yet almost the only things which give such minds a *status* in Literature.

LETTER XLIV.

DEAR SIR, *Nov. 26th,* 1818.

I take the liberty of addressing a Prospectus to you. Should it be in your power to recommend either Course among your friends, you will (I need not add) oblige your sincere, &c.

S. T. COLERIDGE.

"*Prospectus of a Course of Lectures, Historical and Biographical, on the Rise and Progress, the Changes and Fortunes of Philosophy, from Thales and Pythagoras to the Present Times; the Lives and Succession of the distinguished Teachers in each Sect; the connexion of Philosophy with General Civilisation; and, more especially, its relations to the History of Christianity, and to the Opinions, Language, and Manners of Christendom, at different Æras, and in different Nations.*

"BY S. T. COLERIDGE, ESQ.

"Logical subtleties and metaphysical trains of argument form neither part nor object of the present Plan, which supposes no other qualification in the auditors of either sex than a due interest in questions of deepest concern to all, and which every rational creature, who has arrived at the age of reflection, must be presumed, at some period or other, to have put to his own thoughts:—What, and *for* what am I made? What *can* I, and what *ought* I to, make of myself? and in what relations do I stand to the world and to my fellow men? Flattering myself with a continuance of the kind and respectful attention, with which my former courses have been honoured, I have so little apprehension of not being intelligible throughout, that were it in my power to select my auditors, the majority would, perhaps, consist of persons whose acquaintance with the History of Philosophy would commence with their attendance on the Course of Lectures here announced. When, indeed, I contemplate the many and close connexions of the subject with the most interesting periods of History; the instances and illustrations which it demands and will receive from Biography, from individuals of the most elevated genius, or of the most singular character: I cannot hesitate to apply to it as a whole what has been already said of an important part (I allude to Ecclesiastical History)—that for every reflecting mind it has a livelier as well as deeper interest, than that of fable or romance.

"Nor can these Lectures be justly deemed superfluous even as a literary work. We have, indeed, a History of Philosophy, or rather a folio volume so called, by STANLEY, and ENFIELD's Abridgment of the massive and voluminous BRUCKER. But what are they? Little more, in fact, than collections of sentences and extracts, formed into separate groups under the several names, and taken (at first or second hand) from the several writings of individual philosophers, with no *Principle* of arrangement, with no *method*, and therefore without unity and without progress or completion. Hard to be understood as detached passages, and impossible to be remembered as a whole, they leave at last on the mind of the most sedulous student but a dizzy recollection of jarring opinions and wild fancies. Whatever value these works may have as books of reference, so far from *superseding*, they might seem rather to *require*, a work like the present, in which the accidental influences of particular periods and individual genius are by no means overlooked, but which yet does in the main consider Philosophy historically, as an essential part of the history of man, and as if it were the striving of a single mind, under very different circumstances indeed, and at different periods of its own growth and development; but so that each change and every new direction should have its cause and its explanation in the errors, insufficiency or prematurity of the preceding, while all by reference to a common object is reduced to harmony of impression and total result. Now this object, which is one and the same in all the forms of Philosophy, and which alone constitutes a work *Philosophic*, is—the origin and primary laws (or efficient causes) either of the WORLD, man included (which is *Natural* Philosophy)—or of Human Nature exclusively, and as far only as it is *human* (which is *Moral* Philosophy). If to these we subjoin, as a third problem, the question concerning the sufficiency of the human reason to the solution of both or either of the two former, we shall have a full conception of the sense in which the term, Philosophy, is used in this Prospectus and the Lectures corresponding to it.

"The main Divisions will be—1. From Thales and Pythagoras to the appearance of the Sophists. 2. And of Socrates. The character and effect of Socrates' life and doctrines, illustrated in the instances of Xenophon, as his most faithful representative, and of Antisthenes, or the Cynic sect, as the one partial view of his philosophy, and of Aristippus, or the Cyrenaic sect, as the other and opposite extreme. 3. Plato and Platonism. 4. Aristotle and the Peripatetic school. 5. Zeno and Stoicism, Epicurus and Epicureans, with the effects of these in the Roman republic and empire. 6. The rise of the Eclectic or Alexandrine Philosophy, the attempt to set up a pseudo-Platonic Polytheism against Christianity, the degradation of Philosophy itself into mysticism and magic, and its final disappearance, as Philosophy, under Justinian. 7. The resumption of the Aristotelian philosophy in the thirteenth century, and the successive re-appearance of the different sects from the restoration of literature to our own times."

LETTER XLV.

MY DEAREST FRIEND,

The person to whom I alluded in my last is a Mr. T . . . ., who, within the last two or three years, has held a situation in the Colonial Office, but *what*, I do not know. From his age and comparatively recent initiation into the office, it is probably not a very influensive one; and, on the other hand, from the rank and character of his friends, he has occasionally brought up with him to our Thursday evening *conver*—, or, to mint a more appropriate term, *one*-versazione, it must be a respectable one. Mr. T . . . is *Southey's friend*, and more than a literary acquaintance to *me*, only in consequence of my having had some friendly intercourse with his uncle during my abode in the north. Of *him* personally I know little more than that he is a remarkably handsome fashionable-looking young man, a little *too deep* or *hollow mouthed* and important in his enunciation, but clever and well read; and I have no reason to doubt that he would receive any one whom I had introduced to him as a friend of mine in whose welfare I felt anxious interest, with kindness and a disposition to forward his object should it be in his power.

But again, my dearest Friend, you must allow me to express my regret that I am acting in the dark, without any conviction on my mind that your present proceeding is not the result of wearied and still agitated spirits, an impetus of despondency, *that* fever which accompanies exhaustion. I can too well sympathise with you; and bitterly do I feel the unluckiness of my being in such a deplorable state of health just at the time when for your sake I should be most desirous to have the use of all my faculties. May God bless you, and your little-able but most sincere friend,

T. Allsop, Esq. S. T. Coleridge.

This was written just after the utter, and as then it seemed, the hopeless ruin of my prospects. Need I say in that hour of great perplexity what unspeakable solace and support I found in the sympathy and untireable kindness of my revered friend, and in his frank, honest, and every way most excellent house-mate, Mr. Gillman. Charles Lamb, Charles and Mary Lamb, "union in partition," were never wanting in the hour of need: and I have a clear recollection of Miss Lamb's addressing me in *a tone* acting *at once* as a solace and support, and *after* as a stimulus, to which I owe more perhaps, than to the more extended *arguments* of all others. Believe me, my dear son, that in the hour of extreme affliction, of extreme misfortune, there is no solace like the sympathy of an affectionate and gentle woman. *Then*, their sympathy becomes to us strength, it blends with our own sense of sorrow, and we *feel*, rather than are convinced by any process of reason, that it is good. These reminiscences become painful when I think that you cannot now, as I had fondly hoped, pay back in kind attention and ministrations part of the vast debt I owe.

"Hatred of superiority is not, alas! confined to the ignorant.

The best informed are most subject to jealousy, and to unfair representations of new views and doctrines."

"Quoted his short Sketch of Burke from the Biographia Literaria. Burke possessed and had sedulously sharpened that eye which sees all things, actions, and events, in relation to the laws which determine their existence and circumscribe their possibility. He referred habitually to *principles*: he was a scientific statesman, and therefore a *Seer*. For every principle contains in itself the germs of a prophecy; and, as the prophetic power is the essential privilege of science, so the fulfilment of its oracles supplies the outward, and (to men in general) the *only*, test, of its claim to the Title. There is not one word I would add or withdraw from this, scarcely one which I would substitute. I can read Burke, and apply every thing not merely temporary to the present most fearful condition of our country. I cannot conceive a time or a state of things in which the writings of Burke will not have the highest value."

"Observe the fine humanity of Shakspeare in that his sneerers are all worthless villains. Too cunning to attach value to *self-praise*, and unable to obtain approval from those whom they are compelled to respect, they propitiate their own *self-love* by disparaging and lowering others."

"Of all the men I ever knew, Wordsworth has the least femineity in his mind. He is *all* man. He is a man of whom it might have been said,—'It is good for him to be alone.'"

"I have shown in the Biographia Literaria the great evil of too entire domestication. My after-experience would confirm, nay, even extend, this. I incline to think that, unless the husband is abroad the whole day, and therefore only a partaker of his wife's social parties, that in the choice of their associates they should be independent. To exclude all that a woman or a man might wish to exclude from his or her help-mate's society, might leave the rest of little value, and lead to mutual discomfort. The Turkish method is good: they have no difference of opinion in that fine country; but, as our own habits and customs are different, we should seek to make arrangements in harmony with them; and this I think may be accomplished. Why insist upon a married pair—paired not matched—agreeing in the choice of their visitors. The less the independence of married people, especially that of man, is trenched upon, the better chance of happiness for both. Are there any men to whom the wife has a dislike? why should she be annoyed with their presence? Are there women amongst his wife's acquaintance who to him are ungenial, why force them upon the husband's distaste or dislike? I have known permanent aversions, and, what is the same thing, permanent alienations proceed from this cause, all which might have been avoided by each of the parties simply agreeing to see their own friends without the presence or intervention of the other. In the one case the range of the more kindly sympathies may appear to be circumscribed, in the other, dislike is quickly ripened into aversion."

1832.

"I fear that the Revolutionary Spirit which was rebuked by Burke, and derided by Canning, though driven from high places, is not the less active amongst the people. This was my opinion in 1817, and it is still more so now, when the resumption of cash payments has revolutionised our monetary system, and with it has caused the most fearful devastation in the fortunes and general condition of the agriculturists—both labourers and proprietors. If what is charged against Goody

Peel, or Peel the Candid, be true, the epithet "genteelly vulgar" is a term of approval to what I should be inclined to apply to him. To improve his fortune or his prospects by fair means is not denied to Mr. Peel; but to recommend a measure of very doubtful, nay, dangerous policy, merely because it would double his own wealth, when earnestly exhorted by his father against its fearful consequences, is what I dare not believe of Peel (and of him you know I think very meanly), even though charged with it openly, and to my knowledge never denied. The miserable policy of men like Peel will have its reaction during this generation; for them, the problem will be solved, that half is greater than the whole; certainly better for them. The danger does not appear now, nay, at the hour of its arrival, I do not think it will *appear*, to be from within (and I incline to believe that its manifestation *must* be from without); but who can doubt that, if all were right at home, We, this People of ENGLAND, could have any thing really to fear from abroad?

It is quite folly to think that any book, or class of books, can be any longer of *general* Interest. Even Newspapers, the only papers of general Interest as a class, are daily being subdivided. The result of great and constant subdivision is a daily increasing antagonism—or *general* indifference of the whole to the subject of each. It may be you are right in thinking, or rather in hoping, that the greater equalisation, not in wealth, for that is the reverse, but, in intelligence and the external appearance of all classes, and the growing power and ultimate supremacy of the middle classes, will cause greater mental activity, which must result in a daily increasing, and ultimately in universal, benevolence. I have entertained views not dissimilar, as you well know, and they are now held, in some form or other, by all good men; but I doubt whether any good can come from the use of evil or antagonist means. Benevolence and kindly feelings towards all that has life, must precede intelligence and mental activity, in those at least who are to effect any great changes in our social condition. Owen of Lanark fulfils this condition, as all his life has been devoted to extend and improve the happiness of those under his control or within his influence. He has also the most indomitable perseverance, and has attested, by a Life devoted to the most disinterested objects, the purity and singleness of his purpose. With these qualities, what might not such a man have effected, had he not wilfully stumbled over religion, which was not at all in his way, and thus impaired greatly his power of doing good.

I recollect writing a very long letter to Mr. Owen, and conjuring him, with tears in my eyes, to avoid this rock; this vexed question of Fate and Freewill; of which less seems to be known, by those who argue upon it, than of any other subject of difference.

> " The Priesthood grossly cheat us with free-will;
>   Will to do what, but what Heaven first decreed?
> Our actions then are neither Good nor Ill,
>   Since from eternal causes they proceed:
> Our passions, fear and anger, love and hate,
> Mere senseless engines that are moved by fate;
> Like ships on stormy seas without a guide,
> Tost by the winds, are driven by the tide."

These lines of Dryden seem to me to express the doctrine and its results better than any other I recollect. It is true the illustrations are now varied, but nothing has been added to the argument either in force or variety."

With reference to the early project of Coleridge, Southey, and others, to form a community on the banks of the Susquehannah, a project, or rather a principle, the practical application of which seems now in some form or other likely to be tried, I gratify myself, and, I doubt not, shall interest others, by the following brief notice from the Friend:—

> " Truth I pursued, as Fancy led the way,
> And wiser men than I went worse astray."

"From my earliest manhood I perceived that if the people at large were neither ignorant nor immoral, there could be no motive for a sudden and violent change of Government; and if they were, there could be no hope but of a change for the worse.

* * * * * *

"My feelings, however, and imagination did not remain unkindled in this general conflagration (the French revolution); and I confess I should be more inclined to be ashamed than proud of myself if they had. I was a sharer in the general vortex, though my little world described the path of its revolution in an orbit of its own. What I dared not expect from constitutions of Government and whole nations, I hoped from Religion and a small company of chosen individuals, and formed a plan, as harmless as it was extravagant, of trying the experiment of human perfectibility on the banks of the *Susquehannah;* where our little Society, in its second generation, was to have combined the innocence of the patriarchal age with the knowledge and genuine refinements of European culture; and where I dreamt that in the sober evening of my life, I should behold the Cottages of Independence in the *undivided* Dale of Industry.

> 'And oft, soothed sadly by some dirgeful wind,
> Muse on the sore ills I had left behind.'

"Strange fancies! and as vain as strange! Yet to the intense interest and impassioned zeal, which called forth and strained every faculty of my intellect for the organization and defence of this scheme, I owe much of whatever I at present possess,—my clearest insight into the nature of individual man, and my most comprehensive views of his social relations, of the true uses of trade and commerce, and how far the *wealth* and relative *power* of nations promote or impede their welfare and inherent strength."

I have now done. I have placed before you memorials of one of the Greatest and Best Men of this age; in great and varied attainments, in the power of placing scattered Truths in harmonious combination, and of illustrating them out of the Stores of a vast Intellect, by far the most Wonderful Man of his Time.

In these Letters you are admitted, as it were, into the Inner shrine; you hear him commune with his own Soul. I indulge the hope that these volumes may not be without their response from the minds of those who yet, in early youth, seek earnestly, nay anxiously, for Truth; that Truth the test of which is Consistency—the Harmony of the whole with the Parts, and of each Part with the Whole. The human face divine is blurred and transfigured by being made the impress of the Mean and the Selfish; not unfrequently the most intensely selfish, when falsely held to be most beneficent or benevolent.

Read the Faces of all you meet in your next half hour's walk. How many are there, the expression of which satisfies you, that they are happy or possess the conditions of well Being? And why is this? Is it not chiefly from the minds of all men having been trained to be unjust, to seek to become possessed of the labour of others without giving an equivalent, and being made to consider the greater or less extent to which each can carry this practice, as the test of their respective talent? It is this mental robbery, this desire to possess without deserving; of wishing the end and overleaping the means, which is now soon to find its retribution. Look at those beautiful women, beautiful, though, as you plainly see, restless and disquieted? And why restless or disquieted? Have they not Food, Shelter, and Clothing? Yes, these they possess in abundance and variety; in an abundance and variety far beyond the reasonable (I had almost said the *un*reasonable) needs of Human Beings. But they are disquieted because, slaves as they are to the External, the Adventitious, and the Unnecessary, they require yet more of that of which they have already too much, just in the sense that the too much of Drink or of Food to-day leads to the too much of to-morrow. What would be said of a society or a people of whom it was believed —known, that those were held in highest honour who exacted and destroyed the greatest amount of labour? And yet is not this our case? Would not a man at the present time, who purchased a suit of clothes every day, which he destroyed at night, be held as a sort of Divinity by those who uphold the present application, or misapplication, of labour? And yet this very people, or rather their self-constituted instructors who hold, the greater the destruction the greater the benefit, shrink from the more rational proposition of Lord Castlereagh, of employing the "surplus population! in digging holes one day and filling them up the next" as an absurdity. The true principle—at least that which appears to me such—is founded in *eternal justice*, as far as those words have any definite meaning: it is, that no man shall receive more than he gives; that no man shall have rights (the very term being its best confutation) which do not belong to all; such Rights invariably becoming Wrongs alike to those for whose advantage they are exercised, and those at whose expense they are purchased.

And now, my dear children, once more farewell! The life of exercise which I will not yet, nor perhaps again, call labour, to which I destine you, will, I hope, whatever else of good may result, leave you less of inclination, and *your future* less of necessity, for speculations, which have been, for me, as necessary as they are distasteful. You shall have your own independence, and by so much your well being (and how *great* a part independence constitutes, you cannot yet know) in your own power. Health, springing from, and leading to exercise, and cheerfulness; an utter disregard and dislike of the petty externals which are, from custom and the association of weak minds, held in disproportionate regard, it shall be the endeavour of my future life to secure for you. Believe me, my dearest Children, that the highest wisdom is to be found in Simplicity, whether of Thought or Action, and that all those whom you see Slaves to the External and the Unessential, are necessarily Unhappy. This comes of concealment or suppression.

I do not think it would be possible for men to be selfish, if Truth, literal and verbal Truth, were the rule, instead of the exception. If men and women were accustomed to "sun" their minds, to speak openly their wishes and aspirations, instead of brooding over them until they become parts not merely of the habits, but of the mind itself, we should have little vice and less misery. It is this tendency of an artificial and complicated society to become more and more insincere, which gives me to hope less for the future state and prospects of society than I should otherwise do; though I have faith, not alone in the absolute progression, as a fact apart from the human or conventional better or worse, but in the universal Law of Recoil and Re-action.

THE END.

CPSIA information can be obtained
at www.ICGtesting.com
Printed in the USA
LVHW040022180422
716440LV00005B/504

9 783752 592429